D1553226

Polish Heritage Travel Guide

WITHDRAWN

Polish Heritage Travel Guide

TO U.S.A. & CANADA

Jacek Galazka, EDITOR-IN-CHIEF

Albert Juszczak, Ph.D., MANAGING EDITOR

POLISH HERITAGE PUBLICATIONS

Published by Polish Heritage Publications
75 Warren Hill Road
Cornwall Bridge, CT 06754

Distributed to the trade by
Hippocrene Books, Inc.
171 Madison Avenue
New York, NY 10016

ISBN 0-7818-0035-8

Cover and book design by Marek Antoniak

Printed in the United States of America

Editorial Committee

Henry Archacki, *New York, New York*
Clyde R. Bell, *Stillwater, New York*
Stanley Z. Biernacik, *Hamburg, New York*
Joan Bittner, *Hamtramck, Michigan*
Stanislaus A. Blejwas, *West Hartford, Connecticut*
Alfred F. Bochenek, *McLean, Virginia*
Edwin Brzezinski, *Crestwood, Missouri*
Stanley Ciesielski, *Baltimore, Maryland*
Florence Clowes, *Danielson, Connecticut*
Zofia Deskur, *Endwell, New York*
Eugene E. Dziedzic, *Utica, New York*
Robert Dziublowski, *Brooklyn, New York*
Stefan Eminowicz, *Scottsdale, Arizona*
Diana T. Gaza, *Clark, New Jersey*
Barbara Zajaczkowska-Haller, *Endwell, New York*
Zdzislaw A. Jachulski, *Sterling Heights, Michigan*
Henry V. Janoski, *Scranton, Pennsylvania*
Julian S. Jurus, *Port Washington, New York*
Frank Kajencki, *El Paso, Texas*
Krzysztof Kamyszew, *Chicago, Illinois*
Stas Kmiec, *Long Island, New York*
Al Koproski, *Stamford, Connecticut*
Leonard Kosinski, *Aiken, South Carolina*
Jerzy Koss, *New York, New York*
Anna Kwiecinska, *Northampton, Massachusetts*
Ellen K. Lee, *South Laguna, California*
Marcia Lewandowski, *Detroit, Michigan*
John Loga, *Somers, New York*
Elzbieta Lyra, *Warsaw, Poland*
Franciszek Lyra, *Warsaw, Poland*
Krystyna Olszer, *New York, New York*
Cecilia D. Patalita, *DeWitt, New York*
Donald E. Pienkos, *Milwaukee, Wisconsin*
Michael F. Pietruszka, *Buffalo, New York*
Edward Poniewaz, *St Louis, Missouri*

James S. Pula, *Saratoga Springs, New York*
Stanley R. Radosh, *Amherst, Massachusetts*
Denise Restout, *Lakeville, Connecticut*
Anita Richards, *Bolton Landing, New York*
Theresa B. Romanowski, *Philadelphia, Pennsylvania*
Kathryn G. Rosypal, *Chicago, Illinois*
Danuta Schneider, *Chicago, Illinois*
Jonathan D. Shea, *New Britain, Connecticut*
W. C. Shoemaker, *Kosciusko, Mississippi*
Stanley & Eleanor Slusarczyk, *Prospect, New York*
Wanda Sobczak, *Scranton, Pensylvania*
Stanislaw Stolarczyk, *Toronto, Canada*
Ita and Jerzy Straszak, *Ottawa, Canada*
Tom Tarapacki, *Buffalo, New York*
Wanda Tomczykowska, *San Francisco, California*
Joseph S. Wardzala, *Derby, Connecticut*
Nicholas Westbrook, *Ticonderoga, New York*
Ellen Wierzewski, *Chicago, Illinois*
Slawomir Wroblewski, *Chicago, Illinois*
Lawrence R. Wujcikowski, *Pittsburgh, Pennsylvania*
Joseph L. Zazyczny, *Wayne, Pennsylvania*
Ludwik Zeranski, *McLean, Virginia*
Frederick S. Zimnoch, *Northampton, Massachusetts*
Stephanie Zimolzak, *Glen Lyon, Pensylvania*
Helena Ziolkowska , *Chicago, Illinois*
Gene Zygmont, *Torrance, California*
Indexer: Teresa Juszczak

Advisory Committee

Col. John R. Elting (U.S.A. Ret.), *Cornwall-on-Hudson, New York*
Ewa Gierat, *Bethlehem, Connecticut*
Mark Kohan, Editor, POLISH-AMERICAN JOURNAL, *Buffalo, New York*
Gen. Thaddeus W. Maliszewski (U.S.A. Ret.), *Jupiter, Florida*
Walentyna Janta Polczynski, *Elmhurst, New York*
Eugene Rosypal, *Chicago, Illinois*
Wladyslaw Wantula, *Richmond Hill, New York*
Eva A. Ziem, Editor, LANGUAGE BRIDGES, *Richardson, Texas*

Prologue by Stanislaus A. Blejwas, Ph.D.

Since its birth, the United States had been constantly present in Polish minds. Kosciuszko and Pulaski distinguished themselves in the American Revolution, Poles followed the debates over the Constitution, and the names of Washington, Franklin, Jefferson and Hamilton were invoked in Polish debates, political polemics, and literature. Early Polish images of America were both simple and varied. There was the exotic, primeval America of the Indian and the early settlers. The nobleman and poet Tomasz Kajetan Wegierski was drawn to the colonies in 1783, no doubt influenced by J. Hector St. John de Crevecoeur's *Letters From An American Farmer,* which according to Wegierski, presented an "enchanting picture of the happy life of the inhabitants of English America." After the Revolution, America became the Republic where freedom and equality mingled with simplicity of manner and industriousness, giving birth to a democratic society without class distinctions. For Poland, which lost its freedom at the end of the Eighteenth Century, America was a needed Utopia, a proof of what man could achieve when free and his own lawmaker upon a virgin land. At the same time, early Polish travelers did not fail to note the double standard of American democracy when they encountered the plight of the Blacks.

The historian, Jerzy Jedlicki suggests that the function of the American presence in the Polish mind has been to compensate for all those things missing at home. While Poland lay partitioned, America symbolized freedom and the Rights of Man. In the early nineteenth century, nobles, freedom fighters, and political exiles discussed America, but few visited. As he embarked on his two-year journey in 1876, the Polish writer Henryk Sienkiewicz remarked: "The man departing for America is still a rarity among us." But while in America Sienkiewicz observed the early foundations of a permanent Polish presence in the young republic, coming across Radom, Illinois; Krakow, Missouri; Polonia, Wisconsin; New Posen, Nebraska; Panna Maria, Texas, and visiting Chicago. As peasant immigrants arrived in ever growing numbers, America became a new homeland. Sienkiewicz observed that Polish emigres in France might criticize France, but "it would be dangerous to speak disparagingly of the United States to any Pole residing here. He does not cease to love his former fatherland, but after Poland he loves most the United States."

The Polish presence and heritage in America begins with a handful of Poles who landed in the Jamestown Colony on October 1, 1608, on the good ship *Margaret and Mary*. While the Jamestown settlement did not survive, the "Polonians" are remembered as hard workers. Furthermore, they successfully argued for the franchise in the newly formed House of Burgesses. These early settlers were followed by a handful of others scattered about in the early colonies and rapidly absorbed by the surrounding society prior to the American revolution. The arrival of Pulaski and Kosciuszko begins a Polish political emigration to America. They left Poland because of unfavorable political conditions after the first Partition in 1772, and they participated in the colonists' revolution for freedom. Pulaski organized a cavalry and made the champion's ultimate sacrifice. Kosciuszko marshalled his engineering skills to fortify Bemis Heights and assure the American victory at the Battle of Saratoga, the Revolution's turning point. Other political exiles and emigres followed Pulaski and Kosciuszko in the years preceding the American Civil War and the January 1863 Insurrection, but their numbers were small. The Polish presence in the American consciousness was a faintly imprinted memory of a few heroic individual participants in a common struggle against despotism in the battle for the right of every nation to freedom and independence. These memories, however, were to be less important to American society than to a new generation of Polish emigrants that began to reach America in the 1850s.

It was the Great Peasant Immigration, comparable in importance to the Great Emigration after the November 1830 Insurrection, which imprinted a Polish presence upon the New World. Beginning with the arrival on Christmas Eve, 1854, in Panna Maria, Texas, Polish peasants swelled the immigrant flood from southern and eastern Europe in the years after the Civil War up until Congress adopted exclusionary immigration legislation in 1924. America became the subject of that most popular form of national literature, emigrant letters.

In the rush to America, the peasant immigrants created their own urban villages in the great industrial states of the Midwest, and, subsequently, in the Atlantic states of Massachusetts, Connecticut, New York, New Jersey, Pennsylvania, Delaware, and Maryland. While Poles settled in every state of the Union, they were most numerous where there were jobs, for this was, as Sienkiewicz found, an immigration "in search of bread and freedom". America offered what was unavailable at home. The peasant immigrants worked in steel mills, factories, and mines; only a tenth ever made their way to the farms. As they settled, they organized themselves, developing a remarkably complete series of community institutions; over 950 Roman Catholic and Polish National Catholic churches, numerous parochial schools, insurance fraternals, a Polish language press, and host of sports, cultural, social, and political organizations. By 1930, the U.S. Census counted over 3,000,000 first and second generation Polish Americans.

The buildings the immigrants erected to house their community life incarnate their contribution to America's Polish heritage. The churches are often on a grand scale, their size challenging a bishop's cathedral church and other elegant Christian structures. They are a testimony to faith, for God must be worshipped in a great house. They are also an assertion of the Polish presence. God's Polish house had to rival American churches. The immigrant, despite enormous difficulties and often exploitative working conditions, manifested pride in his accomplishments in "Ameryka," pointedly reminding his American neighbors by the size and beauty of his Polish church that he was just as good as any other citizen, and here to stay. Every Polish church, school, national home, and sports hall is physical testimony to the Polish presence in the New World.

Community organizations and institutions preserved and stimulated the immigrant's Polishness, and at the same time eased him onto the road to Americanization. During World War I, Polish immigrants demonstrated faithfulness to their homeland and Poland's independence. They donated generously to charitable relief and over 20,000 returned across the ocean to fight in General Jozef Haller's Blue Army. At the same time, they confirmed their loyalty to their new homeland, purchasing American war bonds and serving in even greater numbers in the American Expeditionary Forces.

When Poland's independence was regained on November 11, 1918, Polish immigrants rejoiced. At the same time most understood that they had become Americans. Too much was invested in America to return to Poland. In the 1920s and 1930s immigrants and their children, now that Poland was sovereign, focused on their domestic affairs. Democratic and Republican political and citizenship clubs sprang up, and the emerging Polish Americans sought recognition through politics. To confirm their status as equal and valuable citizens, Polish Americans invoked their past, raising local monuments to Pulaski and Kosciuszko, and adding to a growing list of public monuments to the Polish and American heroes dating back to the Kosciuszko statue erected in 1904 in Chicago and the Kosciuszko and Pulaski monuments dedicated in 1910 during the Polish National Congress in Washington, D.C. Bridges and skyways, avenues, streets, and even American postal stamps, were also symbols of the politics of recognition.

The community was reaching middle age, looking forward to a prosperous future, and new cultural organizations reflected the changes. The Kosciuszko Foundation was founded in 1925, and Polish Americans opened their own national attic in 1935 when the Polish Museum in America was organized. In 1926, the Polish Arts Club of Chicago was established, later becoming a charter member of the national American Council of Polish Cultural Clubs founded in 1948. The cultural interests of Polish Americans were reaching beyond their parents' popular folk culture to Poland's artistic, musical, and literary heritage, which the second and third generation wished to know more about. Modrzejewska, Kochanska-

Sembrich, the de Reszke Brothers, Paderewski, and Rubinstein were, after all, well known to American audiences.

An unintended consequence of World War II was the broadening of America's Polish Heritage. A new generation of political emigres and soldier exiles arrived. Included in their ranks were many of Poland's most distinguished scholars, musicians, and artists. Determined to preserve Polish learning and her modern history, this intellectual immigration gifted America with individuals who found new careers in American academia or in the professions; with the Polish Institute of Arts and Sciences in America, founded in 1942 and which counts three Nobel laureates among its members; with the Jozef Pilsudski Institute in America, organized in 1943; and with new veteran and scouting organizations.

After 1956 a consumer immigration arrived, and after the imposition of Martial Law in December, 1981, the Solidarity immigration appeared, which, in addition to political exiles and emigres, includes many talented cultural figures.

America since 1939 remains, as it was in the nineteenth century, a haven and a promised land for Poles. By 1980, there were more than 8,000,000 Polish Americans of all generations living in the United States.

The Canadian-Polish community numbering 254,485 according to the 1981 federal census, shares common bonds with the American-Polish community, but also possesses its own distinctive history. Prior to 1915, a handful of political exiles, including the distinguished Sir Casimir Gzowski, made their way to Canada. The majority of the immigrants, however, were like their American counterparts, farmers and unskilled laborers, most of whom settled on the prairies. Among the best known Polish Canadians were the Kashubs, who settled in Renfrew County, Ontario beginning in the 1850s. During the interwar years, Polish laborers came to farms in Western Canada, to the forests of northern Ontario, and to the mines of Alberta, Ontario and Quebec. After World War II, there was, as in the United States, a new immigration of political emigres and soldier exiles. Seeing themselves as the Polish nation in exile, they also altered the nature and increased the size and organizational complexity of the Polish-Canadian community. A consumer immigration from

Communist Poland followed them after 1956. These new arrivals were opposed to the Polish political system and dissatisfied with living conditions there. Finally, since 1980, Canada possesses its own Solidarity immigration, including many well-educated individuals and professionals.

The rural Poles who settled in Canada before 1915 carried with them an image of Poland as an oppressed country, their own Polish identity, and, like their fellow Poles in the United States, a sense of themselves as the "fourth" and the only free "province" of the Polish nation. The historian Robert Harney observed that in the years from 1880 to the 1930's, the North American Poles had only a limited sense of the significance of the Canadian-United States border. Canadian Poles received some of their religious leadership from the American side of the border, read the Polish papers of Chicago or Buffalo as well as their own, and shared some common fraternal links and a Polish patriotic consciousness. After World War II, the difficulties of adjustment for the emigre-soldier generation were eased not only by the existence of the pre-war Polish-Canadian organizations, but also by the efforts of the national organizations in Montreal and Toronto, which drew them into the North American Polish community with its comforting sense of shared experiences, common religious faith, and political patriotism. And Canadian Polonia, like its American counterpart, has contributed its share of artists, writers, academicians and educated professionals to a pluralistic New World country.

Each immigrant generation and every individual immigrant leaves a mark in North America, thus enriching the Continent's Polish heritage. The physical sign posts are the bronze monuments, steel bridges, concrete streets, stone churches, brick schools, national homes, museums, fraternal lodges, culture centers, and Falcon nests. These structures incarnate and house the human spirit of a nation and its immigrant children and exiles.

North America's Polish heritage is not monolithic, nor can it be discovered and enjoyed on one trip, in a single place, or in a single day. This guide will facilitate your discovery of that legacy.

Stanislaus A. Blejwas, Connecticut State Professor and Professor
of History Central Connecticut State University

Publisher's Preface

Few people are aware of the extensive contribution of Polish-Americans to our country. Polish-Americans seem to have slipped quietly through the history of the United States, with a profile as flat as the wide plains covering most of their forefathers' native land. Yet their contributions have been many. This guide, in addition to providing interesting, informative, and stimulating sites for tourists to explore, also serves to introduce Americans to a part of their heritage, which is vastly unknown to them. As a tourist visiting various parts of America, you will be excited, uplifted, and in some instances deeply moved and flattered to get to know first-hand about some of the great and wonderful things your fellow Americans of Polish descent have accomplished on behalf of us all.

Publisher's Introduction

This is the first attempt to collect information of help to the traveler in search of Polish heritage in North America. Wherever you live and wherever you travel, visiting the sites listed will give you a deeper understanding of our past.

We have a special request to all our readers. We tried to be as comprehensive and accurate as possible. Nonetheless, since this is the first edition of this book, which will be updated from time to time, please let us have your comments and suggestions.

Please understand, however, that we have omitted many sites that cannot be visited by tourists (e.g. private libraries & collections of art), and most of the businesses, which normally advertise in the "yellow pages." Clubs and associations, which do not have facilities for tourists are also not listed.

The purpose of this book is to guide readers to sites, which are tangible landmarks of Polish heritage in North America. It does not, however, permit us to dwell on hundreds of other intangible aspects of the Polish contribution to America and Canada: the achievements of Polish scholars, scientists, writers, artists, engineers, teachers, entrepreneurs, and professionals in many fields. Nor can we list the many Polish churches, which mark the trail of Polish immigration. There are some 800 Polish Roman Catholic Churches and scores of Polish National Catholic Churches to be found in North America and many, if not most of them, are repositories of ethnic life and art. Whether noted in this book or not, such churches merit a visit and often are centers of local Polish-American and Polish-Canadian ethnic life.

No one can work on a book like this without becoming more conscious of the vast canvas of Polish-American endeavors and more proud of Polish-American achievements. This journey along the Polish Heritage Trail has already been rewarding beyond all expectations.

This guide would not have been possible without the tremendous support generously given by Polish-American organizations, the press, and countless individuals who as advisers, volunteer editors, photographers, and researchers spent many hours gathering, writing or compiling information. We thank them all, most sincerely.

The Editors

How to Use This Guide

If you look in the Index of Names and Sites, on p. 237 you will find the sites listed alphabetically, with page numbers given. Turn to the appropriate page numbers for a complete explanation of each site and how to get there. Alternately, you may wish to explore the various sites in a particular state or town in that state. In this case, please turn to the Table of Contents (p. xvii to xx), where the listings are grouped alphabetically by state. For full background information on major figures (Kosciuszko, Pulaski, etc.) read all entries listed under that name.

Table of Contents

Tourist Sites in U.S.A.

ARIZONA

Phoenix

FACTS AND FIGURES

There are several dynamic Polish-American cultural and social organizations in the state of Arizona. Phoenix most probably has the largest Polish-American population of any city or town in the state.

Even though the approximately seventy Poles who went to Arizona at the end of the last century came in search of their fortune, most Poles who eventually settled in this state did so to retire. Nonetheless, beginning with the 1970's, a growing stream of young and relatively recent emigre professionals from Poland have made Arizona their home.

WHAT TO SEE

THE PULASKI CLUB

Also known as the POLISH HOME OF PHOENIX, it is located at 4331 East McDowell Road, in Phoenix. It was organized in 1940 to preserve Polish history, language, and customs for the children of the Polish-American citizens of Phoenix. The Club recently celebrated its Golden Anniversary of service. There is

1

a library on the premises with many volumes of Polish literature, history, as well as children's books. The club members meet every second Saturday of the month for a business meeting followed by a social featuring Polish food and music. If you're passing through the city, and would like to join in the social part, or would like to know what hours and days of the week the Club is open to the public, please call (602) 924-0796.

HOW TO GET THERE

Take McDowell Road East to 43rd Street or the Freeway to 44th Street, then North to McDowell Road.

CALIFORNIA

Anaheim

FACTS AND FIGURES

There is nothing particularly Polish about the city of Anaheim. But it does contain at least one noteworthy monument to Polish artistic genius which we discuss below. While in town, visit The Helen Modjeska Park for a picnic lunch. It can be reached from St. Catherine's Military School Chapel by going South on Harbor to Ball Road, West to Nutwood, South for 1 block.

There is a large statue of Helen Modjeska in Pearson Park, Harbor Boulevard at Cypress Avenue (Sycamore is North boundary, Cypress is South boundary). To get there take # 5 to Lincoln exit-East on Lincoln to Harbor, then North to Cypress. Also, # 91 to Harbor Blvd, then South on Harbor to Sycamore.

WHAT TO SEE

SAINT CATHERINE'S MILITARY SCHOOL CHAPEL

It was designed by the Polish-American architect J. George Szeptycki. The murals and stained glass windows inside the chapel are the handiwork of the famous Polish-American artist Jan Henryk de Rosen. The chapel was completed in 1956.

Freeway #91 to Harbor Boulevard exit. South to 215 N. Harbor Boulevard. Or, Freeway #5, exit Harbor Boulevard, and North to 215 Harbor Boulevard.

Glendale

WHAT TO SEE

FOREST LAWN MEMORIAL PARK-HALL OF THE CRUCIFIXION-RESURRECTION

The largest religious painting in the world is displayed in the Hall of the Crucifixion-Resurrection at Forest Lawn Memorial Park, 1712 South Glendale Avenue.

1) Forest Lawn Memorial Park-Hall of the Crucifixion-Resurrection. Glendale, CA

2) The Crucifixion of Christ by Jan Styka (Central section). Glendale, CA

This panoramic canvas, 195 feet long and 45 feet high, was conceived by the famous Polish patriot, pianist, and statesman, Ignacy Jan Paderewski, and painted by the great Polish artist Jan Styka. Since it was installed at Forest Lawn in 1951, nearly 20 million people from all over the world have seen this moving portrayal of Christ's crucifixion. All the biblical characters associated with the crucifixion are part of the panorama. The figures

3

are all life-size and number 2,000. Every one of the 800 seats in the Hall is equipped with a listening device, so viewers can follow the 20 minute recorded lecture as a light beam moves across the painting, highlighting the more important figures shown. Open from 10 a.m. to 4 p.m. Admission free; donations of $1.00 per adult accepted.

HOW TO GET THERE

Take Golden State Freeway to Los Feliz Boulevard (which further on becomes Los Feliz Road), which ends at Glendale Avenue. Take a right onto Glendale Avenue, go to Cathedral Drive, and from there you can easily locate the Hall of the Crucifixion.

Los Angeles

FACTS AND FIGURES

There is a well-organized Polish-American community in Los Angeles, and it is culturally very lively. Poles and Polish-Americans have been associated with Los Angeles since well before World War II.

WHAT TO SEE

1) OUR LADY OF THE BRIGHT MOUNT ROMAN CATHOLIC CHURCH

The church, at 3424 West Adams Boulevard,which was designed and built by the architect J. George Szeptycki, contains a mosaic of Our Lady of Czestochowa by Polish-American artist Stefan Mrozewski. Behind the main altar there is a fresco painting which was commissioned in Italy, *The Stations of the Cross,* and donated to the church by the Polish-born actress Pola Negri, and by Margaret West.

2) THE POLISH LENDING LIBRARY (MILLENIUM LIBRARY)

The Polish Lending Library in Los Angeles was established in 1935. Today it is called the Millennium Library in honor of the worldwide 1966 celebration of 1,000 years of Christianity in Poland. The library contains books in Polish as well as books about Poles, Polish-Americans and Poland written in English and other languages. The collection currently numbers over 5,000 volumes. It includes history, biographies, literature, geography, music, and drama. It is housed in the basement of the church.

HOW TO GET THERE

(1) Take the Santa Monica Freeway to Arlington Avenue, go South (right) onto Arlington to Adams Boulevard. Take a right onto Adams Boulevard. The church is on your left a few blocks down.

San Diego

FACTS AND FIGURES

San Diego has a small and culturally dedicated Polish-American community. There are several Polish-American social, civic, and cultural organizations in and around San Diego.

WHAT TO SEE

POLISH COTTAGE

The Polish American Association of Southern California and other Polish-American organizations together run and maintain the Polish Cottage in Balboa Park. It is under the sponsorship of the House of Pacific Relations.

The Polish Cottage is open every Sunday afternoon. Displays of Polish art and crafts are shown, and Polish food specialties are served. There is no admission charge to the Park or the area. Once or twice a year, special Polish cultural programs are held for the public in front of the cottage.

HOW TO GET THERE

Use Freeway Number 5 (San Diego Freeway) or Freeway Number 163 (Cabrillo Freeway). There are many signs for Balboa Park, which has the best zoo in California, in addition to the showcases of various national cultures.

San Francisco

Prince Andre' Poniatowski, Baron Jan Henryk de Rosen, Helena Modjeska, Paderewski, Captain Alexander Zakrzewski, and Casimir Bielawski are some of the great Polish names that in various ways have been connected with the growth and development of Northern California since the early part of the nineteenth century. Captain Bielawski arrived in San Francisco in 1853 and worked in the U.S. Land Office for 45 years. He became the first President of the new Polish Society in California, in 1863. Prince Andre' Poniatowski founded, in 1897, a power company, which is known today as the Pacific Gas & Electric Company (which brought electricity to San Francisco in 1902). He and his wife lived in the Crocker Mansion, which burned in the 1906 earthquake. On its site stands Grace Cathedral.

WHAT TO SEE

1) THE POLISH CLUB

The Polish Club is at 3040 22nd Street (South of Mission Street). It opened in 1926 as The Polish House. The Club is open for Polish cultural and historical programs and commemorations. For information on the schedule of activities you can call the Polish Arts and Culture Foundation at 415-474-7070.

2) GRACE CATHEDRAL

Grace Cathedral (Episcopalian). On top of Nob Hill, on the site of the former Crocker Mansion.

The Western and Northern arcades of the cathedral are decorated with the murals of the Polish-American artist Jan Henryk de Rosen. These famous murals depict the Nativity, the first Anglican service in California, St. Augustine, and King Ethelbert, St. Clare, Father Junipero Serra, and other famous persons connected with the Anglican church and its history in California.

The main sanctuary gates and the grille of the Chapel of Grace in the Cathedral are the work of the "Cellini of Wrought Iron," the Polish artist Samuel Yellin. The altar rail was crafted by his son after the elder Yellin's death in 1940.

3) THE POLISH ARTS AND CULTURE FOUNDATION

The Polish Arts and Culture Foundation, 1290 Sutter Street, at Van Ness Avenue, telephone 415-474-7070. It contains the only collection in the world of the paintings of Stefan Norblin, Polish aristocrat and world-renowned artist, court painter to the Maharajahs of India and to the King of Iraq before World War II, portraitist, among others, of Bank of America founder Giannini and other San Francisco luminaries.

HOW TO GET THERE

(1) Take Highway 101 to 17th Street, make a left onto South Van Ness Avenue, proceed to 22nd Street.
(2) Corner of California and Taylor Streets in downtown San Francisco. It stands across the park from the Fairmont Hotel.
(3) Take Highway 101 (Van Ness Avenue) to Sutter Street and (heading North) take a left(a very short distance) to 1290 Sutter. It's about one mile North of the Civic Center.

Santa Ana

FACTS AND FIGURES

The Bowers Museum contains a large Helena Modjeska memorabilia collection. Even though this is the only Polish-American heritage site in Santa Ana, it is well worth the sidetrip. Helena Modjeska was, after all, not just a well-known Polish actress. She was the most famous Shakespearean actress of the nineteenth century, and she left an indelible mark on American dramatic culture and appreciation of Shakespeare.

WHAT TO SEE

THE BOWERS MUSEUM

The Bowers Museum has the largest collection of Modjeska memorabilia in the world. Included are photographs, books, clothing, programs, costumes, and personal effects. There is also a large oil painting by the 19th century Polish painter Jozef Chelmonski, which the artist presented to Modjeska as a wedding gift. Chelmonski made his fortune in Paris and London, getting large sums of money for his realistic troikas in full gallop and other scenes from Poland, the Ukraine, and Russia. Hours are 10:00 a.m. to 5:00 p.m. Call in advance (714) 567 3600

HOW TO GET THERE

Take the Santa Ana Freeway (Number 5). Exit on 17th Street, Santa Ana. Go West 3 blocks on 17th street to Main street, then North on Main, three blocks, to the museum.

Santiago Canyon, Orange County

WHAT TO SEE

ARDEN: HELENA MODJESKA HOUSE AND GARDEN

Helena Modjeska House and Garden is a tribute to the great Polish actress Helena Modjeska, (in the original Polish spelling: Modrzejewska; 1840-1909), who lived in Orange County, California, for almost thirty years. She was a social and cultural pioneer in California and was generous with her money to various religious and charitable causes. She was widely respected and loved by her fellow Californians, as her funeral procession in Los Angeles in April, 1909, attested, when thousands of people lined the streets to bid her farewell.

Modjeska's century-old house, Arden, still stands in its live oak grove on the banks of Santiago Creek in the foothills of the Santa Ana Mountains. The historic home now belongs to the County of Orange, which is now engaged in extensive renovation and historic preservation projects.

The actress and her husband, Karol Bozenta Chlapowski, lived in the house from 1888 to 1906. The home was designed by Stanford White and is the only surviving example of his style in California. Helena Modjeska had named her rustic retreat "Arden" for Shakespeare's Forest of Arden, setting for his pastoral play, "As You Like It."

In l992, the house and its 14.4-acre gardens were designated as a United States National Historic Landmark.

The purpose of the park is to provide a cultural, educational, and recreational opportunity in an historic setting which depicts the life and personality of Modjeska.

The Helena Modjeska Foundation, Post Office Box 9582 Newport Beach, California, 92658; (714-499-2995 or 714-768-8907) is an independent organization set up to assist the County of Orange to acquire authentic period furnishings and to create a Helen Modjeska House Museum. It publishes a newsletter to keep members and contributors informed of special events to be held in the house.

3) Arden - Helena Modjeska ranch home, about 1898. Santiago Canyon, CA

The park is open to visitors five days a week, including weekends, from 10:00 a.m. to 4:00 p.m. There is an entrance fee. For reservation information, call the Heritage Hill Historical Park: (714) 855-2028. Off-site parking with shuttle bus service. No separate fees (apart from park entrance fees).

HOW TO GET THERE

Take the Freeway Number 5 (San Diego Freeway) to the El Toro exit, then East on El Toro Road (S-18) to Modjeska Canyon Road and a staging area. All visitors must have reservations, either as a group or as individuals. Shuttle buses will be provided from the off-site area to the site.

Stanford

Stanford University is a world-famous seat of learning and research. It has an oustanding collection of books and documents on Poland, Polish history, language, music, science, and culture.

WHAT TO SEE

HOOVER INSTITUTION ON WAR, REVOLUTION, AND PEACE

The Witold S. Sworakowski Collection on Poland at the Hoover Institution on War, Revolution, and Peace, Stanford, CA 94305, is a magnificent and unique collection of documents from recent Polish history. Named after the first Curator of the Polish Collection, the late Witold S. Sworakowski (1903-1979), it is the largest source of documentation on recent Polish history outside of Poland. The holdings include over 200 archival and manuscript collections, 50,000 volumes of books, and 3,000 titles of periodicals and newspapers relating to Polish history from the late 19th century until today. Within the collection, there are 500 boxes of documents from the Polish Foreign Ministry files for the years 1925-1945. There are 54 boxes of papers from the Polish Embassy in the Soviet Union during the war years, including many documents reflecting the search for the missing officers from the camps in Kozielsk, Ostaszkow, and Starobielsk, over 15,500 prisoners who were massacred on Stalin's orders in 1940. There are 100 boxes of documents from the Polish Armed Forces files in World War II, including the papers of General Wladyslaw Anders and the Polish Second Corps. There are 272 boxes of papers given to the Hoover Institution by Leopold Labedz, an eminent Polish journalist. Jan Nowak's papers deposited here will not be available during his lifetime. Some of these documents may be accessible for viewing to visitors. The vast majority of these documents are not catalogued, and are not readily available.

Please contact in advance to determine accessibility if you are not a researcher.

HOW TO GET THERE

If you are in San Francisco, take Highway 101 South to the Stanford exit. If you called ahead, you will have precise directions to the collection. Otherwise, ask for the collection's location once you get on campus.

Yorba Linda

JOHN PAUL II POLISH CENTER

The recently established JOHN PAUL II POLISH CENTER, a Roman Catholic Church is filled with artifacts central to Poland's religious experience over the centuries, and a Polish souvenir and book shop. The Center is actually established as a "Mission" in service to the Polish American community, much of which is composed of newcomers who have established new lives for themselves and their families over the last decade. Address: 3999 Rose Drive, Yorba Linda, CA.

COLORADO

Pinewood Springs

FACTS AND FIGURES

Of the 1.4 million Poles who emigrated to the United States during the so-called Great Emigration of 1899 to 1915, 974 settled in Colorado—compared with 338,347 in Pennsylvania and a mere 30 in Alaska! It is known for sure that two were Roman Catholic priests. Otherwise, the presence of Poles in this beautiful state has not been widely recorded. Nonetheless, there is a strong Polish-American community in Denver today, with smaller concentrations across the state.

VILLA TATRA

If you've decided to take a ride to Estes Park or to Rocky Mountain National Park, you should certainly stop in at the Villa Tatra. It was founded and is run by Polish-Americans proud of their Polish mountaineer heritage. The Villa Tatra is not just a restaurant serving ethnic Polish food, it is also a place to buy various mementos from Poland. Most importantly, the entire building, both inside and out, is built in the "Podhale" style, with a unique and beautiful mix of wood and stone. In addition, there is an art gallery of Polish and East European art.

HOW TO GET THERE

If travelling from Denver, take Highway 36 North. Continue through Boulder past Lyons until you come to Pinewood Springs, which is 6 miles outside of Lyons. If you want to reserve a place, call in advance: 303-823-6819.

CONNECTICUT

FACTS AND FIGURES

When Polish poet and essayist Julian Ursyn Niemcewicz visited Connecticut in 1797 and praised the "bold spirits" of its traders and the simplicity and industry of its citizens, he also noted "everyone is from one stock, everyone is descendant of the English." By 1910, however, Yankees accounted for only 35.5% of the State's population. The remaining 64.5% of the population were European immigrants, most of whom arrived after the Civil War. In 1870, there were only 83 Poles in Connecticut, but by 1930 the figure was 133,813, 13% of the State's population. In the 1990s Americans of Polish origin, some 300,000, are 9% of Connecticut's population. While some of the very early settlers may have been refugees from the January Insurrection of 1863, the majority of Poles who flooded after 1880 were peasants in search of "bread and freedom." They provided the cheap labor for the State's mills and factories, and also made Connecticut an important Polish American center.

The Connecticut State motto: *Qui Transtulit Sustinet* - (He Who Transplanted Still Sustains) was realized by Polish immigrants. The immigrants erected with their own funds and on their own initiative 24 Roman Catholic and 9 Polish National Catholic parishes, as well as schools, branches of all the major Polish American fraternal organizations, Falcon nests (The Falcons is a Polish fraternal organization dedicated to physical fitness), and Polish homes and monuments.

Ansonia, Bloomfield, Bridgeport, Bristol, Colchester, Cromwell, Derby, East Hartford, East Haven, Elmwood, Enfield, Glastonbury, South Glastonbury, Hamden, Hartford, Kensington, Manchester, Meriden, Middletown, Milford, New Britain, New Haven, Newington, Norwich, Plainville, Rockville, Rocky Hill, Salem, Shelton, Southington, Stamford, Terryville, Thomaston, Torrington, Vernon, Wallingford, Waterbury, West Hartford, Wethersfield, Willimantic, Windsor, Windsor Locks; these Connecticut towns and cities, scattered throughout the State, all contain Polish settlements, active a century or more after their founding.

Ansonia

WHAT TO SEE

GEN. DAVID HUMPHREYS HOUSE
HISTORICAL MUSEUM

Ansonia is the hometown of local Revolutionary War hero General David Humphreys. The Polish patriot, revolutionary leader, and youngest general in Washington's army, General Tadeusz Kosciuszko, was a friend of Humphreys'. Kosciuszko was a guest in Humphreys' home on Elm Street in Ansonia. That home is now the Gen. David Humphreys House Historical Museum at 37 Elm Street. Thanks to the Kosciuszko Historical Society of nearby Derby, there is also a Kosciuszko Room in the museum, and it contains correspondence between the two friends as well as other interesting Kosciuszko memorabilia, including books, paintings, mementos, and personal objects that belonged to the Polish-American hero.

The museum is open to the public Monday through Friday, 9a.m.-4:30p.m. You can also see it by appointment. Call (203) 735-1908.

If you are coming from New York City, take I-95 to State Highway 8 (exit 27, past Bridgeport), go past Shelton to exit 15, take a left (North): onto Derby Avenue; where it forks, take the right fork (Elm Street). Go to 37 Elm.

Bethlehem

The name of this Christmastown in Hebrew means House of Bread. It is therefore most appropriate that Christmas cards with Oplatek (wafer) should be available here, sold at the Abbey Fair in August, the Christmastown Festival in early December, and by mail all year round from the Polish-styled Domek on Flanders Road. One mile North of the famous Benedictine Abbey Regina Laudis, it is the headquarters of a one-woman industry of Scouting (in more sense than one), writing and publishing (*Polonia Vademecum, Historia Harcerstwa w Stanach Zjednoczonych*). Ewa Gierat is an indefatigable participant in good causes and Polonia activities. If you happen to be near Bethlehem, give her a call at (203) 266-7967. The town is in Litchfield County, at the crossroads of Rte 132 and 61.

Enfield

FACTS AND FIGURES

Poles first arrived in the Thompsonville section of Enfield in 1902, recruited as part of a scheme by the management of the Bigelow-Hartford Carpet Company to break up a strike for higher wages. They were also, like the Italians, imported to fill jobs at times when the carpet mill was expanding. The immigrants, mostly

14

from Galicia(Southern Poland), organized the Society of Free Krakovians in 1904, and in 1915 the parish of St. Adalbert was formally established.

The Polish presence in Enfield was enhanced in 1932 when the sixth American province of the Felician sisters was established on the Longview estate, and our Lady of Angels Convent subsequently opened.

WHAT TO SEE

1) ST. ADALBERT'S CHURCH

St. Adalbert's Church, 90 Alden Avenue, (203) 745-4837. The present church, a brick structure with limestone and artificial granite trimming, was dedicated on July 8, 1928. Its most dramatic feature is the 90 foot high bell tower, which begins as a square and ends at the top with an eight-sided roof. The style of the church is Romanesque, characterized by rounded arches, and at each end of the building there is a rosette window. The church is reported to be patterned on an unknown church in Poland, from where the pastor, the Galician Rev. Stanislaw Federkiewicz hailed.

2) FELICIAN SISTERS ARCHIVES

The Felician Sisters Archives are located at Our Lady of Angels Convent, 1315 Enfield Street. (203) 745-6305 or 745-7791. These archives have been designated as the main depository for all Felician provinces in the United States, Poland, and elsewhere. They contain biographical materials about the individual sisters, history and souvenir books from parishes, schools and other institutions staffed by the Order, and internal records and publications.

HOW TO GET THERE

Take I-91 North from Hartford to Route 5. Take Route 5 (which becomes Enfield Avenue) North into Enfield. Our Lady of Angels Convent is on the right. To reach St. Adalbert's, proceed further along Route 5 to Alden Street, and turn left.

Hartford

FACTS AND FIGURES

Connecticut's capital is a leading center of insurance and the head-quarters of the aerospace conglomerate, United Technologies. It is also the home of a Polish community dating back to the 1870s which found work at Colt Firearms, Allen Manufacturing, Capewell Manufacturing, Emhart, and Atlantic Tool.

After World War II, Polish emigres arrived. Urban renewal and economic mobility encouraged the earlier first and second generation Poles to migrate to the suburbs of East Hartford, Wethersfield, Newington, Glastonbury and West Hartford. Many return on weekends for functions at the Ss Cyril and Methodius parish and the National Home, and for the annual Pulaski Day Parade on the second Sunday of October.

WHAT TO SEE

1) SS CYRIL AND METHODIUS CHURCH

Ss Cyril and Methodius Church, 63 Governor Street, tel. (203)522-9157. The present church was dedicated in 1917. It was erected in 1902. The present neo-Gothic structure is decorated with traditional Polish iconography. Two White Eagles were placed on the roof of the presbiterium, "bearing witness to the Polish founders of this house of worship." The church also includes a chapel to the Black Madonna.

4) Polish National Home. Hartford, CT

5) Pulaski Monument. Hartford, CT

2) THE POLISH NATIONAL HOME

The Polish National Home, 60 Charter Oak Avenue, Pulaski Plaza, tel. (203)247-1784. This superb example of Art Deco architecture is included in the National and State Registers of architecturally significant buildings. Designed by Henry F. Ludorf of Hartford, it is the city's most exuberant Art Deco building. The Home's exterior still retains its bas-relief decoration, bronze grill work, light features, and bronze doors typical of the geometricized art deco. Guests at the Home have included Richard Nixon and George Bush. The Home remains a meeting place for Polish clubs.

3) GENERAL CASIMIR PULASKI
MEMORIAL MONUMENT

General Casimir Pulaski Memorial Monument. Pulaski Plaza. The dream for a memorial to General Pulaski goes back to 1946. But it was only realized during the Bicentennial Celebration of 1976. The local Polish-American citizenry collected the funds, and nationally recognized sculptor Granville W. Carter of Baldwin, Long Island, fashioned the bronze monument. The overall statue, including the pedestal, rises 22 feet, and was the first heroically-proportioned equestrian commission in the United States in twenty years. The magnificent portrayal of the Revolutionary War General represents him astride his horse, pointing the way to battle and victory with his sword. This monument joins the very elite rank of important public bronzes on display in the continental United States.

HOW TO GET THERE

(1,2&3) Take I-91 to Hartford, to I-484 and turn South (left) onto Columbus Blvd. Then go one block to Charter Oak Avenue, turn right and go one block. The Polish National Home will be on your right. The Pulaski Monument is two blocks further down on Pulaski Mall (Main Street between Charter Oak Avenue and Sheldon Street). The SS Cyril & Methodius Church is within a block of the Polish National Home.

Lakeville

FACTS AND FIGURES

Sinclair Lewis and Wanda Landowska—it would take a long time to figure out such a combination. Nonetheless, they both inhabited the same house in Lakeville, Connecticut, though at different times and in different eras. Sinclair Lewis lived there in the 1930's while married to Dorothy Thompson, and Landowska lived there at first intermittenly and later permanently, from 1947 until her death in 1959 at the age of eighty.

Landowska was one of the greatest pioneers in music in our century. A Catholic, and a Pole of Jewish ancestry, she brought back to full professional competence the art of the harpsichord, which had lain dormant for well over a century, while keyboard artists lavished their time, talent and ambitions on the piano.

WHAT TO SEE

LANDOWSKA CENTER

Formerly known as Oak Knoll, the house is now called the Landowska Center. The house has a very impressive wood-panelled great hall and staircase. There is a huge stone fireplace built into the wall at the base. The acoustic quality of the parlor is so outstanding that RCA used to send their men and equipment to the house from New York City for recording sessions with Landowska.

6) *Wanda Landowska Center (Oak Knoll). Lakeville, CT*

Pictures of the world-famous harpsichordist line the walls, including photos with her house guests, many of whom were the most distinguished men and women of their day in their respective fields.

The Center contains Landowska's annotated scores, her instruments, and various other memorabilia of her great career. It may be seen by appointment only. Please call Denise Restout, Wanda Landowska's companion of 26 years, as well as her student: 203-435-9308.

HOW TO GET THERE

If you're travelling on I-95, get off at exit 15 in Connecticut, which will get you onto U.S. Route 7, and head up to Lakeville by taking a left onto State Route 112. Then, make a right onto U.S. Route 44 which goes right into Lakeville. The Landowska Center is on Route 44 and is on Connecticut's Historic Houses list.

Meriden

The "Silver City," Meriden was for many years the home of such famous cutlery firms as the Meriden Britannia Company, International Silver, and William Rogers Manufacturing. Polish immigrants from Prussian Poland first settled in Meriden in 1880. Followed by peasants from Austrian and Russian Poland, these immigrants in 1891 erected Connecticut's first Polish parish, St. Stanislaus. In 1980, there were 9,582 individuals of Polish ancestry in Meriden, 17% of the city's 57,118 citizens. Prominent in Meriden's political, economic, and athletic history, Meriden's Poles have left their physical mark upon the city with a church (1908), school (1915), community center (1937), and a Pulaski Monument (1934).

WHAT TO SEE

1) ST. STANISLAUS CHURCH

7) St. Stanislaus Church. Meriden, CT

St. Stanislaus Church, corner of Olive and Akron Streets, tel. (203) 235-6341. Dedicated on Labor Day, September 7, 1908, the red brick Lombard church (Roman style) reflects the tastes of long-time pastor Msgr. Jan Ceppa (1906-1948), who studied in Italy. The church seats 900. On the right altar's side hangs an interesting canvas of Our Lady of Czestochowa painted by the Galician artist Jan Tabinski from Rzeszow, and which was the gift of the second pastor, Rev. Tomasz Misicki.

8) Pulaski Monument. Meriden, CT.

2) PULASKI MONUMENT

The monument, on Broad Street, stands across from the cemetery of Meriden's Revolutionary War veterans. The handsome six-foot bronze statue of Pulaski standing, hand on the hilt of his sword, rests on a foundation of 20 tons of concrete stone and Vermont Barry granite, and is the work of parishioner Juliusz T. Gutzwa. The plinth reads: "Meriden Polonia." The dedication on October 7, 1934, accompanied by a parade of 5,000 and a crowd of 20,000, was attended by Gov. Wilbur Cross and Mieczyslaw Marchlewski, the Polish Consul General from New York. The Inscription on the monument reads: "Casimir Pulaski

Polish-American Patriot Aided the Colonies in Their Fight for Liberty Dying Gloriously In Action."

HOW TO GET THERE

From I-691 take Rt 8 to Rt 5 (Broad Street) South. Go past 3 lights, and the Pulaski Monument will be on the esplanade in the middle of Broad Street. At the fourth light, take a right onto Olive Street, and go two blocks to St. Stanislaus Church.

New Britain

FACTS AND FIGURES

Incorporated in 1850, New Britain became a major manufacturing center and is still the headquarters of Stanley Tools. Polish immigrants, primarily from Eastern Poland, began to settle in the city in the 1880s, and in 1895 Connecticut's second Polish parish, Sacred Heart, was erected under the influential and controversial pastor, Msgr. Lucyan Bojnowski. Bojnowski created a nearly complete urban village, erecting two churches (1895, and the present stone structure, 1904), a school (1910), a religious order (Daughters of Mary of the Immaculate Conception - 1904), a cemetery (1912), orphanage (1923), a home for the aged (1925), a Polish language weekly (*Przewodnik Katolicki* 1907-1966), approximately 25 parish societies, and several business enterprises.

Dissatisfaction with Bojnowski's pastoral style led in 1927 to the founding of a second parish, Holy Cross. The Polish National Catholic Church of the Transfiguration was established in 1942. Other important community centers include the Gen. Jozef Haller Veterans Post and the Pulaski Democratic Club on Grove Street, and the PNA Hall on Ward Street.

New Britain remains the most important political center of the Connecticut Polish-American community. The first Pole to be elected to the State Legislature (Lucjan Maciora,1928) Congressman-at-Large (Boleslaus J. Monkiewicz, 1938), and mayor of a major Connecticut city (Henryk Gwiazda, 1946) were all victories for New Britain Polish-Americans.

New Britain, because of the availability of jobs, has continually been a point of entry for new immigrants from Poland. After World War II, political emigres and displaced persons arrived, and in 1980 erected the first Katyn Monument in the United States at Sacred Heart Cemetery. In the l980s refugees from Martial Law in Poland arrived, and many joined Solidarity International, a human rights organization which erected a monument to Rev. Jerzy Popieluszko at Walnut Hill Park in 1989.

The New Britain campus of Connecticut State University, Central Connecticut State University, has been home to a Polish Studies Program since 1974. In 1984, CCSU inaugurated an historical archive and research center concerning Connecticut's and New England's Polish-Americans. This is the first effort in New England to preserve and record the history and contribution of Polish-Americans to Connecticut and to New England.

WHAT TO SEE

1) SACRED HEART CHURCH

Sacred Heart Church, 163 Broad Street, tel. 203-229-0081 or 225-4278. Dedicated on February 28, 1904, this stone edifice reflects the eastern Polish roots of many of the original settlers. Built in the form of a Gothic cross, the church is 160 feet long, 78 feet wide, and 170 feet high. Erected with gray-blue granite stone on the outside, on the inside it is decorated with white sand marble.

(Next to the church on Grove Street are the Gen. Jozef Haller Post of the Polish Army Veterans' Association of America Stow. Weteranow Armii Polskiej, tel. 229-6155 and the Pulaski Democratic Club).

HOW TO GET THERE

If coming from the South (New York), take I-95 to exit 48 to I-91. Exit at State Route 72, which will get you into New Britain, where you pick up State Route 71 (Stanley Street) which crosses Broad Street.

2) HOLY CROSS CHURCH

Holy Cross Church, corner of Farmington Avenue and Biruta Street, tel. (203) 229-2011. The present church was openened in

1942. It was built in pure Norman gothic style in the form of a cross with a 175 foot tower. There is a richly carved oak gothic altar, and on both sides of the church, a series of colored stained windows depicting scenes from the life of Christ and Polish saints and patrons. In the back vestibule next to an icon of the Black Madonna there are two modern stained glass windows, one depicting St. Maximilian Kolbe and the other Pope John Paul II.

HOW TO GET THERE

Coming from either New York or Boston on I-84, take exit 37 (Finemann Road). Follow Finemann Road, which becomes Farmington Avenue, toward New Britain.

3) KATYN MONUMENT

Katyn Monument, Sacred Heart Cemetery. Take the Osgood Street entrance, to the veterans' section of the Cemetery. This simple but eloquent black granite monument, which reads : "Katyn 1940" was dedicated in May, 1980, "In Memory of Our Comrades in Arms-Polish Prisoners of War Who Were Massacred By The Soviet Russia at the Katyn Forest In The Spring, 1940." The monument was the initiative of the Gen. Jozef Haller Post No. 111 of the Polish Army Veterans' Association of America.

Sacred Heart Cemetery is located on a plot of some 200 acres on Osgood Hill. On this property, which was purchased in a far-sighted move by Fr. Bojnowski, stand the buildings of the former Polish orphanage and home for the aged, the mother house of the Daughters of Mary, Mary Immaculate Academy, and a modern nursing home, Bojnowski Manor. On the Sunday before All Souls Day, there is an afternoon procession from Sacred Heart Church to the Cemetery, where Mass is celebrated. On that evening, "Polish Hill" as the cemetery is sometimes called, glows with thousands of candles that have been lit at the graves of ancestors, in the Polish tradition.

HOW TO GET THERE

If coming from New York or Boston, take I-84 to exit 37 (Finneman Road). Take Finneman Road, which becomes Farmington Avenue, toward New Britain. At the light at Osgood Avenue, turn right up the hill.

9) First Katyn Monument in the US, Sacred Heart Cemetery. New Britain, CT.

4) POPIELUSZKO MONUMENT

Popieluszko Monument, Walnut Hill Park. Located in the Park's upper section, this modernistic steel sculpture was designed by Henry Chotkowski. It was dedicated on June 11, 1989. Next to the monument is a granite stone with the inscription *"Zlo dobrem zwyciezaj"* (Conquer Evil With Good). The inscription goes on to note that the monument is dedicated to the Solidarity martyr, Rev. Jerzy Popieluszko, "Who Gave His Life To God And To The Goals Of Solidarnosc -Human Rights, Justice, Peace And Freedom For Poland And For All Mankind. May This Eternal Flame Of Liberty And The Memory Of His Courage And Sacrifice Burn Forever In The Hearts Of All Freedom Loving People." Rev. Popieluszko was murdered by the Polish communist security service in October, 1984.

25

From New York or Boston take I-84 to State Route 72. Follow 72 to the Columbus Boulevard exit. At the light at the end of the exit, turn right and follow the road to the next light at West Main Street, just to the right.

10,11) Popieluszko Monument, Walnut Hill Park. New Britain, CT

5) THE POLISH-AMERICAN ARCHIVES

The Polish-American Archives at Central Connecticut State University. Corner of Wells Street and Sefton Drive. Located in the University's Elihu Burritt Library, the Archives contain minute books, legal papers, and correspondence of fraternals, parishes, church organizations, veterans' groups, priest associations, cultural and scholarship organizations, social and athletic clubs, and political clubs. There are also the papers of former presidents of the Connecticut District of the Polish American Congress, photographs, a collection of histories and souvenir books of Polish parishes and societies throughout New England and the Northeast, unpublished community studies, and political and other memorabilia.

A unique aspect of the archives, formerly known as the Polish-American Archives and Manuscript Collection, is a collection of nearly 40 Polish American newspapers on microfilm, including such regional papers as *Przewodnik Katolicki* (New Britain) and *Kuryer Bostonski* (Boston).

The Archives welcomes and actively solicits donations of material regarding the Polish-American community of New England and elsewhere.

The Archives are available to students, scholars, genealogists, and to the general public. If you are planning to stop by when school is not in session, please call (203) 827-7524 or 827-7469 in advance.

CCSU also houses the Polish Studies Program, and, next to the archives, the Polish Heritage Book Collection, which numbers over 8,000 catalogued volumes.

HOW TO GET THERE

From New York or Boston, take I-95 to I-91, then take State Route 72 to State Route 71, Stanley Street. On Stanley Street head North until you reach the traffic light on Wells Street where the university begins. Continue straight on to the next right, which is Wells Street, and turn right.

From New York or Boston on I-84, take exit 40 to New Britain Avenue, which runs through the West Farms Shopping Malls. Follow New Britain Avenue, which becomes Stanley Street, to the light at Stanley and Ella Grasso Boulevard. Proceed straight to Wells Street, and take a left.

6) POLISH GENEALOGICAL SOCIETY

Polish Genealogical Society of Connecticut, 8 Lyle Road, New Britain, CT 06053, (203) 229-8873. The Archive and Resource Center contains works on Polish-American family history, Polish immigration history, copies of theses, and other unpublished community studies, as well as several hundred histories and commemorative booklets of Polish parishes in the Northeast. The largest archival collection is that of gravestone inscriptions from nearly 300 cemeteries in the Northeastern United States and several locations in Poland. The Archive also houses several manuscript collections, records of Polish organizations, photographs, and a sizeable obituary collection. The repository is open by appointment only; call (203) 229-8873.

Stamford

Home to some of the Polish-American community's most culturally and politically active members, Stamford, is one of the important centers of Polish-American life on the East Coast. Poles started
arriving here at the end of the nineteenth century.

WHAT TO SEE

1) THE FREEDOM BELL

The Freedom Bell at the Holy Name of Jesus Church, 4 Pulaski
Street. In case you get lost among the tiny streets in this old
Polish neighborhood, the phone number of the parish is (203)
323-4967. The church is approaching 100 years of age. The
magnificent bell in its tower was purchased from the Polish
Government after the 1939 World's Fair where it was on display
in the Polish Pavilion. The Icon of the Black Madonna which
can be seen inside the church, is an exact replica of the famous
Black Madonna Icon which hangs in the church of the Pauline
Fathers in Czestochowa, Poland. This replica was also one of the
artifacts in the 1939 Polish Pavilion at the World's Fair and was
purchased for the church in Stamford.

Also remarkable is the Parish Rectory, which was built in 1852/
53 for a Charles Quintard and was almost immediately sold by
him to Duncan Phyfe, the famous New York cabinet maker. This
rectory remains one of the great architectural gems of Stamford
and is an outstanding example of the Italian Villa style, an American interpretation of the villas of the old Roman countryside. The
building was purchased by Holy Name of Jesus church in 1909.
The Bell is rung daily.

2) POLISH AND SLAVIC INFORMATION CENTER

If you want more details about the Polish-American community's
history and current activities in Stamford, including Polish shops
and restaurants, go to the Polish and Slavic Information Center at
36 Pulaski Street.

3) KOSCIUSZKO PARK AND MONUMENT

Kosciuszko Park and Monument is the largest waterfront park in Stamford. Take Washington Boulevard south to Dyke Lane. The Park has a monument to general Tadeusz Kosciuszko, and sits in the middle of the oldest part of the Polish-American community in Stamford.

HOW TO GET THERE

Take I-95 to Exit 7 and go South to find the three sites listed below.

West Hartford

FACTS AND FIGURES

Poles began to move into this old Yankee town after World War II, but in small numbers. West Hartford is home to one of Connecticut's prominent Jewish communities, many of whose members have roots in Poland and Russia.

WHAT TO SEE

1) STATUE OF NOAH WEBSTER

There are no Polish organizations or institutions in West Hartford. Nonetheless, there is a handsome, modernistic statue of Noah Webster, 13 feet tall, which was sculpted by the Polish-American artist Janusz Korczak-Ziolkowski from a single thirty-two ton block of marble. Before accepting the commission to carve Chief Crazy Horse in South Dakota in 1947, the sculptor lived in West Hartford for several years.

Korczak-Ziolkowski's proposal to carve a memorial to West Hartford's most famous native son was accepted by the Town Council with the proviso that the funds be raised from the public. In the end, the artist had to raise much of the funds himself. He offended local opinion in the summer of 1941 by carving without a shirt, with alleged profanity, and working at night, while a local clergyman criticized him for working on Sundays. Ziolkowski maintained that he was a victim of prejudice, frequently being referred to as a "Polack." The artist had the last word. On the book at Webster's side is an inscription of a letter from Webster to John

Jay: "For you I labored, not for my own day, that by the Word men should know brotherhood. My fellow men! You have not understood, since each of you would go his separate way."

Ziolkowski's South Dakota commission turned into his life's work. He was buried there, in 1982, 35 years after he had begun the great mountain carving.

12) Noah Webster Statue by Korczak-Ziolkowski. West Hartford, CT

HOW TO GET THERE

The statue is on the corner of South Main Street and Memorial Drive, next to the Old Town Hall. Main Street can be reached from exit 41 (South Main Street) on I-84.

FLORIDA

FACTS AND FIGURES

Like most Americans, Polish-Americans came down to Florida to retire. They came mostly in the 1950's and on, though some had settled earlier. There are many Polish-American residents of Florida in St. Petersburg, Clearwater, and a few other places on the West Coast, and on the East Coast they are scattered throughout, though mostly concentrated in Miami, Ft. Lauderdale, and Lake Worth-Pompano Beach. Nowadays, a working immigration has hit Florida: Poles from Poland arrive, working as maids, butlers, chauffeurs, and cooks in the estates of the wealthy, and also in various professions, as well as in their own businesses.

The vast majority of Floridians of Polish descent worked hard all their lives at honest, though often back-breaking labor, in the steel mills of Gary, Indiana, the factories and stockyards of Chicago, the textile mills of New England, and elsewhere. Now in the autumn of their lives, they have come down to live in the sun and warmth of the southern climate. They spend a lot of time in the company of their fellow Polish-Americans. Consequently, there are some outstanding Polish social clubs: in Lake Worth, Ft. Lauderdale, Hollywood, and Miami. They serve good food and drink, and feature amiable social dancing with an occasional guest performer.

Miami, though, is where the most serious, continuous Polish cultural activity takes place.

Miami

WHAT TO SEE

THE AMERICAN INSTITUTE OF POLISH CULTURE

The American Institute of Polish Culture, Inc. on 79th Street Causeway in Miami is the major and only full-time cultural organization of the Polish-American community in Florida. Throughout its existence, this Institute has originated several interesting and important cultural initiatives. The Institute has a lending library with over 2,000 volumes and also sells books, which it has published on Polish cultural subjects. The books are in English. The Institute is open daily and visitors are always welcome.

The founder of the Institute, Mrs. Blanka Rosenstiel, is herself an accomplished vocalist, painter, and sculptor.

HOW TO GET THERE

Take I-95 into Miami to 79th Street exit, heading towards Miami Beach. The Institute is located at 1440 79th Street Causeway (it'll be on your right hand side if you are heading toward Miami Beach). There is parking in the rear of the building.

GEORGIA

Savannah

FACTS AND FIGURES

In 1779, American forces were engaging the British in the southern colonies, especially in South Carolina and Georgia. It was Autumn, and the American army, under General Lincoln was marching against the British in Savannah. But an American deserter betrayed the American plans to the British, and General Casimir Pulaski, the heroic young Polish Count who had volunteered for America's fight for independence, fell wounded, leading the cavalry charge.

He died of gangrene two days later aboard the American brig Wasp. There was a commemorative service for him in Charleston. His grave has never been found.

WHAT TO SEE

THE PULASKI MONUMENT

Upon receipt of the news of Pulaski's death, the United States Congress, on November 29, 1779, appointed a committee to design an appropriate monument for the young hero — Pulaski died at the age of thirty-two. But the wheels of government grind slowly. . . Lafayette, the great French hero of the American Revolution, and friend of Pulaski, laid the cornerstone for the monument in Savannah in 1825, almost half a century after Congress initiated the gesture.

13) The Pulaski Monument as reproduced on the cover of "Pulaski March" published in 1879 in Savannah for the Centennial Celebration

Aside from the Pulaski Monument, which is a prominent Savannah point of interest and can easily be located in the city, there are also memorabilia at the Georgia Historical Museum in Savannah, chief among, which is the ball of grapeshot which was extracted from Pulaski's fatal wound.

HOW TO GET THERE

If you are taking I-95 south, get off at Exit 18 (Route 21), which will take you directly into the historic district. Take a right onto Whitaker Street and another right onto Old Louisville Road, one block to West Broad Street. That is the location of the Greater Savannah Exposition and Visitor Center. They will give you the precise location of the monument and of other Pulaski artifacts in the city, as well as brochures and maps.

If you are heading North on I-95, get off at Exit 14 onto Interstate 17 North, which will take you straight to West Broad Street (at the fork, take I-175).

HAWAII

Honolulu

By some estimates there are some 700 Poles living in Hawaii and many more Polish-Americans. Almost one hundred of these "Polish Hawaiians" are associated in the Chopin Society of Hawaii, a two-year old cultural organization whose members have been responsible for an impressive number of Polish events in the heart of the Pacific.

In February 1990, the first ever Polish Films Festival took place in Honolulu. Other functions included a meeting with a visiting Polish poet Ernest Bryll and a concert by the popular entertainer Krzysztof Krawczyk. Lt. Col. Paul Stankiewicz (Ret.) leads the Chopin Society, and two of its founder-members, Mrs. Bozena Jarnot and Robert Dziublowski, have set up a travel agency, Hawaii Polonia Tours, for Polish tourists from all over the world. The Chopin Society's address is: P.O. Box 11384, Honolulu, HI 96828. Telephone (808) 955-4567.

ILLINOIS

Chicago

FACTS AND FIGURES

The Metropolitan New York area may contain the largest Polish-American community on the North American continent, but Chicago and its immediate suburbs are definitely the most visible as far as Polish-American organizational and political activity is concerned.

Prior to World War II, and going back to the latter part of the 19th century, Chicago was the mecca for many Poles seeking work, unable to eke out a living in their own country. After World War II, came the second large wave of immigrants, those who refused to live under a Communist government, and those who had fought with the Allies against the Germans in World War II and decided to opt for freedom in America.

People from all these immigrations have combined to promote political and humanitarian activities through the Polish American Congress, centered in Chicago and Washington, D.C.

The Polish Roman Catholic Union of America dates from 1873. The Polish National Alliance of the United States of North America (PNA) appeared in 1880 in Philadelphia but soon thereafter moved its headquarters to Chicago. The Polish Women's Alliance of

14) Polish Roman Catholic Union of America building which houses the Polish Museum in Chicago

America held its first meetings in 1899 in Chicago at St. Adalbert's Church. Between them, these three organizations today form the backbone of the organized Polish-American community in the United States.

The neighborhood most intensely identified with the Polish-American community in Chicago runs along the axis of Milwaukee Avenue. In the 1930s, and through the '60s the nexus was the "Polonia Triangle"; the crossing of Ashland, Division, and Milwaukee Avenues. The only Polish lay organizations remaining in that proximity today, are the headquarters of the Polish Roman

35

Catholic Union of America and the Polish Museum of America and its library. Be sure to visit historic churches in the vicinity: Holy Trinity Church, St. John Cantius, and St. Stanislaus Kostka.

WHAT TO SEE

1) POLISH MUSEUM OF AMERICA

The Museum is at 984 North Milwaukee Avenue. Founded in 1935, it is one of the oldest and largest ethnic museums in the United States. Located in the center of the first Polish neighborhood in Chicago, it aims to promote the knowledge of Polish culture and history. Its special mission is to promote Polish and Polish-American art in its paintings, graphics, and sculptures by well-known artists.

15) Polish Museum in Chicago - Main Exhibit Hall

The museum contains the largest public collection of Polish art in the United States. Especially the interwar period paintings and sculpture, which were exhibited in the Polish Pavillion during the World's Fair in New York in 1939 are the most significant.

A new addition, Room of Polish Immigration to the United States, is scheduled to be opened in 1992.

The Museum has an extensive collection of personal effects from the great pianist and statesman, Ignacy Paderewski, and from

17) Polish Museum in Chicago - Paderewski Room

Helena Modjeska (Modrzejewska), the foremost Shakespearean actress of her day. In the Paderewski Room, you can not only see extraordinary rarities such as a famous golden watch given to Paderewski by the New York's Polish Army Veterans, incrusted with seventy-five diamonds and playing his minuet G-dur every hour. You can also listen to his original recordings and watch documentary clips with his public appearances.

16) Polish Museum in Chicago - Art Gallery

The Kosciuszko Collection presented in part on a permanent display consists of a great number of his letters and documents, original paintings as well as extremely interesting personal memorabilia.

There are also numerous permanent exhibits featuring Polish folk costumes, holiday traditions, folk art, as well as military objects, including full armor from various periods of Poland's history.

There are many exhibits throughout the year in addition to lectures, movie and slide presentations, concerts, theater performances, and meetings with artists, scholars and others dedicated to Polish culture from all over the world.

18) Polish Museum in Chicago - The Kosciuszko Collection

If you visit Chicago in the last week of September, don't overlook the Polish Film Festival organized by the Polish Museum of America together with the Film Center of the Art Institute of Chicago, the largest program of promoting Polish film.

If you come in the first week of April, you may hear distinguished soloists in programs of Polish classical music during Polish Music Salon.

In the last week of October, the museum hosts the annual Salon of the Polish Art Book where you may meet publishers of Polish art books and learn about their recent offerings.

In May, during Chicago International Art Expo, the world's largest art exposition where the PMA has its booth in the non-for-profit section, there is Polish Artfest in the museum showing many classics and new faces in Polish contemporary art (a spectacular opportunity for buyers!)

A gift shop in the museum sells, at very reasonable prices, crystal, amber jewelry, wooden carvings, and other items imported from Poland.

The hours are 12:00 noon to 5:00 p.m. daily. Admission and parking are free, though a minimum donation of $2 is suggested to help maintain the museum. Guided group tours are available by reservation. Wheelchairs are available but should be requested in advance. The number to call for all reservations is (312) 384-3352. The museum is a regular stop on Chicago's Culture Bus Route.

2) POLISH MUSEUM LIBRARY

Also located at 984 North Milwaukee Avenue, the Library adjoins the Museum and is part of it. It is a resource for scholars and non-scholars alike interested in the historical and cultural fabric of Poland and of the Polish-American community. It contains over 60,000 volumes in Polish and English, 250 periodicals, collections of Polish music records, discs, and video cassettes. It is considered one of the best Polish-subject libraries outside Poland. The Library specializes in information about Polish genealogy and heraldry. Researchers are allowed access to the research files of the Polish Genealogical Society. The archives are open by appointment only.

There is a small art book store in the Library where you can buy any book on Polish culture or art at unbeatable prices. If the book you want is out of print, the book store offers you a free of charge book search.

Library hours are Monday and Friday from 1:00 p.m. to 7:30 p.m; Tuesday, Wednesday and Thursday from 10:00 a.m. to 6:00 p.m.; Saturday from 12:00 noon to 5:00 p.m. If you need to make an advance reservation, please call (312) 384-3352.

HOW TO GET THERE

From downtown, take Kennedy Expressway North; exit at Augusta Boulevard, cross Milwaukee Avenue and turn left into the Library parking lot. Coming from the North, take the Kennedy

Expressway South, exit at Division Avenue and turn right. Turn left onto Milwaukee Avenue. The Museum is at the second traffic light.

3) THE POLISH HIGHLANDER COMMUNITY CENTER

The Polish Highlander Community Center (Dom Podhalan) stands at 4808 South Archer Avenue, on Chicago's Polish South Side. This building is a magnificent example of Highlander carpentry. It was built as a mountain chalet, by hand, from carved wooden

19) The Polish Highlander Community Center in Chicago

beams and interlocking wooden joists. There is a restaurant, bar, meeting rooms, and a banquet hall. The wooden tables and chairs in the restaurant were also hand-carved by Highlander craftsmen in the United States. No two chairs are exactly alike! There are many cultural activities throughout the entire year especially on weekends (dances, art exhibits, and folk dancing contests).

The hours are 10:00 a.m. to 9 p.m. daily. If you want to call to make sure you can squeeze in for dinner and a tour, the number is (312) 523-7632.

The Polish Highlanders (Gorale) inhabit the mountains at the southern end of Poland. They are fiercely independent, brave, loyal, and often artistically gifted. They are also well organized in the United States, and the Polish Highlanders Community Center is one of their proud achievements in America.

HOW TO GET THERE

From downtown, take the Dan Ryan Expressway South to the Stevenson Expressway West, and exit onto Kedzie Avenue going South. At the Archer Avenue intersection, take a left onto Archer Avenue and go up a short distance to the Polish Highlander Community Center. About two blocks before you reach Archer Avenue heading down on Kedzie Avenue, you will pass the International Polka Museum.

4) INTERNATIONAL POLKA MUSEUM

Located at 4145 South Kedzie Avenue. Costumes, photographs, and various other memorabilia are on display for the many lovers of this dance and music form. Though associated with Polish-Americans, and though most of the outstanding Polka bands have been founded and staffed with Polish-Americans, the dance itself is Czech in origin. Tel. (312) 254-7771. See above for directions.

5) COPERNICUS CULTURAL AND CIVIC CENTER

Located at 5216 West Lawrence Avenue. The Copernicus Foundation of Chicago (established in 1971, thanks to Polish-American community leader Mitchell P. Kobelinski) purchased, redesigned, and renovated the old Gateway Theater in 1980. The original 1929 theater lobby was transformed into a three-story space which houses classrooms, halls, and offices. The Solidarity Tower, which is a replica of the Royal Castle Clock Tower in Warsaw, Poland, was erected in 1985.

The Copernicus Center's activities include: Polish classes, social events, lectures, and exhibitions. The 2,000 seat auditorium is used for movies, concerts, theater performances, and fundraising events.

If you want to participate in any of the events organized at the Center, call in advance: (312) 777-8899.

*20) Copernicus
Cultural and Civic
Center - Solidarity
Tower- Chicago*

HOW TO GET THERE

From downtown, take the Kennedy Expressway north and follow
the left fork where it splits into the Edens Expressway. Continue
along Kennedy Expressway till you see the highway sign showing
the exit for the Copernicus Center. Follow Lawrence Avenue a
short distance (under the railroad bridge) to the Copernicus Cultural and Civic Center parking lot.

*21) Copernicus
Cultural and Civic
Center - Gateway
Theater- Chicago*

6) THE POLISH NATIONAL ALLIANCE OF THE UNITED STATES OF NORTH AMERICA

Located at 6100 North Cicero Avenue, this is the largest and most influential Polish-American fraternal organization. It is an important political and cultural factor in the Polish-American and the American community as a whole. Every major American presidential candidate makes sure to visit this national headquarters of the organization. There are many events sponsored by or in conjunction with the PNA at its headquarters site. Call in advance to find out. While the headquarters serves almost exclusively as the administrative center of the organization, it does have some very interesting items and artifacts on display connected with the political and cultural life of the Polish-American community. Tel. (312) 286-0500.

HOW TO GET THERE

From downtown, take the Kennedy Expressway North, and follow the Edens Expressway at the split (bear right). Go to Touhy Avenue exit, and then turn right onto Cicero Avenue, and head South for approximately one mile to the PNA headquarters. It will be on your right. Parking is in the rear of the building.

7) POLISH WOMEN'S ALLIANCE MUSEUM

At 205 South Northwest Highway, Park Ridge, Illinois. The Polish Women's Alliance is the largest Polish women's organization in the United States. It is a living symbol of the crucial role of Polish women in the development and maintenance of Polish-American communities, churches, and organizations. The organization was established in 1899. The museum contains many interesting items, many of them reflecting the history of the Alliance. There is also a library which includes a good number of rare Polish books. Tel.(708) 693-6215.

HOW TO GET THERE

Take the Kennedy Expressway North, get off at Central Avenue and go a very short distance North to the intersection with Milwaukee Avenue which almost immediately splits into Milwaukee

Avenue and Northwest Highway. Bear left onto Northwest Highway. You will see the Polish Women's Alliance national headquarters building on your right, shortly before you come to downtown Park Ridge. There is parking in front of the building.

8) STATUES OF TADEUSZ KOSCIUSZKO AND OF NICHOLAS COPERNICUS

22) Copernicus Statue on Solidarity Drive in Chicago

23) Kosciuszko Statue on Solidarity Drive in Chicago

Located along Solidarity Drive, which leads from South Lake Shore Drive to the Adler Planetarium. Tadeusz Kosciuszko, the American Revolutionary War Hero, and Nicholas Copernicus, the father of modern astronomy, are both honored by the citizens of Chicago in this beautiful spot, which features magnificent vistas of Lake Michigan and the downtown skyline.

HOW TO GET THERE

From downtown, take Lake Shore Drive South and bear left toward Solidarity Drive, which leads into the Adler Planetarium.

9) POLISH VILLAGE

One of the most intensely Polish parts of America is concentrated on Milwaukee Avenue from Kimball to Addison Avenues. At the very epicenter of all this activity is the newly-christened Polish Village. It encompasses the area immediately surrounding the parish of St. Hyacinth's (Swietego Jacka). This section of town is bisected by Milwaukee Avenue, and its very heart lies in the region from Diversey to Belmont Avenues.

There are many Polish-style bars, restaurants with Polish fare, delicatessen stores, stores carrying books, magazines, clothes, shoes, housewares, and other products manufactured in Poland, located along Milwaukee Avenue going far north, and east and west of the intersection of Belmont and Central Avenues.

There are at least half a dozen well-known Polish restaurants in Chicago, some of them going back a generation or two. In recent times, one of the most popular is Orbit Restaurant; 2940 N. Milwaukee Avenue. The proprietor, Tadeusz Kowalczyk, is a walking encyclopedia of information about the Polish Village.

24) "Polish Village" in Chicago

Chicago's many Polish restaurants run the gamut from the expensive and haute cuisine " Mareva" on Milwaukee Avenue only a block away from the "golden triangle," to the modestly priced "Zofia's" in Niles, Illinois, just northwest of Chicago but also along Milwaukee Avenue.

Across from Zofia's there is the largest of Polish American cemeteries, St. Adalbert's, where more than one half million persons of Polish heritage have been laid to rest since the end of the 19th century. Most interesting are the many impressive monuments erected in an age (before 1950) when people visited cemeteries as a regular pastime. Information can be gained from the cemetery personnel. Located in Niles, Illinois, on Milwaukee Avenue.

10) POLONIA BOOKSTORE

At 2886 North Milwaukee Avenue. A particularly well-stocked book shop carrying a wide variety of Polish book titles and magazines, as well as Polish interest books in English. Professional help, trained by Mrs. Mira Puacz, the owner. You can order what you need if they don't have it. This is the largest book store dedicated to Polish and Polish-interest books in America. Tel. (312) 489-2554.

HOW TO GET THERE

From downtown, take the Kennedy Expressway going North. Get off at the Belmont Avenue exit and go West a short distance to Milwaukee Avenue. Park wherever you can, and take a leisurely walk South with our Guide in hand.

11) GLOBE BOOKSTORE

At 6005 West Irving Park Road, 2nd floor. Polish books, antiques, gifts. Also has a reading room /cafe. A good spot to browse and meet people. Tel. (312) 282-3537.

HOW TO GET THERE

From downtown, take Kennedy Expressway going north and exit at Irving Park Road . Go West (turn left) to Austin Avenue. Street parking available.

12) WOODEN GALLERY

Run by proprietor Jerzy Kenar; 1007 North Wolcott. An original, off-beat kind of place. Tel (312) 342-2550.

From downtown, take Kennedy Expressway going north and exit at Augusta Boulevard. Cross Milwaukee Avenue and follow Augusta West to Wolcott (1900 West). Street parking available.

13) CONSULATE GENERAL OF THE REPUBLIC OF POLAND IN CHICAGO

Located at 1530 North Lake Shore Drive, Chicago, IL 60610, the building is one of the finest surviving examples of the grand mansions, which once lined Lake Shore Drive at the turn of the century. Originally built for a Chicago manufacturer Bernard A. Eckhart and purchased by the Polish Government in 1974, the building is on the list of Gold Coast historical monuments in Chicago.

In the new era of Poland's independence, the Consulate has become a major cultural center. There are meetings, lectures, concerts, exhibits, as well as film showings. Polish artists arriving in Chicago are introduced at press conferences, and visitors attending film showings can often meet the directors. The Consulate offers a range of exhibits and video films, which can be borrowed; please write for the catalog of available offerings. Call (312) 337-7951 or 337-8166 (Fax (312) 337-7841) for information on cultural events.

INDIANA

Merrillville

THE SHRINE OF OUR LADY OF CZESTOCHOWA

The Salvatorian Fathers constructed the Shrine in 1982/83 on the grounds of the Salvatorian Fathers Monastery . The focal point of the newly constructed church is the huge 8ft by 12ft painting of Our Lady of Czestochowa, painted by Wlodek Koss of the Koss Family Artists of New York. Also in the church there is a panorama of statues representing the major historical figures, such as Jesus Christ, the Polish kings, and various saints.

The Shrine is located at 5755 Pennsylvania Street, Merrillville, IN. 46410. For directions and all other information, call (219) 884-0714.

25) *The Shrine of Our Lady of Czestochowa, in Merrillville, IN*

MARYLAND

Baltimore

FACTS AND FIGURES

Of the two hundred sixty-five thousand Polish-Americans living in Maryland, over sixty-five thousand live in Baltimore. This is an old Polish community. General Casimir Pulaski was probably the first Polish resident of Baltimore. From April to July, 1778, Pulaski made the city his base of operations while he recruited volunteers for his independent cavalry corps, which became known as the "Pulaski Legion." The first Catholic parish established by Polish newcomers was St. Stanislaus Kostka (1877); Holy Rosary Parish was founded in 1887. Baltimore is one of the largest and busiest ports in the United States. For over forty years it has received the merchant vessels of the Polish Ocean Lines. Gdynia, Poland's great sea port, and Baltimore have been designated "Sister Ports."

1) THE PULASKI BANNER

During his stay in Baltimore, Pulaski visited Bethlehem, Pennsylvania, where he commissioned the Order of Moravian Nuns to make him a banner for his legion. After Pulaski's death, the banner was brought to Baltimore by Pulaski's friend and aide, Captain Paul Bentalou. The banner is in the permanent collection of the Maryland Historical Society, 201 W. Monument Street. In 1976, the Polish Heritage Society of Maryland commissioned Sister Irene Olkowski of the Polish Order of Sister Servants of Mary Immaculate to make a replica of the banner based on the original. This authentic replica is also a part of the Historical Society's permanent collection.

2) THE PULASKI MONUMENT

At the intersection of Eastern Avenue and Linwood Avenue, which is the heart of Baltimore's Polish community, stands an enormous marble bas-relief monument honoring General Casimir Pulaski. Dedicated on October 15, 1951, the monument was designed by A.C. Radziszewski, a respected Baltimore architect of Polish descent. The heroic-sized bronze bas-relief shows Pulaski leading a cavalry charge. This bronze was executed by Hans Schuler, a well-known Baltimore sculptor.

HOW TO GET THERE

From the Northeast, use I-95 to Baltimore. From the Delaware-Maryland, line an alternate route is the officially designated "Pulaski Highway" (Maryland Route 40). From Pittsburgh, Pennsylvania and the West, use U.S. 70 or the Pennsylvania Turnpike into the center of Baltimore. From Washington and points South, use I-95 or the Baltimore-Washington Parkway. From the North (Harrisburg, PA and New York points) use I-83 going South. All these roads connect with Charles Street in Baltimore and lead to Monument Street, which is the location of the Maryland Historical Society. All can connect with Linwood and Eastern Avenue, the site of Baltimore's Pulaski Monument.

MASSACHUSETTS

Massachusetts has been the home of Polish immigrants for at least 160 years. Among the earliest were a handful of political exiles from the November 1830 Insurrection against Russian rule in the Kingdom of Poland. They were followed by other political exiles who fled the unsuccessful January, 1863 Insurrection against Russia. These early arrivals, however, were rapidly assimilated. During the last two decades of the l9th century they were succeeded and overwhelmed by the larger peasant immigration originating primarily from Southern and Eastern Poland. The first Polish parish, St. Joseph, was erected in 1887 in Webster. A total of 47 Polish Roman Catholic parishes were founded in Massachusetts, including most recently, St. Andrew Bobola, which was founded in Dudley after World War II to accommodate the post-war political immigration. Additionally, 17 Polish National Catholic parishes were erected. By 1930, 187,063 first and second generation Polish immigrants lived in the Commonwealth.

In addition to finding work in the State's factories and mill towns, Polish peasant immigrants were also attracted to the farmlands of the Connecticut River Valley. Through hard work and thrift, they helped to revive the agrarian economy of that part of Western Massachusetts, becoming prominent citizens in Northampton, Easthampton, South Deerfield, Hadley, Hatfield, Ware, Amherst, Sunderland, Watley, and Deerfield. In 1911, the US Dillingham Commission reported that "the whole valley on both sides of the river, from Hadley on the south to Greenfield on the north, will be known as 'Poland' in the course of time." By 1930, Polish immigrants accounted for 19.4% (7,935) of the state's rural population.

Amherst

The twenty-eight story University of Massachusetts (Amherst) library contains more than three and a half million books, documents, periodicals, and microforms. Of the 60,000 items in the Slavic and East European collection, about 10,000 concern Polish topics. Polish-American Archival documentation has been collected since 1985. For hours and additional information contact the Slavic Bibliographer at (413) 545 0058, the Archivist at (413) 545-2780, or the Reference Department at (413) 545-0150.

WHAT TO SEE

POLISH ARCHIVES AT THE UNIVERSITY OF MASSACHUSETTS LIBRARY

The University Archives is, since 1985, a depository for church histories and jubilee catalogs, personal documents of Polish families, old photos, records of fraternal organizations, newspaper clippings, memoirs, diaries, audio tapes, and similar material. Also gathered are the records of several large manufacturing companies, which employed many Polish immigrants at the turn of the century. There is also some genealogical material available.

Also available are such unusual items as the Michael Kislo notebooks of folk poems and drawings, the Edward Borkowski diary (written when he was 99 years old), the Lesinski collection of more than two hundred postcards and photographs, the Jozef Obrebski "Polesie" papers and photographs, and the St. Kazimierz Society records from the years 1904-1919.

HOW TO GET THERE

You can reach the University via Route 90 (Massachusetts Turnpike) and/or Interstate 91 to Northampton. Then take route 9 East over the Coolidge Bridge through Hadley. Amherst is located 7 miles East of Northampton and about 30 miles North of Springfield.

Boston

FACTS AND FIGURES

Boston is associated with Harvard, which hosts the only fully endowed chair of Polish Studies in the United States, the Alfred Jurzykowski Chair of Polish Literature. There are also two Polish parishes in the immediate region: Our Lady of Czestochowa in Boston and St. Hedwig's in Cambridge.

STATUE OF TADEUSZ KOSCIUSZKO

In Boston Commons, there is a handsome statue of Thaddeus Kosciuszko, the Revolutionary War hero.

HOW TO GET THERE

It's not difficult to find Harvard, or the Boston Commons, once you're in Boston. We recommend taking the subway to see the sights, rather than traveling by car.

Fall River

WHAT TO SEE

KOSCIUSZKO MONUMENT

In Kosciuszko Square in Fall River, there stands a beautiful monument to the hero of two continents, General Tadeusz Kosciuszko. This monument was first dedicated in 1950, and a special plaque concerning the Revolutionary War general was installed forty years later, in 1990, on the 173rd anniversary of Kosciuszko's death. The monument is 22 feet tall, very ornate and a focal point of Polish-American cultural activity in Fall River.

HOW TO GET THERE

If you are coming from Boston, take I-95 to the intersection with 195 and ride it into Fall River. The town is small and the square is easily located.

Northampton

FACTS AND FIGURES

Northampton is a western Massachusetts town that lies in the Connecticut River Valley. Polish immigrants started coming here in the second half of the nineteenth century. They worked in the local textile mills, as well as on the farms. There were produce and tobacco farms, and orchards in the region then, and all of them were very eager to obtain the cheap immigrant labor. The Polish American community became quite strong. Several churches were built, as well as schools. Many of the social organizations founded then are still active today.

WHAT TO SEE

1) THE GRAVE OF AUGUST MALCZEWSKI-JAKUBOWSKI

This very young Polish revolutionary, a participant of the Polish Insurrection of 1831, came to America as an exile in 1834. He was then 18 years old. He had participated in the Insurrection at the age of 15! And he died in America at the age of 21. He was the natural son of the great Polish poet, Antoni Malczewski. There are two testimonials that remain after the young and noble exile. The first is a book titled *The Remembrances of a Polish Exile,* a book, which he published in America. The second is his gravestone and grave. The gravestone inscription reads: "A Polish Exile"(A.A. Tarnava Malchewski vel Jakubowski) Obt. 24 April l837, aged 21 (erected by his pupils).

His grave is at the Bridge Street cemetery on Route 9, about one-half mile East of the town center. But the gravestone, a simple, three-foot-tall marble slab, stands on a town plot across from the house at 14 Parsons Street. The cemetery is usually closed in late fall, throughout the winter, and in the early spring.

2) THE BRIGADIER GENERAL CASIMIR PULASKI MONUMENT

This monument is in the form of a large slab of Vermont granite with a relief likeness of General Pulaski. It was a gift of the local Polish-American societies and was dedicated by Calvin Coolidge on Sunday, October 13, 1929. The small park where the monument stands was renovated in 1976. It is located on Main Street. between the Town Hall and the Academy of Music Theater.

3) THE REMEMBRANCES OF A POLISH EXILE

A reproduction of the book by August Malczewski-Jakubowski is located in Forbes Library, West Street, Northampton, Massachusetts.

Take Route 90 (Massachusetts Turnpike) and Interstate 91. Any of the three Northampton exits will take you to the center of town.

MICHIGAN

Detroit

FACTS AND FIGURES

The once populous Detroit district of Hamtramck, with Joseph Campau Avenue as its main axis, served for over a century as the center of Polish-American activity in Detroit. Due to changes in the automobile industry, and due to increased affluence among the Polish-Americans and their consequent move to the suburbs, Hamtramck is not as vibrant as it once was. But the cultural life and influence of the Polish-American community in the Detroit Metropolitan Area is still felt.

WHAT TO SEE

1) THE DETROIT INSTITUTE OF FINE ARTS

Thanks to efforts of the Detroit Polish-American community, the Institute has a small but growing collection of Polish art, and is the only major American Fine Arts Museum, which makes a conscious effort to promote Polish art and to develop a collection of Polish art.

HOW TO GET THERE

The Detroit Institute of Fine Arts is on Warren Road off Woodward Avenue in downtown Detroit. Take 175/375 to Warren Road, and if you are heading North, go left (West) on Warren Road a short distance.

2) POLISH ART CENTER

This fine art and book store is located at 9539 Joseph Campau in Hamtramck, and carries the largest selection of books in the Detroit area. Mrs. Joan Bittner is the cheery and effective manager.

3) **PEOPLE'S BOOK STORE,** 5347 Chene Street, Detroit, MI 48211. Paul Zukowski is the manager.

Forester

BIALOWIEZA

Named after the primeval forest preserve in northeastern Poland, this is a camping area owned by Polish Scouts of Michigan. One hundred beautiful acres, 15 minutes away from Lake Huron, were purchased in 1964 and have been the site of many meetings and seminars since. Many Polish families have bought lots in the immediate vicinity, forming a community of scouting enthusiasts and supporters.

Orchard Lake

FACTS AND FIGURES

The Polish Seminary and High School at Orchard Lake, as well as St. Mary's College, together with several other notable institutions, form what is known as the Orchard Lake Schools. Located 21 miles Northwest of downtown Detroit, this beautiful campus has been dedicated to religious studies and the preservation of Polish heritage since 1909.

The seminary itself began in Detroit in 1885. Founded by Reverend Jozef Dabrowski, it was the first Polish-American institution of higher learning in the United States. Sts. Cyril and Methodius Seminary was relocated to Orchard Lake in 1909, to the site of a former military academy. There the division occurred into a four year college preparatory high school, a four year college (St. Mary's College), and the four year Saints Cyril and Methodius Seminary.

Other notable institutions and centers of cultural activity, which have developed on the campus of the Orchard Lake Schools include the Center for Polish Studies and Culture, established in 1969 and the National Polish American Sports Hall of Fame and Museum which was founded in 1973 to honor and recognize out

26) Shrine Chapel of Our Lady of Orchard Lake, MI

standing American athletes, both amateur and professional, of Polish descent. It is located in the Dombrowski Fieldhouse. The Museum houses plaques and memorabilia of athletes of Polish heritage who in their time gained fame and glory in a variety of professional and amateur sports over the past seventy-five years. New members are elected into the Hall each year. The mailing address of National Polish-American Sports Hall of Fame is 18280 Sunderland, Detroit, MI 48219.

A more recent addition is the Polish Archives at Orchard Lake, as well as a fine Gallery of Polish Art. It is one of the "must see" galleries of Polish paintings in the United States since it includes

27) St Mary's Preparatory Classroom Building. Orchard Lake, MI

56

paintings by Alfred Wierusz-Kowalski, Wladyslaw Szerner, Zofia Stryjenska, Julian Falat, and others, as well as over 100 examples od naive wood sculpture.

The campus, well known for its floral displays, is especially beautiful in the spring, summer and fall, and visitors are welcome.

WHAT TO SEE

ORCHARD LAKE SCHOOLS

There are several archival and research centers at Orchard Lake: The Center of Polish Culture, The Polish Liturgical Center, The Polish Center for Pastoral Studies, and The Center of John Paul II. The most extensive and dynamic is The Central Archives of American Polonia under Rev. Dr. Roman Nir. This very ambitious project has as its main goal to become the largest archival institute for the Polish-American community in the United States.

Currently, the Archives contain 51,000 manuscripts. They also have a collection of Polish genealogical material which, already surpasses in size all other such collections on the North American Continent. There is the collection of over 1,500 Polish parish and organization jubilee and commemorative books, marking important events in the religious, cultural and civic life of the Polish-American community in North America.

The Archives of Orchard Lake Schools are a depository for historical documentation, including photographs, concerning the three schools at Orchard Lake, as well as regarding Polish research centers from across the U.S.A., and also the collection of biographical data concerning students and faculty connected with the three Orchard Lake schools. The School Archives are housed in three separate collections: Institutional collections, Polish-American collections, and collections pertaining to Poland. Included in these three collections are: manuscripts, periodicals, books, newspaper clippings, photographs, maps, drawings, coins, medals, stamps, audiovisual materials, phonograph records, and tape cassettes. A separate division houses periodicals, which have been published out of Orchard Lake. There are complete sets of such well-known and important publications as *Sodalis, Alumnus, Eagle, Good News, Niedziela,* and others.

The Archives of the American Polonia contains a larger and more varied collection of materials concerning Poles in the United States and other countries. Here are some of the countries represented: U.S.A., Canada, Brazil, Argentina, France, and England. Some of the main categories into which the collection is divided are: political and economic immigration, Polish immigrants to specific states, the Polish theater in America, Polish-American film, anti-Polish jokes, Polish-American writers, artists, activists, and editors.

Polish-American parishes are represented in the Archives through the already-mentioned jubilee books, but also in the form of over 100 monographic studies in typewritten form and 20 doctoral dissertations on Polish parishes in various dioceses in the U.S.A.

Polish-American cultural and civic organizations are represented in the Archives through various source materials, such as monographs, souvenir programs, photographic documentation, bylaws and constitutions, and periodicals published by these organizations, of which 500 are represented in the Archives. Of great interest in this organizational collection are the materials pertaining to various Polish professional organizations, such as associations of Polish-American dentists, doctors of medicine, lawyers, pharmacists, mechanics, butchers, tailors, journalists, church organists, stamp collectors, coin collectors, and others!

One entire collection is devoted to biographies of important Polish-American lay and religious activists.

The archival section on Polonica Americana is also very extensive. It contains imprints, brochures, and pamphlets in English and Polish on Polish subjects published outside Poland.

There is also a sizeable collection of old and rare publications. The 16th century, for instance, is represented with 100 publications. Over 1,000 volumes date from the 18th and first half of the 19th centuries. There are also about 500 publications dating from the 16th and 17th centuries which were printed exclusively in Poland. Many of these publications are not represented even in the most extensive European collections.

Rounding out the Archives are collections of Polish weeklies, dailies, and monthlies, a collection of calendars, as well as one of posters. There is also a newly-started collection of materials pertaining to the Polish Second Corps of World War II fame, and a new General Stanislaw Maczek Museum dedicated to the Polish First Armored Division, which fought on the Western Front in 1944 and 1945. A room dedicated to the Polish scouts in the U.S.A. is a recent addition.

In the Activities building, you can see a panorama of Polish history portrayed in 300 statues of Polish kings, saints, writers, and other notables. Last but definitely not least, in a separate building called the Galeria is the Gallery of Polish Art at Orchard Lake with Marian Owczarski, a sculptor in stainless steel, as conservator and Artist-in-Residence. There are some fine Polish paintings there, including masterpieces by Alfred Wierusz-Kowalski, Julian Falat, Zofia Stryjenska, and others.

The public is invited to the archives and gallery from 8 a.m. to 11 a.m. and from 12 noon to 4 p.m. For inquiries, you may call (313) 682-1885.

HOW TO GET THERE

From downtown Detroit, take I-75 North to exit 72. Go South a few blocks to East Long Lake Road, turn right and follow it past Bloomfield Hills, where it becomes West Long Lake Road, to Orchard Lake Road. Take a right here (heading North), and then the first road left to the seminary campus.

Troy

THE AMERICAN POLISH CULTURAL CENTER

Located at 2975 East Maple, Troy 48083, tel. (313) 689-3636.

Built on a 12 acre site, with a parking area for 300 cars, this imposing complex has four halls, seating up to 750 persons, and two banquet rooms. There is full service catering.

There is the Chopin Exhibit and an antique stained glass skylight. Open from Monday through Friday 9 a.m. to 5 p.m. the Center is on the northwest corner of East Maple and Dequindre Roads, just minutes from I-75, Big Beaver, John R and Ryan Roads. Special evening tours are available on Wednesdays from 6 p.m. to 9 p.m.

MINNESOTA

St Paul

WHAT TO SEE

THE IMMIGRATION HISTORY RESEARCH ARCHIVES

is a part of the University of Minnesota and will be of interest to serious students of Polish-American history. The collection of Polish-American newspapers alone is worth a visit. The Archive boasts extensive files on a wide array of subjects central to the Polish-American community's development over the past century, in particular the activities of the Polish fraternals and those of many local Polish-American communities and community leaders.

Winona

FACTS AND FIGURES

Poles from the south and the north of Poland, from Silesia and from Kaszubia came to settle in Minnesota, and particularly in the fertile areas around Winona. Until recently, the Polish language could be heard on the streets of Winona as frequently as English. Today, this lively town of 25,000 residents, nestled on the limestone bluffs overlooking the Mississippi River in southern Minnesota, is the site of the Polish Cultural Institute. The Institute and its museum were founded in 1975 by the Reverend Paul Breza, who at that time was the chaplain of St. Mary's College in Winona. With the help of local donations, but largely with his own money, he purchased a disused industrial building and refurbished it, donating the first artifacts from his own sizeable collection.

WHAT TO SEE

THE POLISH CULTURAL INSTITUTE

The Polish Cultural Institute has, among other interesting items on display, old Polish wedding dresses, handmade baptismal gowns, a Polish flag, costume dolls, tapestries, prayer books in Polish over 100 years old, and a program from a 1923 Paderewski piano recital. There are over 3,000 volumes of Polish literature, 30 of them of great rarity; 4 of which are the only ones in existence in the world.

The museum itself has been beautifully decorated. For instance, the archives room has a hand-painted ceiling. Over the entrance door is a stained glass Polish eagle crafted by hand. A large collection of Polish memorabilia comes from Winona's landmark restaurant, the Hot Fish Shop. There are cultural and "people" events going on all the time, including the annual Apple Days and kielbasa tastings.

The other important Polish-American organization in Winona, the Polish Heritage Society, cooperates with the museum and institute.

For specific information on events and hours open to the public, please call the Polish Cultural Institute at (507) 454-3431.

HOW TO GET THERE

If you are travelling from Minneapolis-St. Paul, take I-35 South to I-90 East to State Road 43 North. It is then a short distance to State Road 61 into Winona.

MISSISSIPPI

Kosciusko

FACTS AND FIGURES

Kosciusko, Mississippi, is not the only town in America named after the famed Polish and American patriot and war hero who fought in Washington's army as his youngest general. There are in fact 4 towns so named (see the appendix on Polish names in the U.S.A.). It is however the only town, which has a museum dedicated to Kosciuszko.

The area in which the town is situated was ceded to the United States Government by the Choctaw Indian Nation in 1834. The honor of giving the young settlement a name belonged to William

D. Dodd, the first representative of Attala County in the State Legislature of Mississippi. Dodd's grandfather had served with General Kosciuszko in the Revolutionary War, and both were active in the siege of Fort Ninety-Six in 1781 in South Carolina. Mr. Dodd had inherited his grandfather's deep admiration for Kosciuszko and therefore suggested the general's name to the Legislature - he inadvertently omitted the "z"-, and thus it has been ever after, Kosciusko, Mississippi. But the townspeople know very well the correct spelling of the name, which is present in the appellation of the Kosciuszko Heritage Foundation and in the Tadeusz Kosciuszko Museum and Information Center.

Since even Americans without any ties to Poland have seen fit to honor Kosciuszko, it might not be out of place to say a few words about him, in order to illuminate the reasons for the intense loyalty and admiration, which the citizens of the town have for this war hero.

Tadeusz Kosciuszko was born of minor nobility on February 12, 1746, in the Grand Duchy of Lithuania, which had united with the Kingdom of Poland into the Polish Commonwealth back in the fifteenth century. Many Poles and members of the Polish nobility settled there in the centuries after the union, and there were many intermarriages. Kosciuszko attended the famous Cadet School in Warsaw and then completed his military education with seven years of study and research in Germany, Italy, and France. Back in Poland, he was commissioned captain in charge of fortifications. After the first partition of Poland in 1772, when the monarchies of Prussia, Russia, and Austria ganged up on Poland and divided it among themselves, he went to Paris. There he heard of the American Revolution. Intensely sensitive to the needs for political freedom and sovereignty, he immediately came to America and volunteered his services.

He was the first of a host of foreign officers to receive a commission from the Continental Congress to serve in General Washington's army. His talent and skill as a fortifications engineer helped earn him the rank of brigadier general, which he received from Congress in 1783.

General Kosciuszko served in the South in the second half of the War. It was then that he came closely in touch with the institution of slavery. He acquired a deep revulsion for it. In his will, the executor of which was his close friend Thomas Jefferson, he left money for "the purchase, liberation, and education of Negro slaves." After the war ended, Kosciuszko returned to Poland where he became the leader of a revolt against the Russian Empire, which occupied the greatest part of the country. That war, known as the Kosciuszko Insurrection, had an unhappy ending. Though a number of brilliant victories were won against enormous odds, in the end the insurrectionists were defeated. Kosciuszko himself was wounded, captured and imprisoned in Moscow. After two years he was freed by the young and freshly-anointed Tsar Paul, but he had to promise never to return to Poland again. He lived out his days in Switzerland and there is a museum in his honor in Solothurn.

By very happy coincidence, the town of Kosciusko is not just a backwater hamlet. Instead, that original settlement on the famed Natchez Trail has grown into a very important community. It is recognized as the metropolis of Central Mississippi, due to the high culture and prominence of so many of her citizens throughout the town's 150 year history. Its second nickname is the "Athens of the State of Mississippi." No other town in the state has furnished so many distinguished people in law, politics, science, theology, and other fields (including entertainment) as Kosciusko. Most recently, the famous TV hostess Oprah Winfrey hailed from here, and the church, which she attended as a girl, still stands.

WHAT TO SEE

THE TADEUSZ KOSCIUSZKO MUSEUM

The Tadeusz Kosciuszko Museum and Information Center opened in November, 1984, and after only six months, visitors from all 50 states and 25 foreign countries had already registered in its guest book. The mix of exhibits about local history and lore and exhibits about Tadeusz Kosciuszko are an indication of how the Polish and American patriot has become a natural and permanent part of the cultural and historical consciousness of this very American town.

The Center, built and maintained by donations from citizens and friends of Attala County, is located at the geographical center of Mississippi; this makes it convenient for tourists from all directions. It offers a welcome air-conditioned rest, and a cool drink of water compliments of a natural spring bottled water company in Attala County. The memorabilia and exhibits concerning General Kosciuszko are certainly worth seeing.

HOW TO GET THERE

The Tadeusz Kosciuszko Museum and Information Center is located in Kosciusko on the Natchez Trace Parkway at Mile 160 marker.

MISSOURI

Eureka

Eureka is within the St. Louis metropolitan area, which is situated on the banks of the Missouri River in the heart of the Midwest. It includes the City of St. Louis, Missouri; St. Louis County; municipalities on the east side of the river in Illinois, and those within a 40 mile radius of St. Louis. Compared to other Polish-American communities in the United States, the one in metropolitan St. Louis is of medium size. Nonetheless, it maintains a relatively visible and active presence among other ethnic groups in the area. Poles began arriving in the 1830s, and there are new arrivals every year.

WHAT TO SEE

1) THE BLACK MADONNA PILGRIMAGE SITE

The Black Madonna Pilgrimage Site and Grottos-"Devotions in Stone." This amazing and beautiful cluster of seven grottos and the Black Madonna Shrine are the work of one man completed over a span of 22 years. This is not only a religious but also an artistic monument to which thousands of visitors of all backgrounds and faiths come every year-from St. Louis, and from all over the United States and the world.

The saga of this achievement began in 1927, when the Franciscan Friar Father Bronislaus Luszcz arrived from Poland with a small group of fellow Franciscans at the invitation of the local bishop, to found and run an infirmary for poor, elderly men.

The current pilgrimage site was begun in 1938 with a shrine to the Black Madonna, the "Queen of Poland," the patroness of that country. The original icon is in the church in Czestochowa, the holiest religious shrine of Poland. A copy of this famous painting, which is over 1,000 years old, and which some attribute to the hand of St. Luke the Evangelist (making it 2,000 years old), can be seen in the shrine in Missouri.

For 22 years Father Bronislaus did back-breaking labor, hauling oil barrels full of water up the hill to mix with concrete, breaking barite boulders into manageable pieces for the building of the grottos, clearing the trees, leveling the land.

The shrine and grottos are artistically as well as religiously sensitive. Brother Bronislaus used great imagination and creativity to create the shapes he needed. For instance, statued animals such as lambs, and rabbits, especially in the Nativity grotto, were fashioned from large cake molds. And though the friar built and fashioned everything by hand himself, the final work was the result of the efforts of thousands of people from around the world: some tourists donated money, and many women and children donated jewelry and trinkets, which Father Bronislaus used in his designs, embedding them in various patterns in the concrete formations of the various grottos.

The Black Madonna shrine and grottos are a place of beauty and inspiration for all.

HOW TO GET THERE

Take Interstate 44 to the Eureka exit. Turn left at Highway W and drive south to Highway FF. Follow FF to the shrine. It is about 45 minutes from downtown St. Louis.

St. Louis

1) ST. STANISLAUS KOSTKA POLISH ROMAN CATHOLIC CHURCH

This church is on the national register of historic places. It is remarkable for its architecture and interior beauty. The sanctuary features a replica of the famous painting "Golgotha" by the Polish

28) St Stanislaus Kostka Roman Catholic Church. St. Louis, MO

artist, Jan Styka. The painting was done for the St. Louis World's Fair of 1904, and currently is on display in Glendale, California, at Forest Lawn Memorial Park. The stained glass windows in this church are by Michael Olszewski.

HOW TO GET THERE

Located near 20th street and Cass Avenue in North St. Louis. Drive West on Market Street. Turn right on 20th Street and go down about one mile.

29) The Stan Musial Statue. St Louis, MO

3) THE STAN MUSIAL STATUE

If you are in St. Louis, definitely see the full-length statue of Stan Musial, a tribute to one of St. Louis's and baseball's greatest players of Polish descent, or any descent for that matter. It is a popular meeting place for visitors to Busch Memorial Stadium.

HOW TO GET THERE

The statue is three blocks West of the Arch, at Busch Memorial Stadium.

NEW JERSEY

FACTS AND FIGURES

The state of New Jersey has hosted Poles and Polish-Americans since the seventeenth century when Albert Zaborowski (Zabriskie), a Polish noble, came into possession of large tracts of land in northern New Jersey. In December, 1777, Count Casimir Pulaski, at that time already the commander of all of General Washington's cavalry, entrenched himself and his cavalry corps in Trenton. Once there, he began fashioning the foundation of the American cavalry, complete with the first service regulations. By the year 1900, there were 21,510 Poles and Polish-Americans living in New Jersey, and by 1915, there were already 124,832 Poles and Polish-Americans residing in the state. Thus by the latter date, New Jersey ranked 4th in the United States as to size of its Polish population (Pennsylvania was first and New York second, with Illinois third).

Major Polish communities in the state of New Jersey are clustered in the towns closest to Manhattan, of which Jersey City and Irvington are two. But there are also important Polish-American enclaves in Perth Amboy and vicinity, as well as closer to Pennsylvania, in Trenton, and in other areas. As in so many states, Polish life in New Jersey tends to revolve around the church and church-related activities, as well as around organizations and activities that have to do with the preservation of Polish history, culture, and language. While there are many notable organizations and sites of interest to the tourist and traveler, a few of the most recently created ones are identified.

Clark

THE POLISH CULTURAL FOUNDATION

The Polish Cultural Foundation has been chartered since 1973 and is located at 177-179 Broadway. From small beginnings, much enthusiasm and no financial resources, it has expanded to its present size of 40,000 square feet of indoor space on a 3.2 acre tract of land and is still growing.

The Foundation already has a permanent loan collection of Josef Kolinski's large oils of flowers from his "radiation" period, a limited edition of prints of American-Indians by Boleslaw Cybis and other art works. Its Rev. Joseph A. Marianczyk Library contains 8,000 volumes of works mainly in the Polish language, and many are archival in nature. An additional, current journal collection on music, dance, the fine and applied arts and adult education, primarily in English, gives the professional or the student a rich source of comparative studies.

The Skulski Gallery and an additional gallery are actively used for exhibits in a wide variety of media. The Leona Karpinski Music Salon is used for concerts, lectures and receptions. The Main Auditorium serves as a ballroom and for theater presentations while the Banquet Hall is used for smaller audiences. Fourteen classrooms and meeting rooms comfortably accommodate the Foundation's Polish School for children, Girl and Boy Scouts, Polish University Club, veterans' and other associations meeting on various days of the week. The Studies Program provides English and Polish language courses as well as special interest courses for the community. Call before you go, telephone (908) 382-7197.

HOW TO GET THERE

The Polish Cultural Foundation is located at 177-179 Broadway in Clark, New Jersey. It is situated on the corner of Broadway and Prospect Streets. Get off at Exit 135 of the Garden State Parkway and proceed one block down Valley Road to Broadway. Take a right and go down to the Foundation, which will be on your right.

Jersey City

1) THE KATYN MEMORIAL

This impressive bronze and granite monument commemorating the thousands of Polish officers who were murdered by the Russians in the Katyn Forest, Soviet Union, in 1940, is a centerpiece of permanent outdoor exhibits in Jersey City and the region.

30) The Katyn Memorial in Jersey City, N.J. - Sculptor Andrzej Pitynski. Unveiling ceremony on Sunday May 19, 1991

This is the first monument raised on American soil to honor the dead of Katyn. Sculpted by the well-known Polish-American artist Andrzej Pitynski, it stands 34 feet high and has the simple but powerful inscription: Katyn 1940. It was unveiled on May 19, 1991, by Polish Consul General Jerzy Surdykowski.

HOW TO GET THERE

The Katyn Memorial is on Exchange Place in Jersey City. If travelling by train from Manhattan, take the Path line to Exchange Place. If travelling by car from New York, take the Holland Tunnel to Route 1-9, make a left at Henderson Street, and a left onto Montgomery Street to Exchange Place. If you are coming from elsewhere in New Jersey, take the Turnpike heading towards the Holland Tunnel, exit on Route 1-9 at Henderson Street. Make a right turn at Henderson and a left onto Montgomery to Exchange Place.

2) "LIBERATION" MONUMENT AT LIBERTY STATE PARK

This monument, the work of sculptor Natan Rapaport, is a fifteen-foot, two-ton bronze statue, which depicts an American serviceman carrying a survivor out of a Nazi concentration camp. The shoulders of the two figures become one; they share one heart. This monument is dedicated to American servicemen as liberators of oppressed people and all victims of the Holocaust. "Liberation" was unveiled on May 30th, 1985, by Governor Thomas H. Kean.

31) "The Liberation" monument at Liberty State Park, Jersey City, NJ

Polish-born Natan Rapaport began his career at the Warsaw Academy of Art. His most famous monumental work is "Warsaw Ghetto Uprising Monument," erected in Warsaw in 1948.

Lodi

FELICIAN SISTERS

The Felician Sisters, an order founded in Poland in 1855, sent five sisters to the United States in 1874 at the invitation of Rev. Jozef

Dabrowski of Michigan. The Convent in Lodi was incorporated in 1910 after a purchase, a year earlier, of 22 acres of ground.

Today, the Sisters run an accredited women's college, a school for gifted children, an infirmary, and a school of practical nursing. There are many concerts, plays, celebrations, and other festivities held here for which the large auditorium is an ideal venue. The address is 260 Main Street, Lodi NJ, 07644; tel (201) 778-1190

Union

WHAT TO SEE

VOYAGE

This enormous mural, by Polish artist Andrzej Czeczot, measuring 6 feet high by 40 feet long, hangs at the Union, New Jersey branch of the Polish & Slavic Federal Credit Union.

Czeczot is a prominent Polish artist who came to the United States in 1982 from Poland where he was persecuted for activities connected with the Solidarity movement. He is a satirist, painter, and graphic artist famous in Europe and North America. His works hang in major European and American museums. He has done covers for *The New Yorker, GQ,* and other important American magazines.

The mural, which runs the length of the lobby in the Credit Union, depicts the story of the Polish immigration to the United States. Poles have been coming to these shores for over three hundred years. The right side of the mural depicts a 19th century Polish scene. In the center, Poles head for the U.S.A. in boats (in the past) and by jet (in our own time). They are greeted by Polish-Americans with a new car, which symbolizes improvement in material possessions by the Polish-American community. The sun is shown in the form of a gleaming quarter-dollar coin, reflecting the importance of the inspiration of money. And a hot air balloon symbolizes the American desire to rise higher, above one's current station in life. On the far left New York City is visible, shining through the mist, the first stop of the new immigrants. In the foreground, there is a new house awaiting the arrivals.

This highly inspirational and informative mural painting is a powerful representation of the desires, ideas, and feelings of millions of Polish-Americans and Americans of other nationalities as well. Even though it was expressly painted for the Polish & Slavic Federal Credit Union, this is an important painting for all Americans to see.

HOW TO GET THERE

The Polish & Slavic Federal Credit Union of Union, New Jersey is located at 667 Chestnut Street. The telephone number is (908) 688-6596. The Union is open during normal business hours and on Saturdays. Please call in advance if you plan to be in the area for instructions on how to get there. It is close to exit 139A on Garden State Parkway North.

NEW MEXICO

Puerto de Luna

FACTS AND FIGURES

Historic Puerto de Luna was the center of Alexander Grzelachowski's enterprises in the 19th century: merchandising, cattle, and sheep ranching. Grzelachowski was a major figure in those parts and in those days. He associated with the likes of Charles Ilfeld, the Territory's foremost merchant, and with John S. Chisum, New Mexico's cattle baron.

Billy the Kid and the man who sought to capture him, Sheriff Pat Garrett, both used to stop in Puerto de Luna and visit Padre Polaco, as Grzelachowski was affectionately called. Captured by the sheriff in December, 1880, and while in his custody, Billy the Kid ate his last Christmas dinner at Grzelachowski's home. The following July, Garrett killed the Kid at Fort Sumner, New Mexico.

But Grzelachowski's most important contribution to New Mexico history took place at the Battle of Glorietta Pass on March

28, 1862, which was the decisive Civil War battle in the West. The Pole saved a Union force from capture by the Confederates and thus ensured the Union victory at Glorietta.

Grzelachowski was born in Poland in 1824. He came to the New Mexico Territory in 1851, in the company of the future Archbishop of Santa Fe, Jean Baptiste Lamy.

WHAT TO SEE

1) ALEXANDER GRZELACHOWSKI HOME AND STORE

The old store and home was a centerpiece of the town. After all the Grzelachowski descendants had left, the building continued to serve as a home until 1970. Since then, it has served as a warehouse and is succumbing to decay.

2) FIRST COURT HOUSE OF GUADALUPE COUNTY

Constructed of red cut stone, the courthouse stands on land donated by Grzelachowski. When the New Mexico Legislature formed the new County of Guadalupe in 1891, Grzelachowski persuaded the legislators to make Puerto de Luna the county seat. Grzelachowski became probate judge in 1893 and occupied an office in the courthouse. In 1902, the county seat was moved to Santa Rosa and the empty court house became a school. Today, it is a private residence.

3) OUR LADY OF REFUGE CATHOLIC CHURCH

This church served the large Grzelachowski family. It is an active parish today. The church, built in 1892, has a dome in the quasi-Byzantine style, but the windows have elements of Moorish architecture.

HOW TO GET THERE

From Santa Rosa, on 1-40, turn South onto State 91 and go for 11 miles. The paved road winds along the Pecos River to the village.

NEW YORK STATE

Greenpoint, Brooklyn

FACTS AND FIGURES

Greenpoint is a small community in the borough of Brooklyn. It overlooks the East River and lies directly across from the United Nations headquarters in Manhattan. It is home to over 30,000 Polish-Americans, many of them recent immigrants from Poland. Polish is the most frequently spoken language on the streets of Greenpoint.

1) ART OF JACEK MALCZEWSKI

Polish & Slavic Federal Credit Union, 140 Greenpoint Avenue. Open six days a week, Saturdays to 3p.m. The walls of its great hall are decorated with enlarged, faithful reproductions of the sketches of the famous Polish painter Jacek Malczewski. The P & SFCU is the largest Polish-American credit union in the U.S.A. (assets over $260 million).

2) REVEREND JERZY POPIELUSZKO MEMORIAL

Father Popieluszko Square, at Bedford Avenue and Lorimer Street. A granite bust of the martyred priest who died in 1984 as a hero of the Solidarity movement in Poland. This solid granite monument was commissioned by the Polish-American Congress, Southern New York District, and unveiled October 21, 1990. It was beheaded by Communist sympathizers on November 11, 1990, but has since been restored.

3) THE POLISH AND SLAVIC CENTER FOR THE ARTS

Completed in 1991, the Polish and Slavic Culture Center is the newest addition to an impressive array of community services provided over the last 20 years by the Polish & Slavic Center of Greenpoint, Brooklyn, a heavily Polish community of metropolitan New York.

The Center for the Arts holds concerts, artistic exhibitions, and has a fledgling gallery of Polish and Polish-American art. It is a beautiful, neo-Gothic hall which was formerly a Catholic church.

Dinner after a concert or exhibition opening is always possible virtually on the spot, as the Polish & Slavic Center's dining facility adjoins the concert hall and is housed in a brand new space, complete with magnificent skylights. There is also a souvenir boutique where various unique items can be purchased at modest prices.

The Center for the Arts is located at 177 Kent Street in Greenpoint, just off Manhattan Avenue. For information you can call (718) 383-5290.

OTHER POINTS OF INTEREST

There are two Polish language book stores which also carry books in English on Polish subjects:
• Pol-Am Bookstore, 946 Manhattan Avenue, Brooklyn, NY 11222, tel. (718) 389-7790
• Polish Bookstore, 140 Nassau Avenue, Brooklyn, NY 11222, tel. (718) 383-3501.

Lipert Studio, 147 Milton Street; proprietor Mr. Michael Legutko. The best gallery in America devoted exclusively to Polish Art.

HOW TO GET THERE

From Manhattan: Queensboro Bridge to Van Dam, across Pulaski Bridge down McGuiness Blvd. to Greenpoint Avenue. Come up Greenpoint to the intersection with Manhattan Avenue. This is the hub of the town. Park wherever you can. Side streets close to the intersection are best.

From Long Island, Long Island Expressway to the Greenpoint Avenue exit. Take Greenpoint Avenue South to the intersection with Manhattan Avenue.

Buffalo

FACTS AND FIGURES

Poland's first connection with Buffalo goes back to the days of the Holland Land Company of Amsterdam in the Netherlands. What is now Church Street was first named Stadnicki Street in honor of one of the partners of the Holland Land Company, Peter Stadnicki. Though Polish settlers of Jewish heritage (mostly from the Russian-occupied part of Poland) had started settling in Buffalo prior to 1848, the first Catholic Poles came to Buffalo about 1864. A full-fledged Polish-American community did not begin developing until 1873, which is also the year of the founding of St. Stanislaus Parish. Between 1873 and 1922, Polish-Americans established thirty-four Polish parishes in Greater Buffalo and Western New York. By 1908, there were already 60,000 Buffalonians of Polish origin, and by 1940 the head count was 76,465. At first, most of them μengaged in unskilled labor (almost all were uneducated peasants). By the turn of the century, they had established musical, theatrical, literary, and civic associations and societies. By World War II there were 15 singing societies and musical clubs; the Polish-American Business Association had a founding membership of 400; 13 new parishes were organized, as well as a Polish library and a patriotic and physical fitness center (The Falcon Club).

Today, Buffalo is a city with a distinctive Polish flavor. Polish-Americans occupy positions of trust and honor in many professions, including politics, law, and business.

As the Pol-Ams have grown in influence and financial stature, they have spread out from the old neighborhoods. Cheektowaga, for instance, is a well-to-do suburb with a large, middle-class Polish population.

WHAT TO SEE

1) THE POLISH ROOM

It is located at the Lockwood Memorial Library of the State University of New York at Buffalo. The Polish Collection was begun in 1955. It includes books, periodicals, filmstrips, and artifacts. The areas covered include: the contribution of Poles and Polish-Americans in the humanities, the sciences, and the history of the United States. There are over 9,500 volumes in the collection. Along with contemporary materials from the twentieth century, there are historical documents from Poland's past when it was a monarchy. Royal documents and scholarly reference works form the backbone of the collection.

As a visitor from outside the Buffalo area, you should call Circulation for information before you come. The Polish Collection is located in room 529 on the 5th floor of the Library. Regular Library hours during the fall and spring semesters are: Monday-Thursday 8:00 am.-10:45 p.m., Friday 8:00 am. to 9:00 p.m., Saturday 9:00 am. to 5:00 p.m. and Sunday 12:00 noon to 10:00 p.m. The hours differ in the summer. The telephone number for the Circulation department is (716) 636-2815.

HOW TO GET THERE

The Polish Room, SUNY, at Buffalo is located on the Amherst campus of the University. For exact directions to Lockwood Library and the Polish Room make sure to call the Library's Circulation Department in advance of your visit. Call (716) 636-2815.

32) Adam Mickiewicz Monument in the Polish Room. Buffalo, NY

2) THE POLISH COMMUNITY CENTER OF BUFFALO

At 1081 Broadway. Telephone: (716) 893-7222. The PCC is housed in the Dom Polski (The Polish Home). The Polish Home was organized in 1905 to assist Polish immigrants in adapting to their new country.

Of the many activities in the Polish Community Center, two are most definitely of interest to the tourist. The first is the J.C. MAZUR GALLERY, dedicated to Joseph Mazur. Born in Buffalo in 1897, Joseph Mazur returned to Buffalo after completing his studies at the Art Students League in New York City, and began a life-long

33) The Polish Community Center; The statue of Chopin in the Mazur Gallery. Buffalo, NY

career as an ecclesiastical painter. Exhibits of regional and visiting artists are held on a continuous basis. Each exhibit lasts one month, and begins with a reception, which is held every first Friday of the month from 7:30 to 9:30 p.m. The public is invited. Gallery hours are: weekdays from 8:30 a.m. to 4:30 p.m. or by appointment.

There is also a Spring and Fall film series featuring Polish and East European film masters. A literary program hosts readings by nationally renowned authors; this is a program that continues throughout the year. Please contact the PCC for information about readings and films during the time you plan to be in Buffalo, at the number given above.

The Polish Community Center of Buffalo and the Adam Mickiewicz Library and Dramatic Circle are very near each other. If you are downtown, take Broadway to Playter Street. The PCC is at 1081 Broadway. For the Mickiewicz Library, walk from the PCC 4 blocks to Fillmore and turn left. Go down to 612 Fillmore Avenue.

3) THE ADAM MICKIEWICZ LIBRARY AND DRAMATIC CIRCLE

At 612 Fillmore Avenue (at Paderewski Drive), telephone: (716) 847-0839. Organized in 1895, the Circle began producing its amateur theatrical productions the same year. The two-story building on Fillmore serves as a library and center of Polish-American theatrical activity, and as a social center. There are meeting rooms, a casino, billiard rooms, a kitchen, hall, administrative offices, and a library of more than 4,000 volumes, including an absolutely unique collection of more than 400 handwritten scripts of Polish plays. Theatrical and cultural events are sponsored regularly. To find out what the schedule of events is, and to get the correct library hours during your stay in the city, please call (716) 854-5828.

See (2) above

4) THE POLISH ARMY ROOM

It is located in the Cruiser "Little Rock" at the Naval and Servicemen's Park. 1 Naval Park Cove, telephone: (716) 847-1773.

The Polish exhibit was established in 1984 by members of Polish and Polish-American War Veterans' associations. All the items on display have been donated. They include authentic uniforms, documents, medals, flags, photographs, and other artifacts which have been arranged and explained to tell the story of those who fought with the Allies in World War II. Among these, two battle groups stand out most distinctly, the First Polish Armored Division, which fought in Normandy, France, Belgium, Holland, and Germany, and the Polish Second Corps, which wrested the strategic fortress of Monte Cassino in Italy from the Germans when assaults by other battle formations of the Allies failed. Over 1,000 Polish lives were lost in that attack alone.

The many authentic displays at the Polish Museum on board the cruiser are proof of the heroic efforts of Polish soldiers who fought with the Allies in almost every major battle of World War II. There are also documents and other artifacts, which attest to the Polish participation in the Battle of Britain. Polish pilots fighting in the R.A.F. shot down 15% of the German planes destroyed over England. The displays cover a wide geographical area, including the Polish participation in the African Campaign, and the crucial Battle of Tobruk where the Poles distinguished themselves.

You will want to see the exhibits detailing the activities of the Polish Home Army, which culminated with the Warsaw Uprising of 1944. There also interesting artifacts that attest to the courageous and selfless work of the Polish Women's auxiliary, which served with great distinction alongside the men.

This is, to our knowledge, the most extensive collection of documents and memorabilia in the United States concerning the contribution of Poland to the Allied victory in World War II.

HOW TO GET THERE

The Polish Army Room at the Naval and Servicemen's Park, 1 Naval Park Cove. Telephone: (716) 847-1773. The Park is located at the end of Main Street, behind Buffalo Memorial Auditorium. You can take I-190 to downtown Buffalo. If you're coming from the south, take the Church Street exit, go right onto Lower Terrace, and then take another right onto Pearl Street. If you're coming down from the North and Niagara Falls, take the Niagara Street exit, go right on Niagara, then turn right onto S. Elmwood (which becomes Lower Terrace after the Church Street intersection). An alternate route is the Kensington Expressway to downtown and the Goodell Street exit, then bear left onto Pearl Street and continue to the Park. If you want to travel by public transportation, board the Main Street Metrorail to downtown Buffalo and go to the last stop.

5) POMOC

If you've decided to visit the PCC and the Mickiewicz Library, you might as well stop by Pomoc, Inc. at 629 Fillmore Avenue, telephone (716) 893-6880. This Polish-American Travel Agency also sells Polish books and gifts.

6) RUDA'S RECORDS

Record fans, especially of Polka and other Polish-American ethnic music, will definitely want to stop by Ruda's Records at 915 Broadway, just a short walk from the PCC. You can always call to find out if they have what you want at (716) 852-3121.

7) BROADWAY MARKET

You can't be interested in what is Polish and not be interested in Polish food. You may want to try the famous Broadway Market. It's at 999 Broadway, and parking for 1,100 cars is available. Many of the region's most famous names in Polish-style meat products, dairy products, and baked goods are available.

Last but not least, Buffalo has a tantalizing selection of Polish restaurants, probably the best selection outside of Chicago. Polonia Restaurant (716-894-8287) at 193 Lombard Street, open Tuesday to Saturday 11 am. to 7 p.m., is just off Broadway between the PCC and the Broadway Market. Polish Villa is at 2954 Union Road (call 716-683-9460) and also at 1085 Harlem Road (call 716-822-4908). The Polish Gardens is at 1588 Broadway and is open from 11 am. to 9 p.m. for lunch and dinner. On Sunday, breakfast is at 8 a.m. You can call 716-896-3032. And there is the Warsaw Inn at 1171 Broadway, telephone (716) 896-2448, which has lunches and dinner daily.

8) POLISH CARNIVAL

At the beginning of spring, Assumption Church at 435 Amherst Street holds its annual Polish Carnival. Included are Polish films (free admission), concerts, a Gourmet Dinner, and a Carnival

*34) The Chopin
Monument.
Buffalo, NY*

Dance. Call the Assumption Church Rectory (at 716-875-7626),
if you're planning to be in Buffalo at the end of March or beginning of April so you can include the Carnival into your plans.

9) THE CHOPIN MONUMENT

The Monument was the work of Josef Mazur during the 1920s.
Originally placed in front of the Museum of Science it is now,
appropriately enough, in front of Kleinhans Music Hall.

Cheektowaga

WHAT TO SEE

STATUE OF JOHN PAUL II

In 1987, a statue of His Holiness Pope John Paul II was unveiled
at Villa Maria College in Cheektowaga. The statue stands in front
of the College's auditorium entrance, facing Pennock Place. The

35) Statue of John Paul II; Villa Maria College in Cheektowaga, NY

College itself is steeped in Polish-American tradition and was a natural location for the statue honoring one of Poland's greatest sons. The Western New York area has over 350,000 Polish Americans, many of them very conscious and proud of their heritage. Small wonder, then, that the public fund drive for the monument was hugely successful—and over-subscribed, with thousands of donations making up the entire sum needed. If you're in the Buffalo area, definitely go to see this likeness of the Pope.

The Cheektowaga Town Park holds an annual Polish American Arts Festival. It takes place in mid-August. For information on how to get there and the exact dates, call (716) 895-1587. The park is located on Harlem Road, between Genesee Street and Walden Avenue.

HOW TO GET THERE

Villa Maria College can be reached from downtown Buffalo (Niagara Square) by taking Genesee Street. Go down Genesee to Sprenger

Avenue. Take a right onto Sprenger and go down to Heminway Street. Take a left on Heminway and go down to the College.

The College is bounded by Pennock Place on the North and by Ridge Road on the East.

Lake George

MARCELLA SEMBRICH MEMORIAL STUDIO

Marcella Kochanska-Sembrich (she adopted her mother's maiden name, Sembrich, as her stage name) was born in Poland. At the age of 19, she made her operatic debut in Athens. Six years later, at age 25, she made her American debut at the Metropolitan Opera in New York (the year was 1883). This moment in her brilliant career came after she had already been acclaimed the reigning coloratura of the opera stages of Berlin, Budapest, Vienna, London, as well as Spain and Portugal.

36) Marcella Sembrich Memorial Studio. Bolton Landing-On-Lake-George, NY

She was also a celebrated violinist and pianist. It is said that Franz Liszt himself admired her playing. After the Met's 1883-84 season, she returned to Europe, but was back again in 1898, and stayed with the Met until her farewell to the stage in 1909.

She founded the vocal departments at the Juilliard School in New York City and in the Curtis Institute of Music in Philadelphia, where her good friend and fellow-Pole Jozef Hoffman was the director. She has been the most influential teacher of singing in America for 25 years.

She gave her money and her heart to many orphaned African-Americans in the Deep South; she was generous to many causes in her adopted country. And when she made her farewell appearance at the Metropolitan Opera in New York in 1909, after having been its reigning coloratura and lyric soprano for ten seasons, she received a two-hour ovation. The audience included all the greatest operatic talents of the day, including the magnificent Enrico Caruso himself.

President Theodore Roosevelt, moved by her contribution to American arts, but especially by her devotion to many social causes on behalf of the poor and the underprivileged, wrote to her: "I am glad to tell you that all those who know best say that your singing has meant very much indeed to the American people, and I especially thank you for the generous way in which you have used your great gift for every philanthropic and charitable undertaking."

Madame Sembrich had a summer home on Lake George in New York. In order to better accommodate her many students, she had a special music studio built nearby.

The Marcella Sembrich Memorial Studio is a museum of opera and it houses the collections of Mme. Sembrich. It was actively used by her for teaching purposes from 1921 until 1935, the year she died. It has been open to the public continuously as an opera museum since 1937.

On display are such artifacts as portraits, autograph scores, objects of art, trophies, and various costumes, which help make real to the contemporary viewer the rich contributions of Mme. Sembrich to the opera. The museum is open for two months in the summer only: from July 1st through Labor Day. Admission is free. The hours are 10:00 a.m. to 12:30 p.m. and 2:00p.m. to 5:30 p.m. You can call in advance if you wish. The telephone number is (518) 644-9839.

Take the New York State Thruway (Interstate Route 87) from New York City, then take Route 9N exit North to Bolton Landing and the Museum.

New York City (Manhattan)

New York City has an established reputation as the gateway to the promised land, to America. It's no accident that the Statue of Liberty stands in New York Harbor and that the famous Ellis Island Museum is there, too. That museum is dedicated to documenting the gargantuan movement of human beings into the New World. It also includes a Polish section, certainly worth viewing (see below).

The Frick Museum on 1 East 70th (212-288-0700) has the famous painting by Rembrandt, "The Polish Rider" (Lisowczyk) around which some controversy continues to swirl among art historians. There is no question about the historical authenticity of the painting but it may have been painted by Rembrandt and/or his assistants. The Metropolitan Museum of Art, at Fifth Avenue and 82nd Street, has a Turkish carpet captured in 1683 when King John Sobieski defeated the Turks at the gates of Vienna. Call 212-535-7710 for further information on the Museum's hours, special exhibits, etc..

The City, as native New Yorkers call it, or Manhattan, is the nation's greatest agglomeration of cultural activity. For instance, of the more than 22,000 private charitable foundations that exist in the entire United States, more than 1,500 are located in Manhattan.

Though most of the immigrants from Poland that settled in Manhattan were poor to start with, a sizeable number of them, sooner or later, if not in the first generation then in the second or third, did establish a good existence for themselves. They paid heed not only to the need for financial security and education, but also to the need for supporting noble social, civic, and cultural causes.

The Polish presence in Manhattan goes back to the very first colonization of the island by Europeans. When Peter Stuyvesant built Fort Amsterdam, it was commanded for a time by a trusted aide and political ally of his, Captain Daniel Liczko, who was a Polish officer. The captain's daughter, Anna would later marry a mayor of English New York.

The real flood of Polish immigration did not occur until the end of the 19th century. From 1899 to 1915, 1,411,760 Polish immigrants came to the United States through Ellis Island. Of this number, 308,861 settled in New York State, most of them in the City of New York. The New York settlement was the second largest on the continent, topped only by Pennsylvania, where 338,347 settled.

Another large influx of Poles came after World War II. These were the tens of thousands who had fought in the war against the Germans and Soviets and who could not return to their homeland for fear of political reprisals. A third wave of immigration came in the late 1960s. As the economic condition in Poland continued to deteriorate at the end of Party Boss Gierek's regime, a steady stream of Poles started coming. Many of them came as tourists, and with time, were able to overcome the difficulties of obtaining the "green card" (immigrant status) and stayed. They continue to come today.

This constant flow of new blood from the "old country" has kept many Polish-American institutions alive, as the new arrivals still require the services and support that their predecessors did.

The steady arrival of Poles, the reawakening of Polish Americans' interest in their heritage, and the growing awareness of the need to preserve Polish culture for future generations have challenged many Polish American institutions in the '90s.

Four most worthy sites of cultural interest exist in New York City for those interested in Polish culture.

WHAT TO SEE

1) THE KOSCIUSZKO FOUNDATION

This institution, located at 15 East 65th Street, is one of the greatest American success stories in the field of public service and cultural activity. It was founded by Stefan Mierzwa who arrived from Poland as a teenager and received scholarships to both Amherst College and Harvard University. Upon graduating, Mierzwa raised $5,000 for the Polish American Scholarship Committee, later to become the Kosciuszko Foundation.

The Foundation is a monument to Stefan Mierzwa's single-minded desire to give the Polish-American the opportunity to better himself through education. Founded with the chief purpose of providing scholarships and grants for study in Poland, the Foundation, in addition, has programs for Americans to study a year

37) Kosciuszko Foundation. New York City

abroad at the Jagiellonian University, offers domestic scholarships for undergraduates and has instituted the Summer-Sessions-in-Poland Program as well as the new Teaching English-in-Poland Program. Today, in the early 1990s, its total assets are well over $12 million.

The headquarters of the Foundation is an elegant neo-classic town house on Manhattan's East Side. It houses the administrative offices of the Foundation, a library with reference works on

Polish and Polish-American subjects, and a book store, which is one of the best-supplied in America on Polish subjects in English. Its art gallery contains the finest collection of Polish art in the country, including works by Jan Matejko, Jacek Malczewski, Jan Styka, Jozef Brandt, and Olga Boznanska.

38) Main Hall and Art Gallery, Kosciuszko Foundation, New York City

The Foundation offers a rich program of cultural events including author's evenings, lectures, concerts, films and art shows. Its Chamber Music Series held once a month is broadcast live by WQXR.

If you are visiting the city and wish to attend one of these events, call (212) 734-2130 for specific information.

2) THE POLISH INSTITUTE OF ARTS AND SCIENCES IN AMERICA

Located at 208 E. 30th Street in Manhattan. The Institute was founded in 1942 by Oskar Halecki, Bronislaw Malinowski, Jan Kucharzewski, Waclaw Lednicki, Wojciech Swietoslawski, and Rafal Taubenschlag to assure the continuity of Polish culture and learning during Poland's darkest hour. It was officially registered as an association in the State of New York on May 1, 1942. Its founding fathers were Polish scholars and members of the pre-World War II Polish Academy of Sciences. Its purpose was to preserve for future generations Polish scholarship, culture, and

89

39) Polish Institute of Arts and Sciences. New York City

other achievements, which had been targeted for destruction by the Nazis. Over the years the Institute grew into a formidable research organization, as well as a repository of art and documents of Poland. Its quarterly Bulletin of the Polish Institute of Arts and Sciences in America, later reincarnated as *The Polish Review*, continues to be an important force in research concerning Poland and Polish America.

Among the prominent members, past and present, are Zbigniew Brzezinski, Mieczyslaw Horszowski, Artur Rodzinski, Artur Rubinstein, Jerzy Kosinski, Boleslaw Wierzbianski and Kazimierz Wierzynski, and three Nobel laureates Isaac Bashevis Singer, Czeslaw Milosz, and Andrew Schally.

The Institute, now in its own headquarters, continues the work of organizing meetings with prominent scholars visiting New York, exhibits of paintings by young Polish artists and other cultural activities. Once a year, the Institute organizes a general meeting for its members with special sessions devoted to the many subjects of interest to the membership.

The Institute's library as well as its art collection are available to the public for viewing. Please call (212) 686-4164 for specific information on hours of business.

3) THE JOZEF PILSUDSKI INSTITUTE OF AMERICA FOR RESEARCH IN THE MODERN HISTORY OF POLAND

At 381 Park Avenue South, telephone: (212) 683-4342. The Institute is open to the public Monday through Friday from 10:00 a.m. to 6:00 p.m. except on legal holidays. Xerox copies of documents can be made on site upon request for a small charge. There are also books for sale on Polish subjects, especially relating to modern Polish history and the life and work of Marshal Jozef Pilsudski.

The Institute was organized in New York City in 1943, during World War II. From the start it was a joint effort of native Americans of Polish descent and of refugees from war-torn Poland. It was to be the continuation of the Institute for Research in the Modern History of Poland, which had been founded in Warsaw, Poland, in 1923.

Among the founding fathers of the American organization were Poland's former Finance Minister, Mr. Ignacy Matuszewski; former Minister of Education, Professor Waclaw Jedrzejewicz; and the former Minister of Industry and Commerce, Mr. Henryk Floyar Raichman. The scope of the Institute's researches and documentation stretches from 1863, the date of the so-called January Uprising in Poland, to the present time.

The Institute has the second largest collection of Polish historical documents in the United States, second only to the Hoover Institution in California. Many of the Institute's collections are unique. The archives are not limited to Polish history, but include other nations of Eastern and Central Europe. Polish-American history is covered by the "National Committee of Americans of Polish Descent" Archives and by the "Committee of National Defence" Archives, which together contain several thousand documents. Many prominent American scholars have used the resources of the Institute as the basis of their research on modern European and American history. A number of important books have been published as a result of these scientific efforts.

The Institute currently contains in its library more than 16,000 catalogued books, 4,000 brochures and pamphlets arranged by subject, and a periodicals section of over 4,100 titles. The photographic collection contains over 19,600 photographs pertaining to various historical events, important persons, and locations of historical value.

The map collection numbers over 800 maps. There is also a stamp section composed of several collections. Finally, there is a very important film collection of high documentary and historical value, as well as a video-cassette collection of about 200 cassettes. Among these are 60 video-cassettes on persecutions of Poles in the Soviet labor camps. The Institute has a distinguished collection of Polish art, consisting of donations from private individuals. A number of these works of art have been featured in various art publications.

Unlike many similar research facilities, which are open only to scholars and researchers, the Pilsudski Institute is open to the public.

4) THE POLISH CONSULATE GENERAL

40) Polish Consulate General. New York City

41) Jagiello Monument, Central Park. New York City

Located at 233 Madison Avenue, corner of 37th Street, telephone (212) 889-8360. Ever since Poland's declaration of independence from the Soviet Union and the changing of the guard at the Consulate from a Communist to a "normal" Consul General and staff, the Consulate has been outgoing and cooperative in its relations with the Polish-American community. There are currently exhibits of Polish artists, concerts, and other events open to the public. Please call for information concerning the exhibit on display at the time if you plan to be in New York City.

5) THE JAGIELLO MONUMENT

Located in Central Park, North of 79th Street and Fifth Avenue, close to the Metropolitan Museum and the Cleopatra Needle, this statue has an interesting history. Commissioned by Baron Ropp, head of the 1939-40 World's Fair Polish Pavilion, it was created by the Polish artist, Stanislaw Kazimierz Ostrowski in four months! It became "the miracle of the World's Fair" and was moved to its present location in 1946 by permission of Mayor Fiorello La Guardia. The inscription on the monument reads: "Wladyslaw Jagiello, King of Poland and Grand Duke of Lithuania (1386-1434), Founder of a Free Union of the Peoples of East-Central Europe, Victor over the Teutonic Knights at Grunwald. July 15, 1940."

6) UNITED NATIONS

At First Avenue between 42nd and 46th Streets.

The stained glass window on permanent display at the main entrance to the Security Council Chamber is based on the motifs of a painting by the famous Polish artist, Stanislaw Wyspianski (1869-1907). It reflects an artistic manifestation of Polish crafts-manship and is a symbol of great love and concern for children. This piece of art is a gift to the U.N. from the people of Poland on the occasion of the International Year of the Child, 1979, and was created by Jozef and Alicja Olszewski of Warsaw, to a design by Halina Cieslinska-Brzeski of Cracow.

At the main entrance to the Dag Hammarskjold Library, there is on permanent display a large bronze head of Copernicus (1473-1543), the famous Polish astronomer. Sculpted by Alfons Karny, it was a gift from Poland to the U.N. in 1970. Karny is one of the world's greatest sculptors of the twentieth century.

7) POLISH AMERICAN ARTISTS SOCIETY (PAAS) FINE ARTS GALLERY

Located at 19 Irving Place, New York, NY 10003, the gallery is a showcase of Polish talent in the field of painting, drawing, graph-ics, sculpture, tapestry, ceramics, photography, video, film, and performance art. Established in 1986, PAAS has organized over 75 one-man-shows and 7 group shows in its first six years of exist-ence. Artists represented include (in alphabetical order) Maciek Albrecht, Hanna Zawa Cywinska, Andrzej Czeczot, Zbigniew Dlubak, Andrzej Dudzinski, Ryszard Horowitz, Janusz Kapusta, Andrzej Kenda, Zbigniew Krygier, Jerzy Kubina, Roman Kujawa, Jan Dawid II Kuracinski, Stanislaw Mlodozeniec, Rafal Olbinski, Christopher Zacharow, Stanislaw Zagorski, and Krzysztof Zarebski.

For information on current exhibits, or to get on the mailing list, call Andrzej Kenda at (718) 565-5505.

8) IGNACY JAN PADEREWSKI IN NEW YORK

This great pianist and statesman lived in New York for many years and gave numerous concerts at Carnegie Hall. His last residence was at nearby Buckingham Hotel, at 101 West 57th Street, where a commemorative bronze tablet was unveiled on November 15, 1991, on the 50th anniversary of his death. Paderewski died at the hotel, on June 29, 1941. His heart is at the National Shrine of Our Lady of Czestochowa in Doylestown, PA.

43) Paderewski plaque at the Buckingham Hotel, New York City

42) Paderewski by Malvina Hoffman, New York City

Steinway Hall, at 109 West 57th Street, contains a number of memorabilia of the great Polish artist, including a bronze of Paderewski as Statesman by Malvina Hoffman, a portrait by Zuolaga, the mask by Benda as well as several paintings, medals, documents and other memorabilia.

9) SAINT STANISLAUS B & M CHURCH

At 101 East 7th Street, New York, NY 10009. Tel. (212) 475-4576.

St. Stanislaus Bishop and Martyr Church was established in 1872 and has been on its present site since 1901. The centennial of the founding of the parish was celebrated on May 7, 1972, with Cardinal Terrence Cooke as principal celebrant.

During the long-time (42 years!) pastorship of Msgr. Felix Ferdynand Burant, the church became the center for religious and

44) Church of St. Stanislaus B. and M., New York City

patriotic activities of all Poles in New York. The first Pulaski Day parade started from this church. On July 1, 1986, the Pauline Fathers were given the church by John Cardinal O'Connor. Rev. Lucius L. Tyrasinski became the 14th pastor of the church. Now completely renovated, it is one of the most beautiful churches in New York, as well as the only Polish Roman-Catholic church in Manhattan, and the oldest Polish church in the Archdiocese of New York. On June 23, 1991, the Monument of John Paul II was erected in front of the rectory. In the church itself there are two large paintings by Adam Styka: "The Assumption" and "The Ascension."

10) ST. PATRICK'S CATHEDRAL

At 50th street and Fifth Avenue there is a chapel dedicated to St. Stanislaw Kostka, the first one in the left nave. It has a white marble statue of the Polish saint, and nearby, at the end wall of the left nave, a bronze head of Pope John Paul II whose visit to the Cathedral in 1979 is commemorated by a bronze plaque on the exterior wall, to the right of the main entrance.

Each year, on the first Sunday of October, a large Polish flag is displayed on the right side of the main facade of the Cathedral for the annual Pulaski Day parade. The Archbishop of the New York Diocese greets the marchers from the steps of the cathedral. This is the largest such parade in the United States in which Polish American organizations from three states, New York, New Jersey, and Connecticut, take part. There is an incredible array of colorful floats, bands, marching groups, performers; fraternal, cultural, religious, military, and police organizations, schools and parishes; all marching and performing, from 26th to 52nd Street. It is definitely worth a major detour or a separate trip!

The Pulaski Day parade is also saluted by a Polish flag on the Empire State Building at 34th and Fifth Avenue where the illumination that night displays white and red colors of the Polish flag.

45) St. Patrick's Cathedral on Pulaski Day, New York City

46) Empire State Building on Pulaski Day, New York City

47) Polish Scouts marching on Pulaski Day, New York City

48) Pulaski Day in
New York City

11) THE ELLIS ISLAND MUSEUM

The Polish American community had made a sizeable contribution to this project in the hope of securing a Polish exhibit room for its own history. This has not happened yet, but there is a section dedicated to Polish exhibits, which President Lech Walesa visited during his 1990 tour of the United States.

49) President Walesa
visits the Polish
exhibit on Ellis
Island, NY

12) ANDRE ZARRE GALLERY

Located at 154 Wooster Street, the gallery was established in 1974 by a Polish poet, Andrzej Zarre. It has included exhibits by Rafal Olbinski, as well as Franek Starowiejski, Hanna Zawa, and Aleksander Roszkowski. The gallery hours are Tuesday through Saturday from 11 a.m. to 6 p.m. Tel. (212) 353-3456.

HOW TO GET THERE

Since Manhattan is within reach by a variety of forms of transportation, and since all the institutions are within easy proximity of each other, we feel there is no need to give specific directions. In each case, please call in advance to determine if you can see what you want when you are in town.

OTHER POINTS OF INTEREST

There are a number of authentic Polish restaurants in the East Village, on First Avenue between 4th Street and 10th Street. Definitely worth taking in.

13) POLISH AMERICAN BOOKSTORE

The Polish Daily News (Nowy Dziennik) at 333 W. 38th Street has a well-stocked book store, with excellent holdings of Polish language titles. Worth browsing through. Don't be surprised if you bump into some high Polish official visiting from Poland. Call (212) 594-2266 to find out when you can visit the book store.

Port Washington

FACTS AND FIGURES

Port Washington, Glen Cove, Riverhead, Wading River, these are some of the North Shore towns on Long Island that have a sizeable and active Polish population. There is Lech Walesa Place in Glen Cove, named after the famous leader of Poland's Solidarity movement who later became the first President of a free Poland after World War II. There are Polish churches and Polish schools for children to learn about their heritage (the so-called "Saturday" schools), and there are Polish festivals, as in Riverhead where some streets have Polish names, signs indicate the distance from major Polish towns and many shutters are painted Kashubian style!

Of the 308,861 Poles who stayed in the State of New York in the turning years of the last and the beginning years of this century, and who had been part of the great influx from Poland, quite a few ventured out to the easternmost part of the state, to Long Island, where the only viable industry at that time was farming. They took up chicken farming, orchards, and potato farming. The potato farms were mostly in the Riverhead and Wading River area. They worked extremely hard, eventually buying their own farms, and did not mind the backbreaking labor and long hours. They were not wealthy, but they were not dirt poor, either, as they had been back in Poland. After World War II, Levittown was constructed for returning soldiers and their young families-to-be. It became the first large-scale, cookie-cutter residential community in the nation; many followed. The result was a growing interest in the attractions of Long Island living. Soon businesses started following, and by the 1970s and 1980s the Island, as it is called by people in the City, became a "boom 'burb," with developments stretching from one end to the other, throughout the island's entire 120 mile length. The Polish farmers suddenly found themselves millionaires, as well-heeled developers paid them handsomely for their acres, paving them over and building rows upon rows of houses on them.

Farming was not the only industry in which Poles did well on Long Island. One wealthy Polish-American in the construction and real estate business in Port Washington, spurred on by the need for a real center of Polish culture and education about it on the Island, made possible the Polish American Museum of Port Washington.

WHAT TO SEE

THE POLISH AMERICAN MUSEUM

At 16 Belleview Avenue, Port Washington, New York, 11050, tel. (516) 883-6542. Formerly, the Port Washington Public Library, this building contains 15 exhibit rooms, a research library, the Henry Archacki Archives, a gift shop, cultural workshops, a sizeable lecture hall, "Saturday" school rooms, and a kitchenette, as well as administrative offices for the museum. Thirty rooms in all are contained within.

The Archacki Archives, started in 1924, in addition to the Henry and Janina Archacki Polish Collection, also contain several other

50) Polish American Museum in Port Washington, NY

51) Mr. and Mrs. Henry Archacki at the Archacki Archives, Port Washington, NY

collections: Haiman, Kowalczyk, Col Anuszkiewicz, Maj. Gen Stevenson, Er. Rozanski, Edward Pinkowski, the Arthur Colemans, Artur Waldo, The Koss Family Artists collection, Ed Sidor, Stanislaw Szukalski, Andrzej Pitynski, Col. Podbielski, and the Sidwas.

The museum's collection includes artifacts, displays, paintings, documents, and various memorabilia and photographs illustrating the achievements of people of Polish heritage who have made lasting contributions to Poland, America, and humanity.

The museum sponsors art expositions, auctions, stamp and coin exhibitions, concerts and recitals, films, literary workshops, field trips, lectures and seminars, all with education in mind about Poland, Polish heritage, and the history of Poles in America. The gift shop offers genuine articles made in Poland and includes not only mementoes and knick-knacks, but also books, dictionaries, cookbooks, and many other hard-to-find items. The Polish American Museum is a member of the American Association of Museums and the Long Island Museum Association.

HOW TO GET THERE

From New York City, take the Long Island Railroad to Port Washington (last stop on that branch of the train). The exact address of the Museum is 16 Belleview Avenue. It is just two minutes walking distance from the train station, off Main Street.

If you are coming from New York City by car, take the Long Island Expressway to the Port Washington Exit, North, and following the road (Searingtown Road), go to Main Street. Take a left and go down to Belleview Avenue, where you'll take another left to the Museum.

In case you need to call and make sure about directions or the schedule of events and exhibits, the phone number is (516) 883-6542 or (516) 767-1936. The museum is open most days of the week.

Stillwater

SARATOGA NATIONAL HISTORICAL PARK

In 1777, the defense of northern New York was crucial to the success of the American Revolution. To assist in this task, Congress dispatched a young colonel of engineers, Tadeusz Kosciuszko. When he arrived at Fort Ticonderoga (see separate entry), located at the strategically important confluence of Lake George and Lake

103

Champlain, the Pole reported that the fort could not be held unless outworks were built to defend the commanding heights nearby. Unfortunately, the American commander paid no heed to this warning and when the invading British army arrived it occupied the heights and forced the evacuation of the valuable fort—just as Kosciuszko predicted.

During the retreat from Ticonderoga, the Polish engineer's talents were put to use directing the felling of trees, destruction of dams and creation of other obstructions that would inhibit the enemy's pursuit.

General Horatio Gates, commander of the American forces, chose Kosciuszko to establish a position to block a British move toward Albany. The site he chose and fortified at Bemis Heights gave Gates' army a superior position that greatly assisted the Americans in achieving a resounding victory at the Battles of Saratoga. Burgoyne was unable to make his way around the Americans who engaged his forces at Freeman Farm, a mile north of the fortified position.

Burgoyne delayed for nearly three weeks hoping for additional help from other New York forces; yet after one last attempt to outflank the American position and to reach Albany, British forces retreated and were surrounded in camp near Saratoga. There, on October 17, 1777, Burgoyne surrendered the entire British force of nearly 6,000 troops.

The battle changed the course of the American Revolution, persuaded France and Spain to come to the aid of the Americans, and made independence a reality. General Gates commented that "the great tacticians of the campaign were hills and forests which a young Polish engineer was skilful enough to select for my encampment." There is a Kosciuszko monument at Stop 2 on the battlefield tour road.

The Park is open all year around, from 9 to 5; battlefield tours are available from April 1st to December 1st.

HOW TO GET THERE

The Park is 8 miles from Exit 12 on the I-87, also known as The Northway. There are some signs leading to the site. If you come from the South and get off at exit 12, make a right turn to enter

Route 9, cross it on County Road 108. Turn right on Route 9P, on which you proceed until you reach Route 423. Turn right and go to intersection with Route 32. Turn left and go for two miles to the Park. For information call (518) 664-9821.

Syracuse

LE MOYNE COLLEGE

The College is the home of seven paintings and four tapestries, which together form a panorama of 800 years of Polish history: from A.D. 1,000 to A.D. 1791. These priceless works of art hang in the College library and are available for public viewing during library hours.

This magnificent display of Polish art and Polish history was made possible by the generosity of one man Stephen Kyburg de Ropp who at one time taught at Le Moyne College.

The paintings were expressly created for the Polish Pavilion at the 1939 World's Fair in New York. The four tapestries were part of the Polish display at the Paris Exhibition of 1937.

Mr. de Ropp was, prior to World War II, a British subject of Swiss nationality. He was a member of the Board of Directors of the European Organization of International Trade Fairs, and he had been the general manager of the Poznan (Poland) International Trade Fair. Thanks to his credentials, the Polish Government chose him to head a commission that would put together the Polish exhibit at the 1939 World's Fair in New York.

Engaged in the creation of the paintings was the President of the Polish Academy of Fine Arts in Warsaw, a former Polish prime minister, and the Confraternity of St. Luke, a group of painters adhering to the pre-Raphaelite school. They had the task of depicting seven selected events from Polish history. Thousands of historical and technical details were researched, including old coins, medals, costumes, life style, and much more. The research was conducted throughout Europe. Though the project started late in 1938, the paintings were ready by March, 1939, and were shipped to New York.

These masterpieces were all signed by each member of the Confraternity of St. Luke because the artists had worked as a team on the paintings. The four tapestries, which had been shown at the Paris Exhibition in 1937 also were displayed.

In September,1939, Germany invaded Poland and World War II began. The money supply for the support of the exhibit in New York was cut off. De Ropp formed a committee of prominent Americans and the display continued. De Ropp was never paid a cent for his labors, and finally, after the war, the President of the Polish Government in Exile asked that de Ropp take the paintings and tapestries as payment for his generous efforts. Even though he could have made a very handsome profit on the sale of these art works, de Ropp instead donated all eleven works of art to Le Moyne College because he had taught there. It is a Catholic college and therefore has an ambience that suited the celebration of Poland as a Christian and Catholic nation.

The eleven painters who made up the team that created the works of art were: Boleslaw Cybis, Bernard Frydrysiak, Jan Gotard, Aleksander Jedrzejewski, Eliasz Kanarek, Jeremi Kubicki, Antoni Michalak, Tadeusz Pruszkowski, Jan Zamoyski, Stefan Pluzanski,

52) Boleslaw the Brave greeting Otto III. A.D. 1000. Le Moyne College, Syracuse, NY

53) Granting of the Charter of Jedlnia. A.D. 1430. Le Moyne College, Syracuse, NY

and Janusz Podoski. Of these, Boleslaw Cybis made a name for himself in America. His name lives on in an art factory in Trenton, New Jersey, which creates beautiful limited-edition ceramics and other works of art. This center of artistic workmanship is appropriately called Cybis, after its founder.

The eleven painters retired for six months into isolation to do their work. A committee of leading Polish historians formed the subject of each painting and indicated where information could be found to authenticate what was to be in each painting. Each detail in every one of the paintings is historically accurate, right down to the color of the mile and a half long red carpet, which German

54) *The Relief of Vienna. A.D. 1683. Le Moyne College, Syracuse, NY*

55) *The 3rd of May Constitution. A.D. 1791. Le Moyne College, Syracuse, NY*

Emperor Otto III walked on in 1,000 A.D. to the pilgrimage site of the tomb of St. Adalbert in Poland. To achieve this perfection, research had to be done in the archives and museums of Austria, France, Germany, Italy, Poland, and Sweden.

The seven paintings that were finally produced represent the following events:

a) Otto III being greeted by Polish King Boleslaw the Brave on Otto's pilgrimage to the tomb of St. Adalbert at Gniezno. A.D. 1000.

b) The Baptism of Lithuania, A.D. 1386.

c) Granting of the Habeas Corpus Act at Jedlnia by King Wladyslaw IV in 1430.

d) The Union of Poland and Lithuania into one Common-wealth, at Lublin, A.D. 1569.

e) The Warsaw Confederation, A.D. 1573. In this historic event, Polish citizens of different faiths promised each other mutual religious tolerance. All kings thereafter had to swear allegiance to that act granting freedom of religion.

f) The Relief of Vienna by Polish forces under King John Sobieski, A.D. 1683.

g) The May 3rd Constitution, A.D. 1791. This was Poland's democratic constitution, voted by Poland's Parliament, which granted equal rights and other privileges to all classes of men in the nation.

Finally, the four tapestries, each nine by seven feet, have as their theme King John Sobieski and his French-born wife Marysienka. Their love was legendary and the subject of many poems, novels, and works of art. The savior of Vienna and the Holy Roman Empire is depicted together with his queen in the tapestry "King John and His Queen." The three other tapestries are titled "The Angels," "King John on Horseback," and "Viennese Victory."

HOW TO GET THERE

Coming from New York City on the Thruway, get off at Exit 35, take Thompson Road South for about 3 miles to Springfield, go to the right and follow the signs to Le Moyne College. Take the second entrance.

Ticonderoga

FORT TICONDEROGA

Between Lake Champlain and Lake George the French built in 1755 at the outset of the Seven Years' War a fort called "Carillon" to block British presence on Lake Champlain. It was defended successfully by a small French force under the Marquis de Montcalm against overwhelming odds, July 8, 1758. The fort was captured in the Revolutionary War by Ethan Allen and Benedict Arnold, the first American victory in the Revolution.

Tadeusz Kosciuszko played a critical role here during the efforts in 1777 to halt the British advance up Lake Champlain commanded by General Burgoyne. Visitors can still visit the sites of Kosciuszko's engineering efforts at Ticonderoga during the late spring of 1777. (Be sure to visit also The Saratoga National Historical Park to learn more of Kosciuszko's achievements in that year.)

In 1977, assistance from Edward J. Piszek and the Copernicus Society of America was instrumental in enabling Fort Ticonderoga to purchase Mount Defiance, at which time there was a commemorative exhibition on Tadeusz Kosciuszko. Also in that year, Fort Ticonderoga was the "location" for filming a PBS special on Kosciuszko, a bicentennial project sponsored by the Copernicus Society and the Reader's Digest Foundation.

The collection of artifacts related to Kosciuszko came to the museum primarily from Count Alexandre Orlowski. There are 11 commemorative items, which are rotated on and off display. All

56) Aerial view of Fort Ticonderoga Ticonderoga, NY

collections are available to researchers in the Thompson-Pell Research Center, including the Orlowski Collection. Call the Curator at (518) 585-2821 to make an appointment. Also call this number for the latest information on special events, new exhibits, books available in the Museum Shop, information on their "Friends" program, and school services.

There is a great deal of information on Kosciuszko in the museum, which this entry can only report in general outline. Fort Ticonderoga is one of the most beautiful spots in the northeast, and it is easy to see why it played such an important role in the history of this continent. Be sure to visit!

Fort Ticonderoga, Mount Defiance, and Mount Independence are open daily from 10 May to mid-October from 9 am to 5 pm (extended to 6 pm in July and August) Adult admission is $6, children under 10 are free.

HOW TO GET THERE

Fort Ticonderoga is 18 miles east on Route 74 from Exit 28 on I-87. Half a mile West of Fort Ti ferry from Shoreham, Vermont.

Utica

FACTS AND FIGURES

Utica is a large town of approximately 70,000 residents. It is located in central New York State, approximately 100 miles west of Albany on the New York State Thruway (I-90), and 200 miles west of Buffalo. The region is the famous Mohawk Valley. The town is on the old Erie Canal. At the turn of the century, many European immigrants passed through and settled there. Most of the Poles who arrived settled in West Utica and the neighboring suburbs of New York Mills and Yorkville, as well as in East Utica. The immigrants were attracted to the enormous complex of cotton mills where work was relatively plentiful for unskilled labor. Though the cotton mills moved to the southern states in the middle 1940s, the descendants of the Polish immigrants and the old immigrants themselves stayed behind, opening up small businesses and going to work in other industries.

WHAT TO SEE

1) GENERAL CASIMIR PULASKI MONUMENT

Located at the intersection of Parkway and Oneida Streets, south of downtown Utica. The monument's plaque reads: "Brigadier General Casimir Pulaski 1745-1779, Originator of American Cavalry." It was erected in 1930 by a local group of Polish-Americans to honor the Father of the American Cavalry who died fighting for freedom in America and had hoped to contribute to the freedom of the people of all oppressed nations, particularly his native land, Poland.

A local organization, the General Casimir Pulaski Memorial Association, cares for the Monument. On the first Sunday of October it sponsors a celebration and a parade through downtown Utica.

2) THE MIKOLAJ KOPERNIK MONUMENT

Mikolaj Kopernik (Nicholas Copernicus) was the famous Polish astronomer who first gave factual proof that the Earth moved around the Sun and not vice-versa as had been imagined for many centuries before him. A sculpture of him stands at the corner of Genesee and Eagle Streets, just South of downtown Utica.

This monument was erected in 1975 through the efforts of the Kopernik Memorial Association of Central New York in commemoration of the 500th anniversary of the astronomer's birth.

A nationwide contest was sponsored for the monument in Poland by the Polish National Academy of Arts and Sciences. It was won by sculptor Bogdan Chmielewski. The bronze was done in Poland, then shipped whole to the United States. The statue is 21 feet tall.

3) THE HOLY TRINITY ROMAN CATHOLIC CHURCH

The parish was organized in Utica in 1896 by Polish immigrants. It became known as the "Mother of Many Daughters," because the many other Polish parishes in the Mohawk Valley were formed with help from this parish. It is the largest predominantly Polish-American parish in the region.

Masses are celebrated in Polish every day at 7:15 a.m. and on Sundays at 11:30 am. All are welcome for mass and quiet prayer. The Church is located at 1206 Lincoln Avenue.

4) KOPERNIK POLISH CULTURAL CENTER

Located in the Polish Community Center, 810 Columbia Street in Utica. The Cultural Center was established through New York State funding. It is operated by the Kopernik Polish Cultural Center Committee of the Kopernik Memorial Association of Central New York, Inc. It contains a very fine permanent collection of Polish works of art, books, artifacts, and videotapes. There is also a continuously changing display and exhibition of paintings and other works of art.

Books and art objects are available for sale. The Cultural Center is open every Sunday from 2:00 p.m. to 5:00 p.m., except holidays. Admission is free.

HOW TO GET THERE

(1), (2) & (3). If you are coming up from New York City, take the New York State Thruway (I-87) and take the continuation into I-90 to Utica. Points of Interest 1 through 3 are easily locatable from downtown Utica.

(4) From 1-90 turn North onto North Genesee Street and follow it for approximately two miles. Turn right on Columbia Street.

OTHER POINTS OF INTEREST

5) Joseph Furgal's Polish Shop, 617 Henry Street, Utica, NY 13501. The shop sells Polish imports, books, and gifts. To find out if they have anything that you may be looking for, call (315) 732-2434.

6) Skiba's Shop, at the Union (Train and Bus) Station. 321 Main Street, Utica, NY 13501. Polish imports, cards, books, and music. Open daily. Telephone: (315) 797-1650.

Vestal

FACTS AND FIGURES

The town of Vestal is in Broome County, upstate New York. The county includes the cities of Binghamton, Endicott, Endwell, and Johnson City. Approximately 7,000 Polish-Americans live there. They maintain three Polish Roman Catholic parishes: All Saints Polish National Church in Johnson City, St. Casimir's in Endicott, and St. Stanislaus Kostka in Binghamton.

WHAT TO SEE

For the masses of uneducated immigrants who came from Poland, life in the United States was extremely difficult. There was plenty of prejudice and bias against them. They could not speak English and were forced to take the meanest jobs for the lowest pay. The

112

turn of the century was not a time when civil rights meant much as a slogan for social progress. The discrimination, the harshness of life, the inability to communicate adequately with others due to the language barrier-all this contributed to the strength and tenacity with which the Polish-Americans developed and supported their churches and organizations. The magnificent achievement of the Polish-American community in central New York must be seen against that background of ethnic history.

THE KOPERNIK OBSERVATORY

In 1973, the Polish-American community in central New York formed the Kopernik Society to commemorate the 500th anniversary of the birth of Mikolaj Kopernik, the father of modern astronomy. The Society raised a large sum of money from the region, which then allowed it to build the Kopernik Observatory in Vestal, New York. This observatory is the only one thus far in the 20th century, which has been built without support from major donors and government funding. The IBM Corporation donated a 12-inch research quality telescope to the facility. The Kopernik Observatory exists next to the $5 million planetarium complex at Roberson Center; the combination has proven to be one of the best public astronomy facilities in the Northeast.

The whole focus of the observatory and of Roberson Center is an effort to upgrade science education and science awareness in central New York. Since 1973, almost $1 million has been raised for science education programs and facilities. More than 25,000 students, teachers, and visitors take advantage annually of this facility.

The Kopernik Observatory together with state and local educational institutions has spearheaded innovative programs in the sciences for schools all over the region.

Currently, the Kopernik Space Education Center project is underway to expand the original facility. Its aim is to upgrade science literacy and improve job skills, as well as to increase tourism and the economic health of the region.

The very people, whose parents and grandparents could not read and were at the bottom of the economic, social, and educational ladder in their newly-adopted country, are now in the forefront of leadership in education and literacy. Thus, the great Polish astronomer has a most fitting living memorial. Thanks to him, enlightenment continues to spread.

HOW TO GET THERE

Take I-80 or I-88 to the Binghamton area. Pick up route 17 there to Exit 675 (Rt. 26 South), and continue on Rt. 265 for 5 miles. Turn right onto Glenwood Road at the Observatory sign and follow Glenwood Road for about 250 yards. Turn left at the Observatory sign onto Underwood Road and continue for 1.5 miles to the Observatory, which will be to your left. There is plenty of parking available.

West Point

"He was one in a word whom no pleasure could seduce, no labor fatigue and no danger deter. What besides greatly distinguished him was an unparalleled modesty and entire unconsciousness of having done anything extraordinary," wrote General Nathanael Greene, one of the commanding officers in Washington's Army, in 1783, of Tadeusz Kosciuszko. It was this same Kosciuszko who, at General Washington's command, set out in March, 1778, to build a fortress at West Point.

There was great anxiety among the Americans that if the British were allowed to advance their men and warships up the Hudson, they would easily capture great swaths of territory and important towns like Albany. Thus they would have effectively cut the colonies in two by controlling the Hudson River. West Point was a key to the American defense. If it were defended well, the British would be unable to take advantage of the situation. Kosciuszko toiled with his men for two and a half years, and when he had finished. The British took a closer look and merely retreated without firing a shot. The fortress was impregnable. A major victory had been won without the loss of a single human life. West Point, the British knew, was the key to America. Without that key, the tide of the war most definitely turned against the British, and in favor of the Americans. By the beginning of 1781, West Point was completed. The British surrendered at Yorktown in October of that year.

114

57) Kosciuszko Garden. West Point, NY

58) Kosciuszko Monument. West Point, NY

115

1) KOSCIUSZKO GARDEN

The work at West Point lasted from sunrise until sunset every day. Kosciuszko often worked even later than that, poring over his plans, making modifications and corrections. Yet he too had to relax. He found a lovely spot overlooking the Hudson River where he built himself a stone bench on which to rest and contemplate, and where he tended a few plants. That garden still exists today and can be visited at West Point.

2) THE KOSCIUSZKO MONUMENT

Near the garden, stands a pedestal erected and dedicated in Kosciuszko's honor by the Corps of Cadets in 1828. It has a very simple inscription on it: "Saratoga," reminding of that famous battle, which was the turning point of the Revolutionary War. It was won by the Americans thanks to the outstanding fortifications erected there by Tadeusz Kosciuszko. The empty pedestal was complemented in 1913 by a statue, which the Polish-American community commissioned, and which stands atop the pedestal today.

3) WEST POINT MUSEUM

While at West Point, you will of course want to visit the famous museum. West Point is the oldest military post in constant service in the Continental United States. It has been garrisoned since January 20, 1778. After the Colonies gained their victory over the British, battle trophies were stored at West Point. General Washington urged the country to establish a military academy here. The honor of establishing it fell finally to President Jefferson.

Among the tributes to the American Revolution, the West Point museum has on display a sword, which has the telling and moving inscription: "Draw me not without reason, Sheathe me not without honor." It was the sword once held by Brigadier General Tadeusz Kosciuszko.

HOW TO GET THERE

From New York City, you can take Route 9W North to the Thayer Gate, which is the main entrance to West Point. For information call (914) 938-2638.

OKLAHOMA

Mountain Park

FACTS AND FIGURES

Charles Radziminski was born a gentleman in Warsaw, Poland, in 1805. He took part in the November Uprising of 1830 against the Russian occupation of a vast part of Poland. The Uprising was over very quickly, as the Poles were vastly outgunned and outnumbered, though they did have some outstanding generals. Upon the collapse of the insurrection, Radzyminski escaped to America with a group of Polish political exiles. He arrived here in 1834.

His career in his adopted country was quite distinguished. From 1840 to 1846, he served as an engineer with the James River and Kanawha Company of Richmond, Virginia. From 1847 to 1848, he served in the rank of lieutenant with the Third U.S. Dragoons in the Mexican War. He was the Principal Assistant Surveyor and Secretary of the U.S. Boundary Commission from 1851 to 1855. Finally, he was a First Lieutenant with the Second U.S. Cavalry in Texas from 1851 to 1855. He was handsome, brave, and charming. His final years were spent with the cavalry on the western Texas frontier. He met an untimely death in Memphis, Tennessee, on August 18, 1858.

In his honor, his fellow officers named a military base in his name the next month, and it was recognized by the War Department. The camp was abandoned in December, 1859, after it ceased to serve its purpose of containing hostile Indians.

WHAT TO SEE

CAMP RADZIMINSKI MARKER

The site of the camp contains the Camp Radziminski Marker. The marker is inscribed with historical information. The camp itself, however, was located two miles west of it. Nothing remains of the camp itself. The Wichita Mountains are in close proximity to the old campsite. The soldiers of the Second U.S. Cavalry named the tallest peak "Mount Radziminski."

From Lawton, Oklahoma, drive West on U.S. 62 about 30 miles to the junction with U.S. 183. Turn North on U.S. 183 for 5 miles to Mountain Park. The Camp Radziminski Marker is located one mile North on U.S. 183.

PENNSYLVANIA

FACTS AND FIGURES

During the Great Immigration, between 1899 and 1915, 388,347 Poles settled in Pennsylvania. That was the largest number of Poles immigrating to any state in the United States. Yet Poles had been present in Pennsylvania for two hundred years before that, though in vastly smaller numbers. The Great Immigration brought the blue collar workers to Pennsylvania. Before that, the Poles there were more in the category of military men, explorers, and political exiles. Some Poles lived among the Dutch and Scandinavians of the Delaware Valley as early as 1650. Twenty-three Poles from Pennsylvania participated in the Continental Army of George Washington during the War for Independence.

Many of the Poles who immigrated between 1899 and 1915 made their way to the coal fields of Pennsylvania. They settled in such areas as Scranton, Wilkes-Barre, and the Wyoming Valley. They also went to work in the steel mills of Pittsburgh and Johnstown as well as in points further west like Erie, and further east like Philadelphia.

The 1970, census indicated that 1.1 million Polish-Americans lived in Pennsylvania, which was about 10% of all Polish-Americans in the United States.

The life of the Poles revolved around the home, the job, and the church. More than fifteen Roman Catholic Polish parishes were established just in Philadelphia and its suburbs. Though, there was such a heavy concentration of Roman Catholics among the Poles, there were Protestants among them as well, who had settled in the eighteenth and early nineteenth centuries. It was also in Pennsylvania that the first serious schism occurred in the

Catholic Church, with the breaking away of a group of Polish Roman Catholics. They believed that they should be allowed to have mass in their native language rather than in the official Latin, which many of them did not understand. They stood their ground and were excommunicated by the Pope. That breakaway group still exists and contains a healthy number of followers. Since then, the Church has officially recognized the right of different national groups to hear mass in their native languages but reunion with Rome still remains in the future.

The Poles of Pennsylvania were in the forefront of civic-mindedness among their Polish-American brethren. It was in Philadelphia in February of 1880 that the Polish National Alliance of the United States of North America (PNA) was founded. It is still today the most powerful and largest Polish-American fraternal organization. The Polish National Union of America was founded in Scranton, Pennsylvania, in 1908. The Union of Polish Women in America was organized in Philadelphia in 1920. The Polish Beneficial Association was founded in Philadelphia in December 1899. The Polish Falcons of America have their headquarters in Pittsburgh. All of these organizations continue to be very influential in the social and civic life and attitudes of the Polish-Americans of Pennsylvania and beyond.

Given the Pennsylvania Poles' tremendous activity in so many areas, it is small wonder that outside of the state of New York no other state of the Union contains so many Polish and Polish-American sites, monuments, and other cultural and civic attractions of interest to the tourist.

Doylestown

THE NATIONAL SHRINE OF OUR LADY OF CZESTOCHOWA

Located on Ferry Road in Doylestown. As you approach it, you will see a gleaming oval structure high on a hill. And later, as you stand on its magnificent terrace, you will have a most beautiful view of the hills and valleys below, far off to the horizon. This place of pilgrimage for people of faith of all national backgrounds is especially dear to the Polish-Americans because it represents the highest expression in America of faith in and devotional expression for the Blessed Virgin Mary. A replica of the miraculous painting, which hangs in the church in the town of Czestochowa, Poland, is the

59) National Shrine of Our Lady of Czestochowa. Doylestown, PA

60) National Shrine of Our Lady of Czestochowa. Original Chapel. Doylestown, PA.

centerpiece of this shrine in Doylestown. Just as the original miraculous painting is guarded and cared for by the Pauline Fathers, so this shrine also is the result of their efforts and in their care.

The National Shrine at Doylestown came into being through the self-sacrifice and efforts of many people. A chief catalyst in this work was Rev. Michael Zembrzuski. It was during his tenure that the major work in preparation for and the actual construction of the shrine took place according to a design by an architect, J. George Szeptycki of Los Angeles.

This magnificent, dignified, and beautiful structure, erected in l966 on the 1000th anniversary of Poland's Baptism, and dedicated by His Eminence John Cardinal Krol in the presence of nearly 100,000 pilgrims, is not just a religious place. The Shrine plays the role of a spiritual Capital of the Polonia. It is an easy confluence of culture and religion, of the progress of the Polish nation's spiritual and lay history. There are many mementos, plaques, and inscriptions commemorating events and moments of importance in the religious, cultural, and historical life of Poland and the Polish-American community. The stained glass windows,

61) The Heart of Ignacy Jan Paderewski in the National Shrine, Doylestown, PA

for instance, depict the history of Christianity in Poland and in the United States. Here is enshrined the heart of the great Polish virtuoso and statesman, Ignacy J. Paderewski.

The gift shop is quite large and contains an excellent book store with a wide selection of not only devotional books, as well as biog-

62) Henry Archacki speaks at the official Paderewski ceremony

63) Cemetery and "Winged" Hussar Monument (by Andrzej Pitynski) at the National Shrine of Our Lady of Czestochowa. Doylestown, PA.

raphies of saints, but also works of Polish literature, language, history, and art. There are also such items as imported Polish candy, tape cassettes, amber gifts, and jewelry, and other items of interest. The shrine's cafeteria is open on Sundays from 9 a.m. to 4 p.m.

Also on the grounds of the National Shrine is the cemetery. It is guarded by an imposing sculpture of a "winged" hussar sculpted by Andrzej Pitynski commemorating Poland's greatest battles as well as the massacre in 1940 by the Soviets of 15,500 Polish soldiers in Katyn and elsewhere. Here are buried several hundred Polish-Americans, including some of the great Polish leaders of World War II, and leaders of the Polish-American community's cultural, religious, civic, and social life. The presence here of many Polish veterans and other prominent Polish-Americans gave rise to a popular designation of the cemetery as "The Polish Arlington."

Further back, you will find a small chapel made of wood, close, dank and semi-dark inside, but wonderful in its interior decoration and furnishings. This is the original church. Looking from it to the magnificent structure out front, one cannot help being astonished at the enormous effort, which must have gone into the final product.

Many groups from up and down the east coast, from the midwest and points still further west come to this religious shrine. If you are in Philadelphia or the surrounding area, a visit is definitely in order. Do not miss the art gallery of fine Polish paintings. There are some 30 fine paintings, most of them by the talented Styka family: Jan, Tadeusz and Adam, donated by Wanda Styka, Adam's widow.

On Labor Day weekend, the Pauline Fathers put on a Polish Festival. The Festival extends into the next weekend as well. The food there is sumptuous and there are many joys and pleasures to greet the hungry eye and ear.

The hours are 7:30 a.m. to 5:00 p.m. on weekdays and 7:30 a.m. to 6:00 p.m. on weekends. You may call to make sure: (215) 345-0600.

HOW TO GET THERE

The National Shrine is 25 miles North of Philadelphia. Because driving instructions vary considerably depending on your point of origin, please call the Shrine for detailed information.

Gettysburg

POLISH LEGION MONUMENT

Visitors to the famous battlefield should look for the monument of the "Polish Legion" and the plaque to the Krzyzanowski brigade, both located along Howard Avenue off Route 15 in Gettysburg.

In July of 1863, the fate of the American Union was severely tested. After a long series of defeats over two long years at First Bull Run, in the Peninsula Campaign and the Valley Campaign, at Second Bull Run, Fredericksburg and Chancellorsville, the Northern Army was in retreat and Southern forces were invading the North. The two armies met at Gettysburg, July 1-3, 1863, in what many historians regard as the "high tide of Confederacy," the turning point in the Civil War.

One of the brigades that fought at Gettysburg was commanded by Colonel Wlodzimierz Krzyzanowski. Comprised of five regiments of mostly immigrant troops, the brigade included the 58th New York Infantry, which was known as the "Polish Legion." On July 1, the brigade fought tenaciously, retreating slowly before superior Confederate forces. On July 2, when Confederate infantry breached the Northern line, Krzyzanowski led two of his regiments in a counterattack that halted the Southern advance and saved the Northern forces from defeat.

At Gettysburg, Krzyzanowski's brigade had 669 casualties, over half of the men it brought into combat. This was a higher percentage of losses than the famous "Light Brigade" suffered at Balaclava. But it was not in vain, for the victory at Gettysburg turned the tide of war against the South and saved the Union.

Lattimer

LATTIMER MASSACRE MEMORIAL MARKER

The Congressional Record of September 12, 1972, reads, in part, as follows: "September 10, 1972, was the 75th anniversary of the tragic massacre of 19 striking workers at the Lattimer Mines near Hazleton, PA. On Sunday afternoon the Lower Luzerne and Carbon Counties AFL-CIO Labor Council dedicated a Lattimer Memorial to these striking workers who were of Polish, Slovak, and Lithuanian descent..."

"Coal miners in the villages of Lower Luzerne and Carbon Counties joined a local of the United Mine Workers to combat the existing miserable working conditions. They hoped to improve their lives, abolish company stores, and protect themselves from any exploitation by the coal companies. To seek support from their fellow miners, the strikers marched from Harwood on September 10, 1897. At the entrance of the Lattimer Mines the sheriff of Luzerne County and his deputies fired upon the unarmed union group. This senseless attack killed 19 men..."

The Commonwealth of Pennsylvania has placed a Historical Marker commemorating this sad event. A Polish-American historian Edward Pinkowski gives the full story of the massacre in his 40 page booklet, "Lattimer Massacre".

PHILADELPHIA

1) THE THADDEUS KOSCIUSZKO NATIONAL MEMORIAL

Located at 301 Pine Street, (corner of Pine and Third Streets), in the heart of Philadelphia. After his unsuccessful Insurrection against the Russians, and after spending two years in a Moscow prison,

64) Thaddeus Kosciuszko National Memorial. Philadelphia, PA

125

Kosciuszko was given his freedom on the condition that he would never again step onto Polish soil. On August 18, 1797, his ship docked at Philadelphia, while guns in the forts, which he had built during the Revolutionary War boomed in salute. Because his battle wounds made it virtually impossible for him to walk unaided, a group of his friends came aboard the ship to carry him ashore. Local citizens unhitched the horses of his carriage and harnessed themselves to it. They drew him through the cheering throngs to the house on Pine Street which friends had rented for him. Among the many visitors that he had there were Generals Greene and Gates, and Vice President Thomas Jefferson called on him. His former commander and retired President, George Washington, wrote him a welcoming letter, which ended: "I pray you to believe that at all times and under any circumstances, it would make me happy to see you at my last retreat from which I never expect to be more than twenty miles again."

In the meantime, stirred by all the joyous commotion and publicity surrounding Kosciuszko's return to America, the U.S. Congress remembered that it owed Kosciuszko back pay and paid him with interest. The sum came to $15,000. Kosciuszko now thought of buying himself a farm at Saratoga Springs. As it turned out, Thomas Jefferson's frequent visits to 301 Pine were not only for pleasure. France under Napoleon was fighting a naval war with the United States, and America needed relief. Jefferson, some surmise, asked Kosciuszko to help. Napoleon needed the brave and experienced Polish soldiers in his army, and Kosciuszko was the most respected and beloved Polish military leader. So Kosciuszko sailed to France never to return to America. Within one month of his arrival in Paris, the French navy stopped attacking American ships. Thus, the house at Pine Street is important not just as the great Kosciuszko's last place of residence in the United States, but as the place of his last undertaken selfless act on behalf of a country for whose freedom and peace he had fought years before.

Before he left for Europe, Kosciuszko drew up his last will and testament and asked his friend Jefferson to be its executor. The entire assets that Kosciuszko owned in America were to be used to free and educate black slaves. No doubt based at least in part on this testimonial to Kosciuszko's deep sense of humanity, Jefferson was to later write of him: " He is as pure a son of liberty as I have ever known, and of that liberty which is to go to all, not to the few or the rich alone."

301 Pine Street was built as a boarding house in 1775. Kosciuszko lived there from November, 1797, to May, 1798. By the 1960s the building was just about ready for demolition. Fortunately, the Philadelphia historian, Edward Pinkowski authenticated the historical importance of this building, thus making it possible for Philadelphia industrialist and philanthropist Edward J. Piszek, to purchase the property in 1970 and donate it as a national memorial. In 1972, the U.S. Congress appropriated the funds necessary for the complete restoration and refurbishment of the site.

Today, this national museum contains a very interesting collection of various mementoes, works of art, and documents concerning Kosciuszko. A copy of his will is there, as well as a recreation of the room he occupied, containing the various pieces of furniture he used. There is also a seven minute slide and tape show about him. The House is staffed by volunteers known as Friends of Kosciuszko comprised of Polish Americans from the community. The hours are 9 a.m. to 5 p.m. daily. Admission is free. If you need information, please call (215) 597-8974.

2) STATUE OF GENERAL TADEUSZ KOSCIUSZKO

Another magnificent sculpture, this time in bronze, is the 20 foot high cast-bronze sculpture of General Tadeusz Kosciuszko, which stands on the southwest corner of 18th Street and the Benjamin Franklin Parkway, at the entrance to the Four Seasons Hotel.

This monument was dedicated on July 3, 1979, in a special ceremony. It is a gift from the people of Poland to the people of America on the occasion of the 200th anniversary of American independence. It was the Philadelphia Polish Heritage Society, which gave original impetus to this idea and broadened the appeal so as to incorporate all Polish-American organizations. The Philadelphia City Council supported the project and secured the splendid site.

The artist who conceived and executed this magnificent piece of art is Marian Konieczny, a world-class sculptor whose work is present in the collections of major museums in many countries of the world. The bronze inscription plaque on the monument's base reads:

GENERAL TADEUSZ KOSCIUSZKO
Hero of Poland and the United States of America
From the People of Poland
To the People of the United States of America
Commemorating 200 Years of American Independence

66) Statue of General Tadeusz Kosciuszko. Philadelphia , PA

3) THE TWINS

Created by artist, Henryk Dmochowski Saunders, this is a beautiful sculpture depicting a young mother holding twin babies in her arms. It is located in Section 7, Lot 375 of the Laurel Hill Cemetery on Ridge Avenue in Philadelphia. Dmochowski was a professional, well-known sculptor, who had come from Poland and settled in Philadelphia. The tragic death of his young wife and two children prompted him to create this marble tribute to his deceased family.

128

After the monument was erected in 1858, Dmochowski returned to Poland, where he took part in the January Uprising of 1863. He was killed in a military encounter. The inscription on this monument is just as evocative as the statue itself, it reads:

"We live in deeds - not years;
In thoughts - not breaths;
In feelings - not in figures on a dial
We should not count time in heart throbs.
He most lives who thinks most,
Feels the noblest, acts the best."

*65) The Twins
Philadelphia, PA*

4) THE KOPERNIK MONUMENT

Another memorial of note stands on Eighteenth Street and Benjamin Franklin Parkway, opposite the Cathedral of Saints Peter and Paul in Fairmount Park. This memorial was a purely American undertaking, under the auspices of the Philadelphia Polish Heritage Society, which required the efforts of the Polish-American community of the Delaware Valley and the Philadelphia Art Commission, the Fairmount Park Commission, and the Philadelphia City Council.

67) The Kopernik Monument. Philadelphia, PA

The Kopernik Monument was dedicated on August 18, 1973, during the silver jubilee of the American Council of Polish Cultural Clubs.

The entire project was undertaken, under the auspices of the Kopernik Quincentennial Commemorative Committee, to create a lasting memorial to the great Polish astronomer known in the West by his latinized name, Nicholas Copernicus.

Dudley F. Talcott of Farmington, Connecticut, was selected as the sculptor. He decided upon an abstract form with which to represent the man through his revolutionary idea. The heliocentric system discovered by the astronomer is shown as a stainless steel ring, sixteen feet in diameter, which symbolizes the orbit of the earth; in the center there is a disc, which represents the Sun at the center of the solar system. The Sun sends forth a shower of rays. The Earth's and Sun's orbits are supported on a steel angle which represents the primitive instruments with which Copernicus was able to successfully check his theory. The monument is 24 feet in height.

5) THE POLISH AMERICAN CULTURAL CENTER

is located at 308 Walnut Street, in the heart of Philadelphia's Historic District. The museum was dedicated in August, 1988, at

130

a ceremony attended by John Cardinal Krol of Philadelphia and Vice President George Bush.

The walls of the museum are covered with the portraits of famous Poles, including Pope John Paul II, Lech Walesa, Fryderyk Chopin, Ignacy Paderewski, and many others. Each portrait has beneath it a display case, which contains mementos and artifacts connected with that person. Still other displays are devoted to Polish arts and crafts, including straw art and paper cut outs. The museum also includes displays of Polish jewelry, native clothing from various regions of Poland, and even tools.

Museum hours are 10:00 am. to 4:00 p.m., Monday to Saturday. Admission is free. There is also a gift shop, which is open during regular museum hours. If you want to call to confirm, the telephone number is (215) 922-1700.

6) STATUE OF GENERAL CASIMIR PULASKI

The young Polish hero of the American War for Independence, General Casimir Pulaski, has been duly honored in Philadelphia

68) Statue of General Casimir Pulaski. Philadelphia, PA

with a beautiful bronze figure, which makes up part of the full-round portrait gallery called the Terrace of Heroes. This museum is located on the west side of the Philadelphia Museum of Art on the mall between the museum and the Azalea Garden. Retired General William M. Reilly left in his will a sum of money to erect statues of Generals Richard Montgomery, Friedrich von Steuben, Marquis de Lafayette, and Casimir Pulaski. They stand on either side of the statue of General George Washington, which is located in front of Independence Hall. General Reilly wanted to honor the great Revolutionary War volunteers from Poland, Ireland, Germany, and France. The bronze of Pulaski, created by the sculptor Sidney Waugh, was not dedicated until 1947.

7) THE CENTENNIAL FOUNTAIN

More popularly known as the Catholic Fountain because it was built in 1876 for the Centennial celebration of the Catholic Total Abstinence Union of America, the fountain is located in West Fairmount Park at the intersection of 52nd Street Drive, North and South Concourse Drives, and States Drive. The fountain is 100 feet in diameter and 35 feet tall. Embedded in the fountain's perimeter wall are the medallion heads of seven patriots and supporters of the War for Independence. Two of the medals represent Generals Kosciuszko and Pulaski.

8) THE GESU CHURCH

At 18th Street and Girard Avenue, it is run by the Jesuit Order. Embedded in its sanctuary wall is a beautiful painting of The Blessed Virgin Mary surrounded by a group of figures. The Virgin Mary holds her hands out in blessing. Beneath this painting, an inscription on the wall reads: "Our Lady of Poland, Pray for Us." Church records indicate that the painting was donated by Mrs. George Wood in 1897. The artist is the celebrated Polish painter, Jan Styka (1858-1925). While still a student of Poland's greatest artist, Jan Matejko, he painted the above-mentioned canvas. The year was 1883. The old master apparently approved, because the painting was exhibited the next year in Warsaw, where it received a Gold Medal. In an exhibition in Paris in 1886, it received an Honorable Mention. Finally, the canvas sailed to America to be part of the Chicago World Exposition of 1892, and then it disappeared, to the chagrin of the Styka family, and the artist himself. It next surfaced in the Gesu Church in 1897. Because it was embedded in the wall of the sanctuary, there was no way to remove it, so the Stykas just requested the inscription beneath it that was cited above.

Jan Styka was one of the greatest European painters at the turn of the century. He was not innovative like Cezanne or Monet, but he painted with clarity, vision, and great power. Together with Wojciech Kossak and others, he created a series of huge panoramic portraits depicting important moments in the history of the Polish nation. The best-known in America is the *Golgotha*,which hangs in the Hall of the Crucifixion at Forest Lawn Memorial Park in Glendale, California.

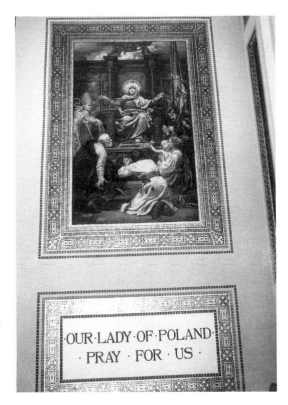

69) Gesu Church, Philadelphia, PA

Styka was born in Lwow (now Lviv in Ukraine), which was then in the eastern part of Poland. He studied in Vienna, Rome, Cracow, and Paris. In 1900, he and his oldest son Tadeusz (known in America as Tade) settled in Paris. His wife, along with their son Adam and their three daughters, stayed behind in Poland so that their children could get a Polish education. They all moved to Paris in 1907. Jan Styka was a very popular painter in Western Europe where he made a lot of money. He had one studio in Paris and another in his villa on the Isle of Capri. He died in 1925 in the home of his daughter Janina in Rome. By then, she was the wife of the Marquis Aurelio Paolucci Mancinelli. Jan Styka lies buried not in Poland, France, or Italy, however, but in the cemetery at Forest Lawn in Glendale, California.

HOW TO GET THERE

(1) and (5) are in the Old City of Philadelphia. It is easy enough to find. Just go to the Visitors' Center, corner of Walnut and 3rd Streets and pick up a Historic Neighborhood Museum Map.

(2) From the Ben Franklin Bridge continue on Rte 30 past Franklin Square and onto Ridge Avenue. Continue to Laurel Hill Cemetery (it will be on your left).

(3) and (4) Coming into Philadelphia across the Ben Franklin Bridge (Rte 30), continue on Rte 30 (which becomes Vine Street), take a left at Broad, go to Cherry, a right on Cherry and go to the Ben Franklin Parkway, where you'll take a right and go to 18th Street.

(6) If you're already on the Ben Franklin Parkway, having seen (3) and (4), continue to the Philadelphia Museum of Art. The statue is located on the Mall between the Museum and the Azalea Garden.

(7) From the Philadelphia Museum of Art, take the park drive north to Rte 30 (Girard Avenue) across the Schuykill River into West Fairmount Park. Take a right onto Parkside Avenue and another right onto 41st Street to the North Concourse Drive (left turn), and proceed to the Fountain.

(8) Assuming you are at the Philadelphia Museum, take the Park Drive North to Girard Avenue, and right onto Girard; take a right onto West College Avenue, a left onto South College Avenue and pick up Girard, taking it to 18th Street and the Church.

Having seen the myriad sites of Philadelphia, you just might want to settle down for a delicious dinner at the Warsaw Cafe at 306 South 16th Street. Though the menu carries items from several countries of Eastern and Central Europe, Poland and Polish food is the dominant theme. The chef, Maria Jarzemska is Polish. Some cognoscenti say that you can get better food at the Warsaw Cafe than you can get in any cafe in Warsaw! Prices are moderate; the food and service are reputed to be superb. For reservations call, (215) 546-0204.

Pittsburgh

FACTS AND FIGURES

The Polish immigrants of the twentieth century to America were attracted, among other cities, to Pittsburgh because there was work to be found in its steel mills. The Polish-American community in Pittsburgh today is still very largely a blue-collar, working man's community. The Pittsburgh Poles are, to a large extent, Union members, forming as they do the rank and file of the various industrial enterprises of that city. Nonetheless, their ambition to gain knowledge and take up positions of greater responsibility in their city, state, and country, is strong.

WHAT TO SEE

1) TOWER OF LEARNING-POLISH ROOM

The centerpiece of the University of Pittsburgh is its famous Tower of Learning, a tall, multi-storied building that houses administrative offices and classrooms. On the ground floor of this imposing structure is a series of rooms that are used as classrooms, but of which each is dedicated to the representation of the culture of a particular ethnic group. Polish culture and the Polish-American citizenry of Pittsburgh is represented there by the Polish Room. Beautifully decorated, with magnificently crafted furniture in a Polish style, it is worth visiting.

At the library of the University you will find the entire Polish language collection from the Polish National Alliance College, which operated in Cambridge Springs , Pennsylvania, from 1912 to 1987. This impressive donation includes more than 100,000 volumes in all.

HOW TO GET THERE

The University of Pittsburgh is just a short ride from downtown Pittsburgh and the Civic Arena. It is located along Fifth Avenue.

2) POLISH FALCONS OF AMERICA HERITAGE CENTER

Located at 615 Iron City Drive, Pittsburgh, PA 15205, telephone (412) 922-2244, in the national headquarters of the organization, a fraternal benefit society. Its first U.S. lodge, or Nest, was organized in Chicago by Felix L. Pietrowicz. In 1894, there were 12 Nests in existence in the U.S., and a national organization was incorporated. Since 1912 The Polish Falcons of America have had their headquarters in Pittsburgh.

Dr. Theophil A. Starzynski, President of the Falcons in 1912, began preparing the organization for any emergencies that might arise. During 1913, he organized Officers Training Schools in Cambridge Springs, PA., Toronto and Camp Borden, Canada, where hundreds of Falcons were trained as officers. These later served in the Polish Army in France and in Poland. When the United States entered the war in 1917 many became officers in the United States Army.

There are 141 Nests as of 1992. The Museum in Pittsburgh has many artifacts of the Polish Falcons' history, including uniforms, a library, and archives. The organization publishes a semi-monthly newspaper titled *"Sokol Polski"* (Polish Falcon) in English and in Polish.

Scranton

Scranton is the national seat of the Polish National Catholic Church in America. For many centuries, Latin was the official language of the Roman Catholic Church. All services were held in Latin. Many church-goers did not know Latin, and consequently felt alienated

70) St Stanislaus Cathedral of the Polish National Catholic Church. Scranton, PA

from their own Church. A growing group of Polish immigrants in America started asking themselves why they could not profess their faith in their own language. A storm was in the offing, compounded by insensitive policies of the Catholic hierarchy towards Polish immigrants in general, and it broke with a vengeance over the heads of the Reverend Franciszek Hodur and his followers. They were excommunicated from the Roman Catholic Church for trying to make their faith a little closer and more comprehensible to their parishioners. That very same premise would become one of the cornerstones of the changes which swept the Catholic Church in the second half of the 20th century.

WHAT TO SEE

1) SAINT STANISLAUS CATHEDRAL OF THE POLISH NATIONAL CATHOLIC CHURCH

The first Christmas Mass conducted entirely in the Polish language was held here in 1901.

Except for the "American Czestochowa" in Doylestown, no other church in America has as powerful position in the religious history of Polish-Americans as does this building. It is a true historic landmark. Many of the religious and artistic furnishings of the church are of great interest and document important moments of the social history of the Polish-American community. For instance, the Polish National Alliance of the United States of North America (called the PNA for short), which is the largest Polish-American fraternal organization in the United States, lent its support to the Polish National Catholic Church for a short period of time (up to about 1907). The sole remaining memento of that support and cooperation is the monstrance, which is still in use at the Cathedral and which was donated by a local branch of the PNA.

2) POLISH NATIONAL UNION OF AMERICA

Located at 1002 Pittston Avenue, Scranton, PA 18505. Organized in 1908 by Prime Bishop Franciszek Hodur, 11 years after the

71) Polish National Union of America. Scranton, PA

founding of the Polish National Catholic Church, PNU is a fraternal benefit society with 25,000 members and assets of $40 million, dedicated to the material and spiritual security of Polish immigrants. PNU is also the publisher of a weekly paper *Straz*-The Guard. The facility includes a shop with Polish souvenirs. Visitors are welcome.

HOW TO GET THERE

Take Route 81 to Exit 52 and take River Street West to Pittston Avenue South, then turn to East Locust Street.

Wilkes-Barre

WILKES COLLEGE POLISH ROOM

At the invitation of Wilkes College a group of women under the guidance of Mrs. Joseph J. Kocyan formed the Wilkes College Polish Room Committee to establish The Polish Room at the college. The Committee engaged Stefan Mrozewski, a leading wood-block engraver, to design the reading and reference room, which is in the style of Zakopane, a city in the Tatra Mountains of Poland.

The Polish Room brings to the library an authentic air of old Poland: tapestries (kilims) which grace the walls, a striking "Mask of Jesus" by the sculptor W.T. Benda, and three cases containing folk art. Through the years, many precious paintings, lithographs, maps, prints and objets d'art were donated or purchased to augment the changing exhibits of the room which includes an extensive collection of art and rare books on Polish subjects.

Resources available to students and the public include: photos, slides, manuscripts, and other data of early Polish settlers in the Wyoming Valley; biographies of outstanding Poles, anniversary booklets of local Polish parishes and program booklets of numerous Polish organizations as well as a rare collection of songs of the Polish miners.

The Polish Room is located in the E.S. Farley Library, South Franklin and South Streets, Wilkes College, Wilkes Barre, PA 18701; (717) 824-4651.

Wilkes Barre can be reached by Route 81, as well as from the Pennsylvania Turnpike. Please call in advance to make sure that the library and the Polish Room will be open when you come.

Aiken

FACTS AND FIGURES

1) JOZEF KAZIMIERZ HOFMANN

Jozef Kazimierz Hofmann was born in Poland in 1876. Six years later, he made his debut as a pianist. In 1885, at the age of 9, he was a soloist with the Berlin Philharmonic Orchestra. He made his American debut, playing to a packed house at the Metropolitan Opera, two years later, in 1887, when he was 11 years old! That American tour lasted 70 days, and in that period of time, he gave 52 concerts! Twelve years later, in 1898, at the age of 22, he settled in America. He was a founder and musical director of the Curtis Institute of Music in Philadelphia. He is also credited with the invention of the air brake and 59 other patents. There is no doubt that in his time he was the finest interpreter of Chopin and one of the most brilliant interpreters of Beethoven and Schumann.

72) Josef Casimir Hoffman Marker. Aiken, SC

Hofmann married an Aiken girl, Marie Eustis, and settled in this South Carolina town with his bride. They opened, in 1919, the Fermata School for Girls, which at first operated on the upper floor of their home. For entertaining, more spacious quarters were needed than their house could provide, and for that purpose the Hofmanns used the Wilcox Inn in Aiken. The Inn is open daily to the public. It is located on Colleton Avenue and Whiskey Road. The Fermata School for Girls is now the Fermata Club, a private club on the site. There is a bronze marker in Aiken honoring its most famous citizen and you can be guided to it, as well as to the old Hofmann home, by stopping in at the Dom Polonais.

2) DOM POLONAIS

The Dom Polonais is home to the Polish Heritage Association of the Southeast-Aiken: "PHASE-A" for short. Its headquarters is open daily from 10 a.m. to 12 noon and from 2 to 5 p.m. It contains books and materials dealing with Polish history and current events. Many items are also available for purchase. There will shortly be a Polish reading room and an archive. Tel. (803) 648-9172.

Len Kosinski, the dynamic president of PHASE-A will personally escort visitors, or make the necessary arrangements to show some special points of interest in Aiken: the Racing Hall of Fame with memorabilia of Henryk de Kwiatkowski, the colorful personality of the racing world; the Fermata Club, and a famous portrait of Mrs. Thomas Hitchcock by Wojciech Kossak (who visited Aiken in the 1920s) at the Aiken Preparatory School at 619 Barnwell Avenue NW (803-648-3223).

HOW TO GET THERE

The Dom Polonais is located at 1018 Hayne Avenue in Aiken. To get to Aiken from I-95 get off at I-20 and past Columbia exit to Highway 1, the turn-off to Aiken.

Ninety Six

FACTS AND FIGURES

The first Southern land battle of the Revolutionary War was fought at Ninety Six on November 19 to 21, 1775. It also turned out to be the final British stronghold in the interior of the State of South

Carolina. In May, 1781, Washington's commander in the South, General Nathanael Greene, began siege operations against the British fortress. His top engineering aide was the Polish engineer, Colonel Tadeusz Kosciuszko. Kosciuszko started digging a tunnel, which became known as "Kosciuszko's Tunnel." The diggings went on secretly at night. Unfortunately for the Americans, a British raiding party discovered the work and the tunnel was never completed. General Greene's siege of Ninety Six ended in failure and he had to retreat. Nonetheless, the British had had enough and they evacuated the fort.

WHAT TO SEE

STAR FORT

The British constructed a star-shaped fort at one corner of the village of Ninety-Six. It was made of massive earthen embankments. The star shape was an advanced European design which was well-nigh impregnable. The fort's embankments and about 35 feet of Kosciuszko's tunnel have survived since 1781. The National Park Service now owns the site which is open to the public. Tours are available for groups as are self-guided tours. There is an on-site Visitors' Center. The site is open to the public daily from 8 a.m. to 5 p.m. Two markers detail Kosciuszko's contributions in the siege.

HOW TO GET THERE

If you are taking I-95, get off at Exit 86, and take Route I-26 West to exit 72. Go South on Route 121 to the town of Saluda, take a right onto Route 178 and at Epworth take a right turn onto the road leading to the National Historic Site.

TEXAS

FACTS AND FIGURES

There were many events of importance for the Polish-American community that have occurred in Texas. There have also been many important Americans of Polish descent who were Texans. Perhaps the single most significant event to occur on Texas soil that is connected with the history of Poles in America is the settlement of Panna Maria.

In Poland, by the second half of the nineteenth century, living and working conditions for the Polish peasantry had become all but impossible. According to ancient practice, the land owned by a peasant was divided among his male children upon his death. Since farming was the only life these people knew, and since industrialization was still some time distant in Poland, there was no outlet, no means of escape to the cities. By the mid-19th century, in many parts of Poland, the land was overworked and the people who worked it could no longer make a living . The situation was desperate. A way out had to be found. That way out proved to be emigration to the "Promised Land," to America.

In 1854, a well-educated Franciscan friar and priest, the Reverend Leopold Moczygemba, persuaded nearly 100 Polish families from Upper Silesia in Poland to come to America in search of a better future. They landed in Galveston and marched west, attacked by disease, rattlesnakes, and even Indians. Many died on the 300 mile journey. They arrived at the future site of Panna Maria, six months after the journey began, just before Christmas of that year. Their first Christmas Eve was celebrated under the oak tree, which still stands today. Along the way they lost most of their meager possessions but the church bell from their Silesian village still tolls in Panna Maria today. Others soon joined them. The settlers built a church and a school, the first Polish church and school on American soil. The church is the centerpiece of the hamlet, which also still exists. Nearby, there are villages named Cestochowa, Helena, Pulaski, and Pavelekville.

The first settlers had quietly hoped to get to California, having heard about the gold rush before their departure. They barely made it to Panna Maria. But today, as if in recompense, there are many oilwells providing the hardy immigrants from Poland "black gold" instead!

Today, the state of Texas is home to 167,000 Americans of Polish descent.

PANNA MARIA

Because the entire town (a very small one) of Panna Maria has kept its Polish character, the whole town is of interest. The Church is, of course, the centerpiece. But the people there are just as important, as

73) Town marker and the church. Panna Maria, TX

74) The historic oak and marker. Panna Maria, TX

is the very atmosphere of this place, which for over 136 years has tried to be faithful to the religion, culture, and language of its forefathers.

75) The historic marker - close-up. Panna Maria, TX

From San Antonio take Route 87 to Route 123 and go South on 123. You will pass the Polish-founded and settled towns of Kosciusko, Pavelekville, and Cestohowa; finally you will come to Panna Maria. The distance from San Antonio city limits is 47 miles, just a small step or two in the huge state of Texas.

El Paso

FACTS AND FIGURES

As a member of the United States Boundary Commission in the years 1851-1855, Charles Radziminski surveyed 330 miles of the boundary between Mexico and the United States. Radziminski arrived in the United States in 1834, the victim of the November 1830 Insurrection against the Russian government. This uprising ended with the defeat of the patriotic Poles who were trying to liberate their occupied country from the Russians. He and 234 other Polish officers of that campaign all came to the U.S.A., seeking asylum. He served in the U.S. military with distinction, and finally became a surveyor for the U.S. Government.

The laying of the foundation for International Boundary Marker No. 1 on the Rio Grande took place on January 31, 1855. Those present included Commissioner William H. Emory, Mexican Commissioner Jose Salazar y Larrequi, Radziminski, and four prominent Mexicans as well as four prominent Americans. A brief document was signed by all present, placed in a glass bottle, and buried 5 feet below the center of the monument.

WHAT TO SEE

INTERNATIONAL BOUNDARY MARKER No. 1

International Boundary Monument No. 1 is located in a small park on the exact boundary between Mexico and the United States. This marker designates the beginning of the boundary between Mexico and the United States from the Rio Grande westward to California (a distance of about 500 miles). There is a historic description on the monument. From the site you can see the Rio Grande cutting the Franklin Mountains at El Paso del Norte (the Northern Pass).

HOW TO GET THERE

From downtown El Paso, drive North on Interstate 10 two miles and exit on Executive Drive. Go West (left), cross I-10 to Doniphan Drive, turn South (left) on Doniphan Drive to El Paso Brick Company bridge. Cross the Rio Grande to Levee Road, turn South (left) and follow the signs to Monument No. 1 Park.

VIRGINIA

Alexandria (see Washington, D.C.)

Jamestown

FACTS AND FIGURES

Jamestown is associated with Captain John Smith, Pocahontas, and tobacco. Few Americans are aware of the vital contribution that Polish settlers made in that first English colony on American soil. It was no accident that Poles were asked to join the Englishmen. Captain John Smith had spent a number of years in Poland. He had fought alongside the Poles against the Ottoman Turkish Army in Hungary. He knew and understood Poles, and valued their industriousness and talents as craftsmen and artisans. That is why a group of Polish glassblowers, pitchmakers, and potash workers came to Jamestown in 1608 on the supply ship "Margaret and Mary." The Jamestown glasshouse and the pitch and potash works were set up by the Poles, and the products they produced were the first exports from America to Europe, except for what the Spanish exported. In just a few years, there were fifty Poles working in Jamestown. They founded the manufacture of resin, potash, glass products (including window panes), clapboard, and frankincense.

Some assert that without the Poles the colony would have surely flopped. Among the original group of colonists, who came from England, only twelve worked. The rest were adventure-seeking gentlemen who were not used to labor, and had no practical skills.

Even more interesting is the political contribution, which the Poles made at Jamestown to civil liberties in America. At one point the English decided to set up a council and to exclude the Poles. The Poles and Hollanders were denied the franchise for the House of Burgesses, and protested, securing for themselves the franchise. The English relented because of the recognized value of the Poles for the colony's economy.

WHAT TO SEE

JAMESTOWN HISTORIC AREA

When you go visit Jamestown and see the glass house and the other centers of industry that were a part of that first colony, remember who made it happen. The marker in the Visitors Center

76) "First Poles" Marker. Jamestown, VA

commemorating the Polish contribution to Jamestown may or may not be back up on the wall; it was taken down during a recent remodelling and has reappeared as of mid-1992. But if you do not see it, ask for it.

If driving down from Washington, D.C. or even further North, take I-95 until just before Richmond, and follow 295 into I-64 toward Williamsburg; at Exit 57 take a right onto Route 199. There should be signs indicating the turn-off to Jamestown via Colonial Parkway; a most scenic 10 mile run. The distance from Washington is about 155 miles, and takes three hours by car. Go to the Visitors Center, where you can pick up detailed information.

(Combine your trip, if you can, with a visit to Williamsburg, which is worth a detour, and Jamestown, 15 miles from Williamsburg).

WASHINGTON

Seattle

POLISH HOME ASSOCIATION- POLISH HALL

Located at 1714 18th Avenue, Seattle WA 98112 (206-322-3020) and founded in 1918, the Association's Polish Hall has always been the center for all activities of the Polish-American community in the Seattle area, and is the home to all Polish organizations. Polish Hall offers its members and guests social functions, lectures and slide shows, dinners every Friday evening, a library of books and videos, and the chance to meet other Polish-Americans. The Association publishes a quarterly news-letter, which includes a calendar of events, listing appearances by Polish lecturers, composers, and writers visiting the Seattle area.

WASHINGTON D.C.

FACTS AND FIGURES

Washington, D.C. itself does not claim very many Polish-American residents, though there is a sizeable and culturally active Polish-American community in the metropolitan area. Many Polish-Americans living there hold government or government-related positions. They include Zbigniew Brzezinski,

National Security Advisor to President Carter and a top advisor to many high U.S. officials since; Jan Nowak, former head of the Polish section in Radio Free Europe and now an advisor to the Polish American Congress. Stefan Korbonski, the last head of the Polish underground state in World War II, author of many books and one of the great heroes of Poland's struggle for independence since 1939, lived in Washington until his death in 1989.

The greatest importance of the Capital to Poland and Polish-Americans stems from its function as the national and international nexus of America. Symbols of American interaction with Poland and of Polish and Polish-American progress through the history of the United States are present in great number throughout the city. The Polish Embassy is a dynamic center of cultural activity now that it represents free Poland and has the full support of Polish-Americans. The national executive office of the Polish American Congress office is a crucial connection to the government centers of the U.S.A. The American Council for Polish Culture has just purchased a home, which will be converted into a center of Polish culture in the near future.

WHAT TO SEE AND HOW TO GET THERE.

1) THADDEUS KOSCIUSZKO MONUMENT

Located at the northeast corner of Lafayette Park on Pennsylvania Avenue, across from the White House. Take the Metro Blue or Orange Line to Mcpherson Square. The Kosciuszko Monument is one of five located in the heart of Washington and dedicated to Revolutionary War heroes. It was fashioned by the Polish sculptor Antoni Popiel and shows a standing figure of Kosciuszko on a high pedestal. The inscription reads: "Erected by the Polish National Alliance of America and presented to the United States on behalf of Polish-American citizens, May 11, 1910." It was dedicated by President William Howard Taft (who could not be present on May 3rd, the anniversary of Poland's celebrated Constitution of May 3, 1791). The statue was paid for by the Polish National Alliance and was designed as a gift from the Polish-Americans to the people of America.

*77) The Kosciuszko
Monument.
Washington, DC*

2) KAZIMIERZ PULASKI MONUMENT

At Western Plaza; corner of Pennsylvania Avenue and 13th Street,
NW. The Metro Blue or Orange Line to Metro Center stop will
get you there. The Pulaski monument is a heroic-sized equestrian
statue over eight feet tall, and shows the founder of the American
cavalry in the uniform of a Polish nobleman and marshal. The
names of Revolutionary War battles in which he participated are
carved on the pedestal. Sculpted by Kazimierz Chodzinski, it was

*78) The Pulaski
Monument.
Washington, DC*

unveiled on May 11, 1910, the same day on which the Kosciuszko statue was dedicated. The statue was paid for by the U.S. Congress and served to at last realize the American government's pledge made in 1779 to erect a monument to the fallen revolutionary war hero. This monument is the center of many Polish gatherings, commemorating important events in Polish history and is seen and admired by thousands of tourists.

3) IGNACY JAN PADEREWSKI MEMORIAL MARKER

The remains of Ignacy Jan Paderewski rested for 51 years in the turret of the Maine memorial at Arlington National Cemetery. (Take the Blue Line Metro to the Arlington Cemetery stop. Location: across Arlington Memorial Bridge on the Virginia side of the Potomac River).

79) Dedication of Memorial Marker to identify resting place of Ignacy Jan Paderewski, May 9, 1963 by President John F. Kennedy. Arlington, VA

He was Poland's greatest twentieth-century pianist who extensively toured the U.S.A. in the first part of this century, and was also Premier and Foreign Minister of Poland in 1919. Paderewski's coffin was moved to Poland in July, 1992 to a crypt in St. John's Cathedral in Warsaw.

4) THE POLISH CHAPEL OF OUR LADY OF CZESTOCHOWA IN THE NATIONAL SHRINE OF THE IMMACULATE CONCEPTION

The shrine is some distance away from the center of town. Take the Metro Red Line to the Brookland-CUA (Catholic University of America) stop. This is the largest Catholic church in the Western Hemisphere, completed in 1959. The famous Polish chapel has been the focal point of many Polish and Polish-American religious and patriotic events. It contains a faithful replica of the Black Madonna, Poland's revered religious icon. The entire chapel is designed by Polish artists. The north apse of the church has a huge mosaic of Christ in Majesty, and several murals done by the great Polish-American artist, Jan de Rosen.

5) THE LIBRARY OF CONGRESS

This is the most important library in the United States if not the world. Its Polish collection is estimated at 150,000 volumes, including the first edition copy of "De Revolutionibus Orbium Coelestium" by Polish astronomer Nicholas Copernicus, printed in 1543 shortly after his death. It established, for the first time in history the correct position of the sun among the planets. This book's findings caused one of the greatest revolutions in science and thought in the last two thousand years. It is on permanent display on the main floor of the Library of Congress.

Take the Metro Red Line to the Capitol South stop. The Library is located off Independence Avenue S.E. , across from the Capitol.

6) THE EMBASSY OF THE POLISH REPUBLIC

Located at 2640 16th Street, N.W. Because the new team at the embassy has made it so much a part of the Polish-American community, we include it in this guide even though strictly speaking it is not a "tourist site." Yet, so many functions and events are held there: film showings, concerts, discussions, and lectures that it is entirely possible for a visitor to Washington to visit also this elegant palace. Built at the beginning of the twentieth century, the palace was purchased in 1919 by Prince Kazimierz Lubomirski who turned it over to the new Polish state. In 1990 Kazimierz Dziewanowski, well known author and journalist, became the Ambassador of new Poland. Be sure to see a few paintings by famous Polish painters such as Falat and Jacek Malczewski, and Paderewski's piano.

7) ST. MATTHEW'S CATHEDRAL

Located at 1725 Rhode Island Avenue, NW, at M Street. Metro Stop Farragut North on Red line. This Catholic Church is the seat of the Archdiocese of Washington; President John F. Kennedy's funeral started from here. Of interest to readers of this guide will be a nine feet tall, 3 1/2 ton carrara marble figure of the Virgin Mary commissioned by Cardinal Baum in 1980 and sculpted by Polish artist, Gordon Kray. It stands in the left isle. There is also an oversize bust of Pope John Paul II, by the same artist. In the baptistry, there are two magnificent mosaics created by the Polish painter, Jan de Rosen.

8) AIR AND SPACE MUSEUM

Located at Independence and 6th Street, it is easily the most popular museum in Washington with millions of visitors each year. The museum holds a number of exhibits of interest. The moon-rover, a vehicle used by the astronauts when on the surface of the moon, was designed by Polish engineer, Mieczyslaw Bekker. The Gordon-Bennett Trophy for winners of pre-war free balloon competitions was won many times by Polish balloonists Capt. Hynek, Burzynski, Wawszczak and others. Also on display is the "Orbiting Space Laboratory Copernicus."

9) THE AMERICAN CENTER OF POLISH CULTURE

New headquarters at 2025 "O" Street, N.W. Washington, D.C. 20036, tel. (202) 785-2320. Located in the Dupont Circle area, the building is now being remodelled and furnished. Small concerts and receptions are already being held on the first floor of the center.

10) POLISH LIBRARY IN WASHINGTON

Located at 1503 21st Street, N.W. Washington, D.C. 20036, the library is open on Tuesdays (7:30 to 9:30 p.m.), Thursdays (1:00

to 4:00 p.m.), and Saturdays (11:00 a.m. to 2:00 p.m.). Of its over 3,000 volumes, 90% arE in Polish (fiction, memoirs, and history). The English language collection has translations from the Polish and a section on "Poles in America." Tel. (703) 356-8120.

RELATED POINTS OF INTEREST

Old Warsaw Galleries. The first Polish fine arts, crafts and book shop in the Washington, D.C. Metro area. It specializes in contemporary Polish artists, and Polish tapestries, and wall hangings (gobelins and kilims).

Metro Yellow Line to King Street; Alexandria stop. Go to 319 Cameron Street in Old Town Alexandria.

WEST VIRGINIA

Harper's Ferry

FACTS AND FIGURES

Cyprian Kamil Norwid spent the years 1853-1854 in America. He was one of the greatest Polish poets and one of the greatest European poets of all time. A number of his poems from that time immortalize America as it was then. One of his passages describes the flowing amber waves of grain as he looked down on them from Brooklyn Heights in Brooklyn, New York. He was a reflective poet, a thinking man's poet, a liberal in the truest sense of the word: a creative artist who believed in the liberating qualities of the human mind. He believed in man's inherent capability to distinguish between right and wrong, between justice and injustice. He was deeply and spiritually involved in the pre-Civil War abolitionist movement in the United States and made John Brown the centerpiece of two of his greatest works.

WHAT TO SEE

NORWID MEMORIAL

An hour drive by car from Washington, D.C. at Harper's Ferry, a beautiful spot, there is a memorial to Norwid. Housed inside the

*80) Norwid
Memorial Marker.
Harper's Ferry, WV*

John Brown Museum of the Harper's Ferry National Historical Park, it is a bas-relief by the Polish-American sculptor from Washington, D.C., Gordon Kray. The sculpture honors Norwid and the Polish tradition of concern for human dignity and personal freedom. The two poems, which Norwid wrote about John Brown and his anti-slavery sentiments are reproduced in the original Polish and exhibited below the sculpture.

HOW TO GET THERE

If travelling by car from Washington, D.C., take Route 270 to Route 340 and Route 340 across the Potomac at Harper's Ferry to the Harper's Ferry National Park. If coming by car from points North of Washington, D.C., take I-95 to I-70 (just North of the Capital) to Route 340, and cross the Potomac down to Harper's Ferry National Historic Park.

WISCONSIN

Milwaukee

FACTS AND FIGURES

Though Wisconsin seems an out-of-the-way place to many Americans — and to many Polish-Americans, it has played an important role in the development of Polish-American history. Stevens Point, Ripon, Pulaski, Arcadia, Independence, Polonia, and Milwaukee are towns either founded by Polish settlers or in which the Poles have had a strong presence for well over a century.

St. Wenceslaus Church in Ripon was founded by the Polish residents of that town, led by the Reverend Wenceslaus Kruszka, an early activist, writer and organizer who was one of the first to recognize the need for Polish-American bishops in the Roman Catholic Church in America. Eventually, his great influence and efforts, which reached all the way to Pope Pius X, did help the selection of the first Polish-American Bishop in the United States, Paul Rhode.

Stevens Point is the decades-old headquarters of the Worzalla family's publishing dynasty, the centerpiece of which is the *Gwiazda Polarna (Polar Star)*, a Polish language weekly which has been read every week for generations by Polish-Americans all across the United States. The town square is decorated with Polish folk art ("wycinanki" designs painted on the walls) and makes for an enjoyable tour. A different sort of attraction is the Stevens Point Brewery, owned by the Shibilski family. There is a gift shop, replete with souvenirs proudly advertising the brewer's Polish roots. Just to the south of town there is a bust honoring Pulaski.

Pulaski, in the northeast corner of the state, near such interestingly named villages as Krakow, Lublin, Polonia, and Sobieski is dominated by the monastery church of the order of Polish Franciscan friars. In Crivitz, the Polish Scouting Organization of Chicago established in 1968 a camping center known as the Norwid Scout Center where scouts can visit and train during the summer.

156

It is Milwaukee, however, which has seen the greatest cultural and political activism of the Polish-American community in the state of Wisconsin. There are no less than 18 Roman Catholic churches established by the city's Polish population.

Milwaukee is home to the Polanki, a group of women who have political clout, which they use for the cultural betterment of the citizens of Milwaukee by making accessible to them the significant aspects of Polish culture. The University of Wisconsin at Milwaukee has one of the most ambitious Polish Studies programs in the United States. There are many other important elements in the chain of events of Polish-American history in Milwaukee, too numerous to mention here.

The Polish immigrant community in Milwaukee settled mostly on the old Near South Side of the city. The first Polish daily newspaper in America was founded in Milwaukee in 1888. It was not until after World War I that Chicago became a more important center of Polish intellectual and political life in America than Milwaukee.

In recent years, Milwaukee has become home to a number of fine modestly priced Polish restaurants, all of them located on the city's South side. These include "Crocus," "Cracovia," and "Polonez" as well as a real "old time" Polish-American hideaway, "Fountain Blue," south of the city.

The Milwaukee County Public Museum is recognized as one of this country's best thanks to its many interesting displays. One of special note here is the Museum's "European Village" exhibit which includes an authentic Polish peasant home rich in artifacts and lore. (Just to the west of Milwaukee is "Old World Wisconsin", an outdoor museum and park dedicated to preserving the record of the state's immigrants who turned to farming as a way of life.) As of 1991, the Polish presence at the Museum is still limited to one farm house, but it is hoped that more will be established in the not too distant future.

Each summer in June, Milwaukee's Polish American community celebrates "Polish Fest," a three-day outdoor music and cultural festival held on the city's "Summerfest" grounds along Lake Michigan. (Chicago's Polish-Americans, not to be outdone, also host their own summer festival, "Festival Polonaise," which takes place in the city's Grant Park in late August)

1) ST. JOSAPHAT'S BASILICA

One of the oldest Catholic churches in the Midwest is Saint Josaphat's Basilica, built in 1901. It is also one of the most architecturally imposing shrines in the United States. This is a major center of religious life for Milwaukee's Polish South Side.

2) KOSCIUSZKO PARK & MONUMENT

Across the street from the Basilica lies Kosciuszko Park. In the Park a magnificent monument to Thaddeus Kosciuszko, funded by the Polish community and dedicated in 1905, remains a center for patriotic parades and manifestations.

Just to the south is Pulaski Park where a statue to Casimir Pulaski erected after 1929 (the 150th anniversary of his death at the battle of Savannah) can be viewed. Yet, another Pulaski statue can be seen in Cudahy, Wisconsin, a heavily Polish American community just south of Milwaukee.

3) ST STANISLAUS BISHOP AND MARTYR CHURCH

A mile to the North, on 6th Street and Mitchell, is Saint Stanislaus Bishop and Martyr Church, another especially beautiful shrine to faith and fatherland which dates back to the 1870s. This "Church of the Golden Domes" features an outdoor mosaic dedicated to the Virgin of Czestochowa that was added to celebrate the Parish's centennial and Poland's one thousand years of Christianity in 1966.

4) POLISH-AMERICAN ARCHIVES

The University of Wisconsin at Milwaukee houses a very important and growing collection on Polish and Polish-American affairs: the Polish American Archives Collection at the UWM Library. It includes a 35,000 photo collection of Polish Milwaukee prior to 1945; an extraordinary and unique collection of the work of photographer Roman Kwasniewski, which presents the life of Milwaukee's Polish-American community in ways not available anywhere else. For those travelers wishing to delve into Polish-American history, and especially into the history of Poles in Wisconsin, this is the best place to visit. Call in advance: (414) 229-5402.

HOW TO GET THERE

St. Josaphat's Basilica is located on the corner of West Lincoln Boulevard and 6th Street. Take I-94 to West Becher Street, go West on Becher to 6th Street (approximately three blocks), then take 6th Street left (approximately 2 blocks) to West Lincoln Avenue and the Basilica. The Basilica is across the street from Kosciuszko Park.

To get to the University of Wisconsin at Milwaukee and the Polish Archives, take I-94 to Locust Street and go East to North Downer, where you'll take a left (North) and go two blocks to Kenwood. The University campus is bounded by North Downer and Kenwood.

Tourist Sites in Canada

PROVINCE OF ONTARIO

Grimsby

FACTS AND FIGURES

The town of Grimsby is about a third of the way between Niagara Falls and Toronto. It is on the southern shore of Lake Ontario.

About 3,000 Polish-Canadians live in Grimsby. There are several Polish organizations: The Polish Association Centre ("Place Polonaise"), The Polish National Association, and a Polish supplementary school where children can learn Polish, Polish history, and culture.

WHAT TO SEE

1) STATUE OF GENERAL SIKORSKI

A statue of General Wladyslaw Sikorski was unveiled next to the Polish Centre on June 7, 1987. This statue was originally erected in the W. Sikorski Park in Milton, Ontario and then moved to Grimsby.

General Sikorski was a Polish hero of World War II and the head of the Polish Army and of the Polish Government in Exile, which had headquarters in London. He distinguished himself in the war between Poland and Russia in 1920 and in 1922 became the Premier of Poland. He was a very strong-minded person with very definite ideas about Poland's place in Europe after World War II. Had he lived, he certainly would have done everything possible to prevent the disastrous turn of events for Poland at the Yalta Conference in 1945. He was killed on July 4, 1943, in Gibraltar in an airplane accident, which may have been sabotage.

2) WAR MEMORIAL

Located next to "Place Polonaise," this monument, dedicated on July 26, 1987, commemorates all the Canadian and American Poles who died in World War II. This memorial also commemorates the contribution made by Polish-Canadians and Polish-Americans towards the regaining of Polish independence in 1918.

HOW TO GET THERE

From the U.S. border at Niagara Falls, take the Queen Elizabeth Way to Grimsby (about 35 miles).

Wilno...Kaszuby...Barry's Bay

FACTS AND FIGURES

"Little Poland in Canada" is located in Renfrew County in the northeastern part of Ontario Province. It is a settlement of descendants of Polish pioneers who came here from the Kaszuby region of Poland in 1859. They were the first Polish settlers in Canada. They chose this area because it reminded them in topography and climate of their native land on the shores of the Baltic Sea. About 5,600 Polish-Canadians live in "Little Poland" and almost all are direct descendants of the original settlers of 1859. Even though they are the sixth generation to live in Canada, they continue to speak the Kaszubian (pronounced kashoo'byan) dialect among themselves. They live in the town of Wilno (population 200) and in the surrounding farms, small towns, and villages scattered within a thirty-mile radius of Wilno: the towns of Kaszuby, Round Lake, Killaloe, and Combermere.

Many Kaszubians live in Barry's Bay (population 1,400), which is about 10 kilometers (approximately 6.5 miles) west of Wilno on

Highway 60. The intensely Polish atmosphere and ambiance of this region has attracted many non-Kaszubian Poles who own summer cottages here. They hail from Toronto, Ottawa, Hamilton, and various areas of the United States, including Chicago. The main area of concentration of this summer colony is on Wadsworth Lake. You're more likely to hear Polish than English in Barry's Bay, especially in the summer months.

HOW TO GET THERE

From Niagara Falls, take the Queen Elizabeth Way to Toronto, where you pick up Route 401 to Route 35/115, and then continue, at the fork, on Route 115 (right fork), which becomes Route 28 past Bridgenorth, and continue on 28 to Bancroft, where you bear left at the fork onto Route 127. At Maynooth bear right at the fork and bear left onto Route 62 at Combermere, which will take you into Barry's Bay.

If travelling from Ottawa, take Highway 17 West to Renfrew, then through Eganville on Highway 60, go about 170 kilometers to Wilno and then another 12 kilometers to Barry's Bay in the direction of Algonquin Provincial Park.

Wilno

WHAT TO SEE

1) SHRINE HILL

This is a lookout point with magnificent views toward the Round Lake Centre. A commemorative information plaque here states that Wilno is the first Polish settlement in Canada.

2) OLD CEMETERY

If you want to get a sense of passing generations and the depth of history which permeates this unique community, definitely visit the old cemetery. It is the oldest Polish cemetery in Canada and contains the last remains of all the original settlers who came here in 1859, as well as the succeeding generations.

3) ST. STANISLAW KOSTKA CHAPEL

The first Polish church in these parts was built in 1875 but it burned down in 1936. St. Stanislaw Kostka's Chapel was built in its place and still stands.

4)THE CHURCH OF MARY, MOTHER OF GOD

It was consecrated in 1937, and contains a faithful replica of the miraculous painting of the Virgin Mary and child, called The Black Madonna of Czestochowa, Poland. The replica was offered to this Canadian church as a gift by President Ignacy Moscicki, the President of the Republic of Poland prior to World War II. There are many other Polish mementoes and commemorative plaques in the church dedicated to the "Queen of Poland."

Kaszuby

WHAT TO SEE

Polish scouting organizations from Canada and the United States have camping grounds in these parts. The scouts have also built many interesting wayside shrines, similar to the kind you still find in Poland today. They are usually located at crossroads.

81) A view of Kaszuby, Ontario, Canada

1) MEMORIAL OF THE MILLENIUM OF CHRISTIANITY OF THE POLISH NATION

This memorial has the inscription "Polonia Semper Fidelis" and over it the emblem of the Polish Crowned Eagle. It was funded by the local Kaszubian population as well as the Polish-Canadians of Ottawa.

82) Poland's Millenium Monument (part). Kaszuby, Ontario, Canada

2) CATHEDRAL UNDER THE PINES

This is an open air altar with a large picture of the Madonna of Czestochowa. A Mass is held every Sunday during the summer.

83) Cathedral Under the Pines. Kaszuby, Ontario, Canada

164

*84) Three Crosses
Mountain. Kaszuby,
Ontario, Canada*

3) THREE CROSSES MOUNTAIN

An excellent lookout point upon the "heart of Kaszuby" i.e.
Wadsworth Lake.

Barry's Bay

WHAT TO SEE

1) POPE JOHN PAUL II OBELISK

It was erected in 1980 to honor Pope John Paul II. It stands on
Karol Wojtyla Street.

2) THE CHURCH OF ST. JADWIGA (ST. HEDWIG)

Built in 1914, it has unique and beautiful stained glass windows funded by the local settlers.

Niagara Falls

About 1500 Polish-Canadians live in Niagara Falls.

WHAT TO SEE

1) INTERNATIONAL BRIDGE

A technical marvel of the time, this railroad bridge connects Fort Erie with Buffalo. It is the work of Casimir Stanislaw Gzowski, a plaque commemorates the designer.

2) SIR CASIMIR S. GZOWSKI OBELISK

It was erected in 1891 to honor the chairman of the Commission of Queens Victoria Park in Niagara Falls. Gzowski's exceptional energy and personality were the mainspring in the creation of this national park that was opened in 1888, and where the obelisk is located.

Niagara-on-the-Lake

From November 4, 1917, Polish volunteers from Canada and the U.S.A. were trained here at the Tadeusz Kosciuszko Military Camp for the General Haller Army in France. 22,395 volunteers were admitted for training; of these, 20,720 were sent to France.

WHAT TO SEE

1) BUTLER'S BARRACKS

Located in Niagara National Historic Park, it has a number of Polish memorabilia, including a painting by famous Canadian artist C.W. Jeffery, depicting scenes from Polish soldiers' army life.

166

85) Polish Cemetery Memorial. Niagara-on-the-Lake, Ontario, Canada

2) POLISH CEMETERY

There is a monument to those who died for Poland's freedom in both World Wars, and an obelisk commemorating General J. Haller.

86) Monument to General Haller. Niagara-on-the-Lake, Ontario, Canada

From Niagara Falls: Highway on the left bank of the Niagara
River, directly north - about 30 miles of very picturesque travel.

Ottawa

FACTS AND FIGURES

Ottawa is the capital of Canada and about 7,500 Polish-Canadians live there. During World War II, priceless treasures from Poland were kept here, including furnishings from the Royal Castle
in Cracow, as well as such irreplaceable national treasures as the
coronation sword of Polish kings, which had been used since the
11th century A.D. The main Polish organizations in the city are:
The Canadian-Polish Congress, The Polish-Canadian Club, The
Committee of Assistance to Polish Missions, The Polish Combatants Association Branch No. 8, The Association of Polish Engineers and Technicians, The Polish Supplementary School, and
The Embassy of the Republic of Poland.

WHAT TO SEE

1) ST. HYACINTH POLISH PARISH

Located at 201 Lebreton North. This Church of St. Jacek, a Polish
saint, is the work of a well-known Polish architect and painter,
Roman Stankiewicz. The stained glass window over the main altar
is the handiwork of Waclaw Czerwinski. The church was consecrated in 1956.

2) MEMORIAL PLAQUE

A plaque commemorating the 26 Canadian airmen shot down by
the Germans while carrying out supply operations over Poland is
located at the Monument Plaza in Confederation Square in the
center of Ottawa. The Canadian airmen flew their missions mostly
during the Warsaw Uprising, trying to support the heroic Poles
who fought there, surrounded by over 20 divisions of the German
Army. The plaque was unveiled in 1964, twenty years after the
Warsaw Uprising. The unveiling was done by Prime Minister

168

Lester B. Pearson. The plaque was funded by the Montreal Association of Former Soldiers of the Polish Home Army.

3) THE CANADIAN TRIBUTE TO HUMAN RIGHTS

Located in downtown Ottawa at the corner of Elgin and Lisgar Streets, is Canada's newest national symbol. It celebrates the principles of the worldwide human community. Started in 1983, it was inspired by the Polish Solidarity Trade Union movement, which was a non-violent struggle for basic human rights. The inspiration of Solidarity led to the award-winning design representing the universality of the struggle. Hundreds of organizations, individuals, businesses, and governments at all levels helped to build this monument. In November, 1989, Lech Walesa took the first steps on the symbolic pathway leading to the ceremonial arch at the center of the tribute. The Canadian-Polish Congress and St. Hyacinth Polish Parish are among the more than forty names listed on a special plaque as major donors. The Tribute was unveiled in 1990, by the Dalai Lama of Tibet.

HOW TO GET THERE

From Toronto: Highway 401 East in the direction of Montreal, and at Prescott, take Highway 16 directly North (about 290 miles).

Prescott

THE BATTLE OF THE WINDMILL

In November of 1838, during the so called "patriot war" between Canada and the United States, a Pole named Mikolaj Gustaw Szulczewski, also known as von Schoultz, a veteran of the 1831 Polish Uprising, crossed the St. Lawrence River from the States into Canada. Adhering to the Polish motto: "For your freedom and ours" he led a detachment of 177 hunters, 6 Poles among them, to free Canada from the English yoke, capturing a mill on the river.

After an engagement of several days' duration, Szulczewski's legion had to surrender to the British regiment surrounding them. The commander Mikolaj Szulczewski was tried, sentenced to death,

87) Site Of The Battle of the Windmill. Prescott, Ontario, Canada

and hanged. This battle is known in Canadian history as "The Battle of the Windmill." The windmill that gave its name to this engagement was built in 1822, and still stands today.

HOW TO GET THERE

From Ottawa: Highway 16 South to Johnstown (88 kilometers) then along the St. Lawrence River on Highway 2, in a south-westerly direction, for 2 kilometers.

Note: At St. Mary's Cemetery in Kingston there is a neglected tombstone with the following epitaph to the hero of the battle: "N. Sholtewski von Schoultz, Native of Poland who died Dec 8, 1838. Aged 31 years."

Toronto

FACTS AND FIGURES

Toronto contains the largest Polish-Canadian community, about 105,000 persons strong. There are three Roman-Catholic parishes, including the largest in Canada (St. Casimir's, with 7,000 members), as well as a parish of the Polish National Catholic Church. Toronto is the organizational and intellectual center of the Polish-Canadian community. This city is the seat of the headquarters of the Polish-Canadian Congress, the Canadian-Polish Research Institute, the largest Canadian-Polish credit union, and numerous other organizations. There are several Polish language newspapers: *Gazeta Echo, Glos Polski* and *Zwiazkowiec,* as well as Polish radio and TV stations.

WHAT TO SEE

1) RONCESVALLES AVENUE

Also known as Polish Street, it has a jocular nickname, Kielbasa Avenue. This is the main Polish artery in town with many of the social, civic, and cultural organizations located here, such as the ZG KPK, the Credit Union, St. Casimir's Church, also Polish shops, restaurants, and service industries.

2) KATYN MONUMENT

Located at the corner of Roncesvalles Avenue and Queen Street. The inscription on it reads: "To the memory of fifteen thousand Polish P.O.W's missing in 1940, camps of Kozielsk, Ostaszkow and Starobielsk in the U.S.S.R." A Virtuti Militari Cross (Cross of Valor-Poland's highest military honor) is engraved in stone on the monument, under which the inscription reads: "Discovery of mass graves in Katyn near Smolensk revealed 4,500 victims murdered by the Soviet security forces." The monument was dedicated on September 14, 1980.

3) STATUE OF HIS HOLINESS POPE JOHN PAUL II

Located at Roncesvalles Avenue next to the Credit Union building. It was unveiled in 1984, during the Holy Father's visit to Canada and his meeting with Toronto's Polish-Canadian community on September 14, 1984.

4) STATUE OF SIR CASIMIR STANISLAS GZOWSKI

Located in Gzowski Park. This very distinguished Polish engineer died in 1893. He served as the chairman of the Commission of Queen Victoria Park in Niagara Falls and was the person most responsible for its creation. He was also the builder of International Bridge, between

Canada and the United States at Niagara Falls, which was completed in 1873 and was considered a technological marvel in its time. Gzowski built many other roads and bridges in Canada as well.

HOW TO GET THERE

From Niagara Falls: Take Queen Elizabeth Way into Toronto. From Detroit: Take the Windsor Tunnel into Windsor, Canada and continue on Route 401 into Toronto. From Ottawa: Take Highway 16 South to Highway 401 West to Toronto.

OTHER POINTS OF INTEREST

5) A Polish book store "Zwiazkowiec" is located at 1638 Bloor Street West.
6) A Polish book store "Glos Polski" is located at 390 Roncesvalles Avenue.

Thunder Bay

FACTS AND FIGURES

Approximately 6,000 Polish-Canadians live in Thunder Bay. They are very active civically and culturally. The community has two Roman-Catholic parishes and lists the following organizations: The Canadian-Polish Congress-Lakehead Region; the Polish Branch of the Canadian Legion, Nos 149 and 219; the Polish Combatants Association, Unit No.1; the Polish Association in Canada; the Marshal Pilsudski Brotherhood Society; the Polish Supplementary School; the Polish Sports Club, and the Polish-Canadian Fishing Club.

WHAT TO SEE

1) THE MILLENIUM MOUND

This is a memorial to the Millenium of Christianity of the Polish Nation. The mound was raised by heaping up the soil from the gardens of local Polish-Canadians. On top of the mound there is a monument with an eagle and the inscription "Poland."

Memorial mounds, called "Kopce" in Polish have a very long and distinguished history in Poland. There are three very famous memorial mounds in Krakow. One is dedicated to Wanda, the half-legendary princess of Krakow who committed suicide by flinging herself into the Vistula River from the ramparts of the royal castle. She did this because she did not want to marry the leader of an invading German army. Her death was the rallying point for her troops, who, outraged, gathered strength and threw back the enemy and won. This mound is very much visible in Krakow. The second famous memorial mound was heaped to honor Tadeusz Kosciuszko, leader of the Kosciuszko Insurrection against the Russian occupiers of Poland. This is the same Kosciuszko who as a young man came to the United States to offer his services to General Washington in the Revolutionary War for American independence. This mound, also in Krakow, is actually a small mountain. The third mound was heaped, just before World War II began, in Krakow to commemorate Marshal Jozef Pilsudski who died in 1935.

These three Polish mounds, as well as the one in Thunder Bay, were heaped cup by cup, hatful by hatful, bucket by bucket. They are the joint effort of a community or a nation, to honor an important event or a great hero. Seemingly, this is the perfect expression of unity and unanimity, of achieving the greatest ends through the most humble means.

2) INTERNATIONAL FRIENDSHIP GARDEN

A park, called the International Friendship Garden, located at the corner of Victoria Street and Hyde Park Avenue, contains a beautiful columnar shrine of Our Lady of Czestochowa (The Black Madonna). It was funded in 1969, by the Polish Women's Club.

HOW TO GET THERE

From Ottawa: Take Highway 17 West, for a distance of approximately 1,465 kilometers (915 miles)!

PROVINCE OF QUEBEC

Montreal

FACTS AND FIGURES

About 35,000 Polish-Canadians live in Montreal. That is the largest grouping of Polish-Canadians in all of French-speaking Canada.

Aside from the Roman Catholic and the Polish National Catholic churches, there are the following Polish organizations in Montreal: the Club of the Polish Western Territories; a Branch of former soldiers of the Polish Home Army (Armia Krajowa); the Polish White Eagle Society; the Polish-Canadian Credit Union; the Association of Polish Airmen; the Polish Combatants' Association, Section No. 7; the Marshal Pilsudski Society of Polish Veterans; the Polish Socio-Cultural Foundation; the Polish Library, the Polish School, and several other clubs and organizations.

WHAT TO SEE

1) THE CHURCH OF THE BLACK MADONNA OF CZESTOCHOWA

The Church of the Black Madonna of Czestochowa was completed in 1947 by the Polish community of Montreal. One of the local guide books describes it: ". . . the marrying of the religious art of the Middle Ages with that of the modern age by talented artists together with the exceptional generosity of the parishioners combined to create a church unique on this continent." The artists were: Father Bernard, a Franciscan priest who was vicar of the church from 1930; architect Zygmunt Kowalczuk; painter Stefan Katski; sculptor Paul Barbaud; and a grandson of Italian sculptors, Sebastian Aiello. The church is located at 2550 Gaston Avenue.

2) THE STATUE OF NICHOLAS COPERNICUS

This statue of the Polish astronomer is a copy of the work by the Danish sculptor, Bertel Thorvaldsen, which stands in Warsaw, Poland. The Canadian replica is a gift of the Canadian Poles to all the people of Canada on the occasion of the centennial of the Canadian Confederation. The monument was unveiled on November 12, 1966, on the ground of Expo '67 in Montreal. It is currently located on the square by the Montreal Planetarium (the Dow Planetarium).

HOW TO GET THERE

(1) & (2) Take Highway 20 to the Planetarium. Otherwise, if coming into Montreal via the Champlain Bridge, take High-

174

way 10 to Highway 20, bearing South on Highway 20 a short distance to the Planetarium.

PROVINCE OF ALBERTA

Calgary

FACTS AND FIGURES

Calgary is the center of Polish activity in the entire Alberta Province, even though the number of Polish-Canadians is only about 1,500. There is one Roman Catholic church, in addition to the following organizations: The Canadian Polish Congress (Calgary); the Association of Polish Combatants, Branch No. 18; the Polish-Canadian Association; the Society for the Promulgation of Polish Culture; the Dramatic Circle, a Polish School; and a Polish Sports Club.

88) Church of the Mother of God, and Statue of John Paul II. Calgary, Alberta, Canada

WHAT TO SEE

THE CHURCH OF THE MOTHER OF GOD, QUEEN OF PEACE

Located at 2111 Uxbridge Drive. It was consecrated in 1968, and was built in the shape of an Indian wigwam. Next to the church is a statue of Pope John Paul II, commemorating his pilgrimage to Canada in 1984.

HOW TO GET THERE

From Ottawa, take Highway 17 West. It changes to Highway 1, the Trans-Canada Highway. The distance is 3,553 kilometers: 2,220 miles!

Edmonton

FACTS AND FIGURES

Edmonton is a very Polish town. There are 26,000 Polish-Canadians living here. Aside from the local church, the Polish organizations represented are: The Canadian-Polish Congress (Alberta Region); the Central Committee of Polish Organizations in Edmonton; the Association of Polish Combatants (Section No. 6); the Association of Polish Defenders of the Fatherland; the Society of Polish Culture; the Society of Eastern Territories of the Polish Republic; and several others. There are a few Polish supplementary schools, including the John Paul II School, which has a bilingual Polish-English program.

WHAT TO SEE

THE MILLENIUM MONUMENT

The Monument to the Millenium of Polish Christianity, funded by the parishoners of the Church of the Madonna of the Rosary, was unveiled in 1966. It is located at 11485 106th Street.

HOW TO GET THERE

To get to Edmonton from Calgary, take Highway 2 North to Edmonton.

176

PROVINCE OF MANITOBA

Cook's Creek

FACTS AND FIGURES

This is one of the oldest settlements in Western Canada. It was settled in the nineteenth century by emigrants from southeastern Poland. The town has about 300 citizens of Polish origin.

WHAT TO SEE

1) THE COOK'S CREEK HERITAGE MUSEUM

The Cook's Creek Heritage Museum is the only museum of Polish immigrants in Canada. It contains items of Polish folklore, farming implements of the first settlers, and similar items. It was opened in 1968. There is a cake sale every Sunday in the summertime. For information call: 444-22-48.

2) ST. MICHAEL'S CHAPEL

The Polish townspeople have built a beautiful chapel dedicated to St. Michael. It was consecrated in 1922. The lovely stained glass window depicting St. Michael was crafted by the artist J. Randal. There is a stone cross with the likeness of the Virgin Mary, crafted in agate.

HOW TO GET THERE

From Winnipeg take Highway 212. The distance is only 25 kilometers that is about 16 miles.

Winnipeg

FACTS AND FIGURES

About 30,000 Polish-Canadians live here. There are three Roman Catholic parishes and one National Polish Catholic church. The organizations represented are: the Canadian Polish Congress (Manitoba Region); the Polish-Canadian Legion, Post No. 34;

the Polish Society of the Holy Spirit; the St. John Kanty Society of Fraternal Assistance; the Polish Gymnastic Society "Sokol"; the Association of Friends of Polish Culture and Arts; the Polish Combatants Association (Branch No. 13); there are also Polish Schools, sports clubs, and a few other organizations.

HOW TO GET THERE

If you're coming up from Minnesota, take U.S. Route 29 (just West of the Minnesota/North Dakota border), which becomes Highway 75 in Canada, and go straight up to Winnipeg. If you're coming from Ottawa, take Highway 17 West, and then the Trans-Canada Highway. The distance is 2,218 kilometers (about 1,386 miles).

WHAT TO SEE

THE CHURCH OF THE HOLY SPIRIT

The church of the Holy Spirit was built in 1899. It is the oldest Polish-Canadian church that has survived undamaged since its original construction. Above the main altar hangs a painting of the Black Madonna of Czestochowa, a faithful copy of the original in Poland. The address: 341 Selkirk Avenue.

PROVINCE OF BRITISH COLUMBIA

Vancouver

FACTS AND FIGURES

About 16,000 Polish-Canadians live in Vancouver. The sole Roman Catholic parish built by the Poles is dedicated to St. Casimir. Organizations represented here include: the Canadian-Polish Congress (British Columbia region); the Polish Society "Zgoda"; the Polish Combatants Association (Branch No. 3); the Polish Engineers and Technicians Association; the Society of Polish Eastern Territories, and a few others, including a Polish (supplementary) School. The University of British Columbia in Vancouver has an excellent Polish studies program.

MEMORIAL TO THE VICTIMS OF
THE MARTIAL LAW

A memorial plaque is built into the wall of St. Casimir Church (located at 1187 East 27th Avenue). It commemorates "Those who died in the defence of democracy during the martial law imposed in Poland from 1981 to 1983." The tablet was funded by the Society of the Friends of Solidarity and was unveiled on December 13, 1983.

HOW TO GET THERE

From the United States (Washington State) take Highway 15 North, 45 kilometers from the border; or Highway 1 from Ottawa -a mere 4,611 kilometers (about 2,882 miles).

Appendix A

POLISH GENEALOGICAL SOCIETIES IN THE U.S.A.

Polish Genealogical Society of Connecticut
8 Lyle Road
New Britain, CT 06053
203-229-8873

Polish Genealogical Society
984 Milwaukee Avenue
Chicago, IL 60622

Polish Genealogical Society of California
P.O. Box 713
Midway City, CA 92655

Polish Genealogical Society of Massachusetts
50 Hastings Heights
Northampton, MA 01060

Polish Genealogical Society of Michigan
Burton Historical Collection
Detroit Public Library
5201 Woodward Avenue
Detroit, MI 48202

Polish Genealogical Society of Wisconsin
P.O. Box 37476
Milwaukee, WI 53237

Polish Genealogical Society of Texas
15917 Juneau Lane
Houston, TX 77040

Polish Genealogical Society of Western New York
299 Barnard
Buffalo, NY 14206

Bialystok Lomza Genealogical Study Group
8 Lyle Road
New Britain, CT 06053

Appendix B

POLISH BOOK STORES IN NORTH AMERICA

The book stores listed below can order Polish interest books in English for you. Some can order Polish language books. In the Polish-American market the definition of a bookstore has to be stretched somewhat to include gift shops, drug stores, etc. All of the book stores listed below have ordered books of Polish interest in the past. Some, which are mentioned in their city listings, have considerable stock and experience. Most also do business by mail.

Almost any American book store in your town will order books published by American publishers if you are willing to wait. The best way to "train" a book store to stock Polish interest titles is to order through it. Once the bookseller sees a continuing market, he may even order for stock. He may also surprise you by telling you about new books on Polish subjects.

Support booksellers because they are an essential link in the flow of information. When you buy, explain your interest so that the bookseller can watch out for books you like. Steer your friends to the book store so that you may become known as a promoter of books.

A word about libraries. Your local library is another treasure. It has books you need, and it can get you-through inter-library loans–just about any book you need. Libraries have limited budgets and have to spend money on books that circulate, the key measure of their success. Libraries are always looking for donated books, particularly if such books circulate. If you donate a Polish interest book to a library, make sure your friends take it out and read it. Next time the librarian may just watch out for a new Polish interest book and order it for the library. Promote your library in all ways possible.

Buy books, give books, above all read books. Make sure your children read books as well.

CALIFORNIA

Szwede Slavic Books
P.O. Box 1214 2233 El Camino Real, Palo Alto, CA 94302

Polish Arts and Culture Foundation
1290 Sutter Street, San Francisco, CA 94109

John Paul II Polish Center
29836 Desert Hills Road, Sun City, CA 92381

CONNECTICUT

John & Mary's Variety Store
180 Broad Street, New Britain, CT 06053

Vistula Supplies
44 Broad Street, New Britain, CT 06051

Old Country Stand
363 Lombard Street, New Haven, CT 06513

ILLINOIS

Globe Books
6007 West Irving Park Road, Chicago, IL 60634

Polonia Bookstore
2886 Milwaukee Avenue, Chicago, IL 60618

Redyk Polish Book & Card Shop
4302 W. 55th Street, Chicago, IL 60632

Watra Church Goods Co
4201 So. Archer Avenue, Chicago,IL 60632

A.S. Wegrzyn
1164 Milwaukee Ave, Chicago, IL 60622

MARYLAND

T & S Distributors
221 South Collington Avenue, Baltimore , MD 21231

MASSACHUSETTS

Modern Mail International
34 Martin Street, Holyoke, MA 01040

182

Edward S. Grzyb & Son
26 Carroll Road, Woburn, MA 01801

MICHIGAN

Ave Religious Store
19229 W. Warren, Detroit, MI 48228

Ksiegarnia Ludowa (Peoples Book Store)
5347 Chene Street, Detroit, MI 48211

A. Mateja Religious Store
7844 Michigan, Detroit MI 48210

Polish Art Center
7539 Jos. Campau, Detroit, MI 48212

Angelus Religious Supplies
641 Diamond, N.E., Grand Rapids, MI 49503

St. Mary's College Bookstore
3535 Indian Trail, Orchard Lake, MI 48324

NEW JERSEY

Polish Cultural Foundation
177 Broadway, Clark, NJ 07066

Mary Ann's Gifts
27 Anita Drive, Piscataway, NJ 08854

P.T.V.N. Video Club
646 Newark Avenue, Jersey City, NJ 07306

Variety Drug
50 Passaic Street, Garfield, NJ 07026

Karpaty Gift Shop
927 N. Olden Avenue, Trenton, NJ 08638

NEW YORK

Pol-Am Store
946 Manhattan Avenue, Brooklyn, NY 11222

Polish Book Center
140 Nassau Avenue, Brooklyn, NY 11222

Po Polsku-Country Book Shop
12 Saranac Avenue, Lake Placid, NY 12946

Polish American Book Store
333 West 38th Street (Fourth Floor), New York, NY 10018

Kosciuszko Foundation Bookstore
15 East 65th Street, New York, NY 10021

Polish American Museum Bookstore
16 Belleview Avenue, Port Washington, NY11050

Karnival Imports
18 2nd Avenue, Pelham, NY 10803

OHIO

Eugenia Stolarczyk
6506 Lansing Avenue, Cleveland, OH 44105

John Kusko Travel
36-63 63rd Street, Cleveland, OH 44105

Boutique Polonaise
2291 Lee Road, Cleveland Heights, OH 44118

Polish Peddler
1754 Boston Road, Hinckley, OH 44233

PENNSYLVANIA

National Shrine of Our Lady of Czestochowa Bookstore
Ferry Road, Doylestown, PA 18901

Podhale Travel Service
3154 Richmond Street, Philadelphia, PA 19134

Polish-American Cultural Center Gift Shop
308 Walnut Street, Philadelphia, PA 19106

VIRGINIA

Old Warsaw Galleries
319 Cameron Street, Alexandria, VA 22314

A'dees Inc.,
2901 South 13th Street, Milwaukee, WI 53215

Gwiazda Polarna
2619 Post Road, Stevens Point, WI 54481

Pride of Milwaukee
306 N.Milwaukee Street, Milwaukee, WI 53202

CANADA

Polish Library
c/o H. Bobr-Tylingo
22 Walton Drive, Halifax, N.S. B3N 1X7

Polish Library
3479 Peel Street, Montreal, QUE H3A 1W7

Polish Bookstore in Ottawa
512 Rideau Street, Ottawa, ONT K1N 5Z6

Polish Voice Bookstore
390 Roncesvalles Avenue, Toronto, ONT M6R 2M9

Polish Alliance Press
1638 Bloor Street, West, Toronto, ONT M6P 4A8

Appendix C

POLISH STUDIES PROGRAMS IN THE U.S.A.

Center for Slavic and East European Studies
University of California at Berkeley
372 Stephens Hall, Berkeley, CA 94720
(415) 642-3230

Center for Russian and East European Studies
University of California at Los Angeles
334 Kinsey Hall
405 Hilgard Avenue, Los Angeles, CA 90024
(213) 825-4060; 825-4998

Department of Slavic Languages and Literatures
Columbia University
420 West 118th Street, New York, NY 10027
(212) 280-4623

Soviet and East European Language Center
Harvard University
1737 Cambridge Street, Cambridge, MA 02138
(617) 495-5852; 495-4038

Polish Studies Program
University of Wisconsin at Milwaukee
P.O. Box 413, Milwaukee, WI 53201

Russian and East European Center
University of Illinois
1208 West California Street, Urbana, IL 61801
(217) 333-1244

Russian and East European Institute
Indiana University
Ballantine Hall 565, Bloomington, IN 47405
(812) 335-7309

Soviet and East European Studies
University of Kansas
Lawrence, KS 66405
(913) 864-4236

Center for Russian and East European Studies
University of Michigan
212 Lane Hall, Ann Arbor, MI 48104
(313) 764-0351

Polish Studies Program
c/o History Department
3094 FAB, Wayne State University
Detroit, MI 48202

Center for Slavic and East European Studies
The Ohio State University
344 Dulles Hall
230 West 17th Avenue, Columbus, OH 43210
(614) 422-8770

Russian and East European Studies University of Pittsburgh
4E-23 Forbes Quad, Pittsburgh PA 15260
(412) 624-1215

Council on Russian and East European StudiesYale University
85 Trumbull Street, New Haven, CT 06520
(203) 436-0250

Department of Slavic Languages and Literatures
Foster Hall
University of Chicago
Chicago, IL

The University of Illinois at Chicago
M/C 306, Box 4348
Chicago, IL 60680

University of Connecticut-New Britain
Department of History
Polish Studies Center
Central Connecticut State University
New Britain, CT 06050

Appendix D

POLAND AND POLES ON U.S.A. POSTAGE STAMPS

89) Stamps issued by the US Post Office to commemorate Poles and Poland

1) The 150th anniversary of the death of General Pulaski (1748-1779) was commemorated on a stamp issued two years late, in 1931.

2) General Tadeusz Kosciuszko was granted American citizenship in 1783 and the 150th anniversary commemorated on a stamp in 1933.

3) The Polish flag appeared in 1943, one of a set of 13 flags of countries overrun in World War II.

4) Ten foreigners were honored in a series called "Champions of Liberty," among them Ignacy Jan Paderewski in 1960.

5) One thousand years of Christianity in Poland was commemorated in 1966 by a stamp picturing the Polish eagle wearing a crown,

90) Postcard commemorating Casimir Pulaski. First day of issue October 11, 1979

which led to protests from the then communist government and refusal to allow mail bearing the stamp to enter the country. A souvenir of the cold-war days.

6) The 500th anniversary of the birth of Polish astronomer, Nicolaus Copernicus (Mikolaj Kopernik;1473-1543) was celebrated by a stamp issued in 1973. Due to unknown influence, the background of the figure in the draft of the stamp showed the national colors of Germany; under protest the U.S. Post Office deleted this!

Appendix E

POLISH-AMERICAN AND POLISH-CANADIAN PRESS

THERE ARE TWO POLISH LANGUAGE DAILY NEWSPAPERS IN THE U.S.A.

NOWY DZIENNIK, with its weekly literary supplement PRZEGLAD POLSKI is published at 333 West 38th Street, New York, N.Y. 10018. It has excellent coverage of events in Poland as well as in the U.S.A. Telephone 212-594-2266. Editor and Publisher: Boleslaw Wierzbianski.

DZIENNIK ZWIAZKOWY (POLISH DAILY NEWS), with its weekend supplement KALEJDOSKOP TYGODNIA ispublished at 5711 N. Milwaukee Ave, Chicago, IL 60646. Telephone 312-763-3343. Editor: Wojciech Bialasiewicz.

POLISH LANGUAGE PERIODICALS OTHER THAN DAILIES

GWIAZDA POLARNA (POLISH AMERICAN WEEKLY), published at 2619 Post Road, Stevens Point, WI 54481. Telephone 715-345-0744. Editor: Malgorzata T. Cwiklinska.

HORYZONTY, published at 1917 Center Street Stevens Point, WI 54481 Editor: Leszek Zielinski.

GLOS, published monthly by Polish & Slavic Federal Credit Union, 140 Greenpoint Avenue, Brooklyn, NY 11222. Editor-in-chief: Andrzej Dobrowolski.

KARIERA, 1116 Lorimer Street, Brooklyn, NY 11222

OKAY AMERICA, 628 E. 14th Street, New York, NY 10009. Editor-in-chief: Renata Gorczynska.

POLISH-AMERICAN PERIODICALS

POLISH-AMERICAN JOURNAL published every month at 1275 Harlem Road, Buffalo, N.Y. 14206. Telephone 716-893-5771. Editor: Mark A. Kohan.

POLISH HERITAGE published by American Council for Polish Culture at 6520 109th Terrace North, Pinellas Park, FL 33565. Editor: Wallace M. West.

POLISH AMERICAN STUDIES, Polish American Historical Association. SUNY-Empire State College, 28 Union Avenue, Saratoga Springs, NY 12866. Editor: James S. Pula.

POLISH DIGEST, 933 A Main Street, P.O. Box 202. Stevens Point, WI 54481.

POLISH CULTURAL NEWS, Polish American Cultural Network, 24212 Park Street, Torrance, CA 90505. Tel. 213-375-8471 Editor: Artur Zygmont.

AM-POL EAGLE, 1335 E. Delavan Ave. Buffalo, NY 14215.

POST EAGLE, 800 Van Houten Avenue, Clifton, NJ 07039.

POL-AM, A Newsletter About Polish American People and Events in Minnesota. 1213 NE Monroe Street, Minneapolis, MN 55413 Tel. 612-789-6445. Editor: Czeslaw Rog.

LANGUAGE BRIDGES QUARTERLY, P.O. Box 850792, Richardson, TX 75085. The only fully bilingual Polish-English literary magazine in the U.S. Editor: Eva A. Ziem.

NEW HORIZON, monthly publication of the Bicentennial Corporation of New York, 333 West 38th Street, New York, NY 10018. Tel. 212-354-0490, Editor: Boleslaw Wierzbianski.

TYGODNIK SWIAT POLSKI/THE POLISH WORLD, a weekly published at 12021 Joseph Campau, Hamtramck, MI 48212. Tel. 313-365-1990. Editor: Ewa Matuszewska-Juocys.

THE SARMATIAN REVIEW, publication of the Houston Circle of the Polish Institute of Arts and Sciences. Three times a year. P.O. Box 79119, Houston, TX 77279. Editor: Ewa M. Thompson.

POLISH REVIEW, published quarterly by the Institute of Arts and Sciences in America, 208 East 30th Street, New York, NY 10016.

POLISH STUDIES NEWSLETTER, published monthly by Albin S. Wozniak, 3433 Gregg Road, Brookeville, MD 20833

PERSPECTIVES, published bi-monthly by Artex Publishing, Inc. P.O. Box 202, Stevens Point, WI 54481. Editor: Leszek Zielinski.

ZGODA, official publication of the Polish National Alliance, published semi-monthly at 6100 N. Cicero Avenue, Chicago, IL 60646. Editor: Wojciech A. Wierzewski.

GLOS POLEK (Organ of the Polish Women's Alliance), 205 S. Northwest Hwy., Park Ridge, IL 60068. Editor: Maria Lorys.

NAROD POLSKI, published by the Polish Roman Catholic Union of America, 984 Milwaukee Avenue, Chicago, IL 60622. Tel. 312-278-3210, Executive Editor: Kathryn G. Rosypal.

POLISH-AMERICAN WORLD, 3100 Grand Boulevard, Baldwin, NY 11510. Editor L. Romalewski.

THE POLISH WEEKLY STRAZ, 1002 Pittston Avenue, Scranton, PA 18505.

HEJNAL, 12205 Rollingsford Dr. Florrisant, MO 63033. Editor:Delphine Z. Kazlinski.

WHITE EAGLE, 56 Pulaski Street, Ware, MA 01082

SOKOL POLSKI—The Polish Falcon (Organ of the Polish Falcons of America), 615 Iron City Drive, Pittsburgh, PA. Editor: Timothy Kuzma.

IN CANADA

GLOS POLSKI, 390 Roncesvalles Avenue,
Toronto, ONT M6R 2M9

CZAS, 1150 Main Street,
Winnipeg, MAN R2W 3S6

ZWIAZKOWIEC 1638 Bloor Street, West,
Toronto, ONT M6P 4A8

Appendix F

THE POLES IN ALASKA

Many contributions of Polish-Americans cannot be captured in a work of this kind because of its emphasis on specific sites. One such case is the story of Poles in Alaska's history.

According to the eminent chronicler of Polish-American history, Henry Archacki, the purchase of Alaska from Russia in 1867 was called Seward's Folly because President Andrew Jackson's Secretary of State William H. Seward dared to spend all of 7,200,000 American silver dollars for a huge patch of wilderness that the Russians had annexed for themselves when virgin land was free. The sale was legitimate and in writing! But Seward needed a translator of the sheaf of Russian documents.

By good fortune who should be in the Land Office in Washington, D.C. but Dr. Henryk Kalussowski, a Polish exile who knew the Russians, only too well! Dr. Kalussowski saw to it that the United States of America, his adopted homeland, was not cheated.

America owned Alaska and soon was waging a war against the American poachers and trappers who moved in there. Major Gen. Carl Schurz became the Secretary of the Treasury. He appointed Brig. Gen. Wladimir (Wlodzimierz) Krzyzanowski-the organizer of New York's Polish Legion-as a ranking Customs Agent. In short order Gen. Krzyzanowski was commissioned to survey the Alaskan situation and crack down on the human vultures, which with the help of the U.S. Army, he did very well.

In 1879 American explorer Dr. W.B. Dall discovered a sizeable island off the lower Pacific coast of Alaska. He named the island after the Polish General in Washington's army, Tadeusz Kosciuszko. 55 years later Prof. Stefan Jarosz was commissioned by the Jagiellonian University of Cracow to explore Kosciuszko Island. After a year of solitary surveys Prof. Jarosz discovered a sizeable lake, which he named Pilsudski Lake.

Frederick Schwatka, an American of Polish descent, son of a Polish exile, was born in Galena, Illinois. He graduated from West Point. Schwatka eventually retired and became an explorer of

Alaska's Yukon River. He was to establish an Arctic record with his dog-sled team that traveled over 3,000 miles of Alaska's wonder lands. Lieutenant Schwatka published two magnificent books: "Summer in Alaska" in 1882 and "Nimrod in the North: Hunting and Fishing Adventures in the Arctic Regions" in 1885, upon which rests his fame. He died in 1889.

If you want to find spiritual warmth in cold Alaska we recommend visiting the Missionary Diocese of Northern Alaska where Michael J. Kaniecki, S.J. (a member of the Jesuit Order) officiates as the Bishop of Fairbanks in a salvaged quonset hut. The Northernmost U.S. Catholic Church, St. Patrick's, of Barrow, Alaska was established here. It is both a visual and a spiritual experience to view the Church today. If there is any uplifting to be done Bishop Michael Kaniecki is ready to get into his monoplane and pay you a visit! The readers of this Travel Guide can airmail greetings to Bishop Michael Kaniecki, S.J.; 1312 Peger Road, Fairbanks, Alaska 99079-5199.

Appendix G

POLES AMONG NOBEL PRIZE WINNERS

by Florence Clowes

Reprinted by kind permission of the *Polish American Journal*

In 1867, a thirty-four year old man invented dynamite in Stockholm, Sweden. He regretted that day for the rest of his life.

Alfred Bernhard Nobel, born in Stockholm in 1833, received most of his education in St. Petersburg, Russia. He returned to Sweden where he began experimenting in his father's factory. He received a patent for his invention in 1867 and set up factories all over the world, which brought him great wealth.

By 1895, he realized the potential danger of his invention and established the **Nobel Prize**, to be awarded annually to those, of any nationality, who "shall have conferred the greatest benefit on mankind," with outstanding achievements in chemistry, physics, physiology or medicine, literature and world peace. A sixth prize in economic science was established in 1969. Nobel endowed the Foundation with $9,200,000 before his death in 1896.

In 1901, the first prizes were awarded, and throughout the years, Americans of Polish descent and Poles themselves have been recognized for their achievements.

PRIZE WINNERS

In 1903, the first Polish person to receive the Nobel prize was **Marie Sklodowska Curie** (1867-1934). She is perhaps the best known of all Nobel prize winners.

Born in Warsaw in 1867, she went to Paris in 1891 to study at the Sorbonne, for women were not admitted to schools of higher education in Poland at that time. She received a degree in physical science (first in her class) and a year later a degree in mathematics (second in her class). She became a research assistant, when she met and worked with Pierre Curie. They married in 1895 and continued experiments together. In 1898, she discovered radium, and together with Pierre and Antoine H. Becquerel was awarded the prize **in physics** for discovering radioactivity and studying uranium. It was the dawn of the Atomic Age!

Henryk Sienkiewicz (1846-1916) was born in Wola Okrzejska, in Podlasie province. He went to school in Warsaw and became a journalist upon graduation. When he was thirty, his newspaper sent him to the United States to cover the Centennial Exposition in Philadelphia in 1876. He stayed two years, during which time he helped locate a communal living area in California for a group of Warsaw writers and artists. He began writing short stories of his travels, sending them to Poland. When he returned to his country, he began writing an historical trilogy, which was published in the newspaper in installments, coming out in book form later. It brought him instant fame. He was awarded the Nobel prize in literature in 1905. This magnificent trilogy now has a new American translation by W. S. Kuniczak. *With Fire and Sword* was issued in May, 1991 and *The Deluge* in November of that year. *Fire in the Steppe* was published in May, 1992.

In 1907, **Albert A. Michelson** (1852-1931) became the first American and first Polish-American to receive the Nobel prize. Albert A. Michelson was born in Strzelno, Poland and emigrated to America with his family two years later. He graduated from the U.S. Naval Academy in 1873, and then studied in Germany. In 1880, he designed an instrument to measure the speed of the earth through ether called a Michelson interferometer. He continued to refine his experiments and in 1907 was awarded the **prize in physics** for his design of precise optical instruments and the accurate measurements of the speed of light he obtained with them. He taught physics at the University of Chicago for most of his career.

Once again we find **Marie Curie** in the limelight; The only person to receive two Nobel prizes. Following Pierre's death Marie took a chair at the Sorbonne, the first woman professor in its history. She continued her research with her daughter Irene as an assistant. She successfully isolated pure radium and discovered polonium, naming it after her motherland. For this she was awarded the **prize in chemistry** in 1911. Having handled radium since 1897, she died from exposure to radiation in 1934.

The second Pole to receive a **prize in literature** was **Wladyslaw Reymont** (1867-1925). He was born to a very poor family in Kobiele Wielkie, near Radom in 1867. He left school at an early age and became a wandering actor. He began to write in 1896, self-taught. *The Peasants,* in four volumes, is a classic traditional peasant novel, with all the traditions, superstitions, and rhythms of nature. It brought him the **prize in literature** in 1924, being considered the best peasant epic in world literature.

Irene Joliot-Curie (1897-1956) was born in Paris the year her mother Marie began her study of radioactivity. She began working with her mother in 1918, at the Radium Institute, where she helped her mother perfect her new medical diagnostic tool, "X radiography," a mobile x-ray unit she took to the battlefront to minister to wounded soldiers. In 1925, she received her Ph.D and married Frederic, an assistant in Marie's lab. They both received the **prize in chemistry** for their work in bombarding various elements with alpha particles, artificially producing radioactive elements. She died like her mother, of leukemia, caused by overexposure to radioactivity.

Tadeusz Reichstein, born in Wloclawek, Poland in 1897, grew to be a scientist and educator. He studied in Zurich, where he received his degree in chemical engineering. He continued on to receive many other degrees, researching in universities in Paris, Switzerland, and England. He has been professor emeritus of the University of Basel, since 1967, and led the Institute of Organic Chemistry. In 1950, he received the **prize in medicine**, sharing it with Philip Hench and Edward Kendall, for their discoveries on cortisone and ACTH.

Marie Goeppert Mayer (1906-1977) was born in Kattowicz, Poland (now Katowice). She studied in Germany, received a doctorate in mathematics, and fled Germany when the Nazis gained power in 1930. She came to the United States with her husband, American chemist, Joseph Mayer. In researching, Marie discovered that atomic nuclei possess shells similar to the electron shells of atoms. J. Hans Jensen made the discovery at the same time, although the two worked independently of each other. The both shared in the **prize in physics** for this in 1963. Their discoveries were instrumental in the perfection of the atomic bomb. She joined the faculty of the University of California in San Diego in 1960 and continued to teach and study there until her death at age 65.

In 1977 **Andrew Schally**, together with Roger Guillemin and Rosalyn Yalow received the **prize in medicine** for their research concerning the role of hormones in the chemistry of the body. He was born in Poland, but received a Ph.D. in biochemistry at McGill University in Montreal and became a research assistant in the field. He came to the United States in 1957, working and studying in many fields: psychiatry, biochemistry, physiology, as well as authoring several books. Presently, he is chief of the Endocrine Polypeptide and Cancer Institute in the VA Medical Center in New Orleans.

Isaac B. Singer (1904-1991) is known the world over for his impassioned narrative art, with roots in the Polish-Jewish traditions. Born in Leoncin, Poland, he left his native land for the United States in 1934. He continually wrote in Yiddish. In 1978, he was awarded the **prize in literature** for his many novels full of Hasidic traditions and nostalgic chronicles of life in nineteenth century Poland.

Two years later, in 1980, **Czeslaw Milosz** also captured the **prize in literature**. Born in Wilno in 1911, Milosz was educated in prewar Poland. He writes his novels and poetry in Polish. His poetry, then considered "avant garde," was first published in 1933, and he became a prolific translator of foreign poetry. In 1946, he entered the diplomatic service of Poland, but broke with the government when he was no longer able to conform to Communist thought. He first went to Paris, then the United States where he remained. He is now professor at the University of California in Berkeley.

Lech Walesa has been known to the public for many years. His rise to fame came about quite differently from any other of the Nobel Prize winners. He was born in 1943 in Popow, Poland, during the war, to very poor parents. However, he became an electrician and in 1967 began working in the Gdansk shipyards.

Immediately, he became involved in politics and the workers' rights movement. In 1980, unemployed, he joined the strikers at the shipyard and was chosen provisional head and spokesman for the newly formed Solidarnosc. In October of that year, he was elected its chairman. During martial law, he was imprisoned with other strikers. The government outlawed Solidarnosc in 1982. The ban ended in 1989, and Solidarnosc was recognized as a legal labor organization. For his efforts to prevent violence while trying to gain worker rights and other freedoms, he was awarded the **peace prize** in 1983.

Lech Walesa's efforts, together with many unnamed heroes, altered the Polish nation, decisively leading the way for a new Europe, just as Marie Sklodowska Curie, the first woman to receive the Nobel prize, and the only woman to receive it twice, opened the new nuclear era with her discoveries.

Appendix H

POLISH PLACE-NAMES IN THE U.S.A.

Elzbieta Lyra, Franciszek Lyra

The origin of place-names in the U.S.A. is as complex and hetero-geneous as American society itself. The intricate geographical no-menclature in this country includes many foreign names, among them some of Polish origin.

We have limited the scope of this essay to places that bear Polish names, and have excluded those settlements that either no longer exist or have been swallowed up by larger ones. We have not paid attention to names such as Stanislawowo or Wojciechowo, com-monly used by the American Polonia, denoting only districts within large urban agglomerations; furthermore, towns whose names have been changed from Polish to American forms were omitted from this analysis.

Towns and settlements bearing names of Polish origin have been correlated with the distribution pattern of Americans of Pol-ish descent in the U.S.A.

This article presents a synthesis of the research that has been carried out so far; the work is by no means complete.

METHOD

There is no source available giving a complete list of all towns and settlements in the U.S.A. The first step in the realization of the project consisted of completing, as far as possible, a list of all the places in the U.S.A. that bear Polish names, or names that might be of Polish origin, making use of geographical dictionaries, monographs on par-ticular counties and states, and other historical material.

Since we consulted a number of old works, some of them pub-lished in the 19th century, it was necessary to check whether particular places mentioned in these works still existed, whether their names had been changed, or whether they had been swal-lowed up by larger conurbations. The "Standard Oil" maps and the "Commercial Atlas" proved to be indispensable sources.

To collect as comprehensive a gazetteer as possible a special questionnaire was devised and sent to libraries, archives, societies, private persons, and post offices in the places under scrutiny. 70% of the letters were answered, but only 45% included any complete and thorough information. A series of visits to about 25 places were also undertaken.

LITERATURE

A work closely related to the subject of this research is a list made by the Rev. Franciszek Bolek, "Settlements founded by Poles in the United States" [3]. This work proved to be very helpful even with its serious deficiencies. It includes a list of places in each state, arranged in alphabetical order. In many instances, the author gives not only the name of a place, but also the county in which it is situated, the year of its foundation and the name of its founder. The author's uncritical approach to the subject matter is a serious drawback to the work; he was unable to resist the attraction of Polish-looking and Polish-sounding onomastic forms that in reality were far from being names of Polish origin. However, Bolek's work constitutes the only attempt so far to list all American place-names of Polish origin. It has provided a source of information on Polish names in the U.S.A. for other investigators such as J. Wasowicz [32].

Substantial material on this subject can be found in the studies of authors concerned with the immigration of Poles to the United States. The following authors deserve mention in this connection: M. Haiman [9, 10], W. Kruszka [15, 16], F. Niklewicz [19, 21] and H. Sienkiewicz. Some works by American philologists and geographers also provide important, though not always complete and reliable information. Among these, the basic work is a bibliography on the history of over 3,000 counties in the United States [24]. Such states as Indiana, Missouri, Nebraska, New York, Ohio, Pennsylvania, and Wisconsin have published monographs.

There are a few works that aim at a synthesis of all American place-names. Although, these have only a limited value for a re-search on Polish place-names in the U.S.A., none of them can be ignored. The most important among them are studies by H. Gannet [7], A. Holt [12], and G. R. Stewart [29].

Furthermore, there exists, for every state, at least one monograph on its geographical names. It should, however, be emphasized that none of them is completely comprehensive when place-names of Polish origin are concerned. The same is true of some general studies that deal with the United States as a whole.

The history of Polish place-names in the U.S.A. may be divided into two periods. The first began at the turn of the 18th century and lasted until the mid-19th century. The second covers the period from the middle of the 19th century up to the present day. The process by which American places acquire Polish names is by no means finished, although it is no longer as productive as it used to be. The Polish names that appeared during the first period resulted from the sympathetic attitude of Americans towards Poland and their appreciation of Tadeusz Kosciuszko and Kazimierz Pulaski. However, though the former has always been extremely popular in the States, only two places and one county bearing his name are to be found there: Kosciusko county in Indiana, Kosciusko in Attala county, Mississippi, and in Wilson county, Texas. Though W. Kruszka mentions another place named Kosciusko in Day county, South Dakota [16], it has proved impossible to establish whether it actually exists. Of the three places called Kosciusko only the one in Texas was founded and named by Poles. The name of Kosciusko in Mississippi originated on the initiative of William Dodd, the grandson of General Dodd who, together with Kosciuszko, had participated in the American War of Independence under the command of General Greene. Before the place was named Kosciusko, it had had several other names: Greenville, Prentice, Pekin, and Paris.

The name of Pulaski appears more frequently on American maps than that of Kosciusko. We were able to find 22 places named after the hero of the battle of Savannah while the existence of another 5 remains to be confirmed. The largest town called Pulaski is situated in the county of the same name in Virginia. Warsaw is the most popular name of Polish origin in the United States. The history of 19 places of this name is known to us at the present stage of our research, and 15 more await more detailed documentation. The capital of Gallatin county, Kentucky, is the oldest of all the places bearing the name of Warsaw.

During the second period the initiative to give Polish names to certain places in the United States came from Polish immigrants. The oldest settlement founded and named by Poles is Panna Maria, Karnes County, Texas. Edward Dworaczyk [5] has written the history of that place and of some other Polish settlements in Texas.

Since the second half of the 19th century, a great number of towns bearing Polish names have appeared on maps of the United States. They usually indicate from which region of Poland a particular group of pioneering settlers came. Names of the following Polish towns appear in America: Cracow or Krakow (five times), Lublin, Opole and Cestohowa (twice), Tarnow, Torun, Radom, Chojnice, and Gniezno (once each).

In addition to Kosciusko and Pulaski, a few American places have been given the names of famous Poles. A settlement founded by the actress Helena Modrzejewska in California appears as Modjeska, since this is the Americanized form of her name. There are four places in Minnesota, Michigan and Wisconsin bearing the name of Sobieski, while in Wisconsin there is a settlement called Poniatowski.

LINGUISTIC ASPECTS

All the place-names of Polish origin which appear on American maps have been subject to assimilation. The Americanization of these names is brought about by the following processes:

(a) translation, for example, Polska-Poland, Warszawa-Warsaw;

(b) orthographic modification, i.e. by leaving out all diacritical marks not to be found in the English alphabet.

In many cases orthographic adjustment has been unnecessary as, for example, in Lublin and Opole, but such names have become adapted phonetically, i.e. place-names of Polish origin have come to be pronounced in accordance with the orthoepic rules of the English language.

(c) contraction, i.e. word-shortening as, for example, Pulaski-Plaski, Modrzejewska-Modjeska.

(d) addition of the-ville ending, for example, Paveleksville, Pulaskiville.

A research worker on place-names in the United States must be particularly sensitive to the phenomenon of homophony. F. Bolek, misled by the sound and orthographic form of some American place-names, interpreted them as being of Polish origin, though in fact they were not. Thus, for example, he included the following place-names in his list:

Polacca (Navajo county, Arizona), Waleska (Cherokee county, Georgia), Hanska (Brown county, Minnesota), and Chokolaskee (Lee county, Florida). All these names, when more closely scrutinized, have proved to be of Indian origin.

AMERICAN PLACES BEARING POLISH NAMES IN RELATION TO THE GEOGRAPHICAL DISTRIBUTION OF AMERICANS OF POLISH ORIGIN

Fig. 1. illustrates the distribution of Polish immigrants in the United States on the basis of absolute figures [13]. The characteristic feature of the geographical pattern revealed is the dispersion of Americans of Polish origin over the whole country, their greatest concentration being in the northeast and a slightly lesser concentration around the Great Lakes. Such states as, for example, Minnesota and Texas are comparatively small centres of the American Polonia if we consider the total number of immigrants in these states. However, they are distinguished by the concentration and homogeneity of the Polish communities, which undoubtedly accounts for the presence of Polish names. Polish immigrants living in Mississippi, Kentucky, Nebraska, and Utah are the least numerous.

The pattern of distribution of places bearing Polish names does not parallel that of the Polish immigration (Fig. 2). They appear mostly in the middle west and in the western areas of the Eastern states. Most of the southern states have only one place with a Polish name in each, with the exception of Mississippi, in which there are three, and of Alabama and Arkansas, in which no places bearing Polish names were found. The westernmost concentrations of settlements with Polish names are found in Texas, Nebraska and California.

There are no Polish place-names in Connecticut, where the percentage of Americans of Polish origin in relation to the total number of inhabitants in particular counties, is the highest in the entire the United States (36.8% in Hudson county), and where the number of Americans of Polish origin per square mile amounts, in the most extreme instances, to 800 persons (Hudson county), 264 (Union county), 241 (Essex county). Similarly, there is a total absence of settlements bearing Polish names in Massachusetts where the number of Americans of Polish origin (136,961) is higher than that in Connecticut (117,663) and in Rhode Island [13]. The lack of Polish names in this part of the country can be explained by the fact that these states were already densely populated and their nomenclature had been established before the process of giving Polish names to American places began. In a state such as New York, for example, Polish names appear only in its western area, which has a relatively low number of Polish immigrants.

Concentrations of places bearing Polish names are to be found in Texas and, to a lesser extent, in the southern part of Illinois and the central part of Wisconsin. Other Polish names are scattered all over the south and middle west.

If we compare the two maps, it can clearly be seen that there is no close correlation between the distribution of Polish immigrants and Polish place-names. The existence of Polish place-names depends less on the absolute number of Polish immigrants living in a given area than on the degree of ethnic homogeneity of their environment, and on certain factors that have no connection with Polish immigration. Thus, for example, Texas, in which 18,000 Americans of Polish origin live at present, has eight places bearing Polish names, whereas New York with 700,000 Americans of Polish origin has only three.

Hitherto research has revealed that 67 places with Polish names exist in the United States (Fig. 2.). Their distribution is as follows: Illinois-8, Texas-8, Nebraska-7, Ohio-5, Wisconsin and Minnesota-4 in each, Michigan, Kentucky, New York and Mississippi-3 in each, Virginia, North Dakota, Missouri and Indiana-2 in each, and one to be found in each of other states.

The data provided by the questionnaire survey helped to establish that, out of the 67 places bearing Polish names, 37 were founded by Poles and 23 by Americans, while in 7 cases it was impossible to establish the nationality of the founders.

50 places from a list of 228 place-names no longer exist. The geographical distribution of the places that have disappeared strikes

us as very interesting, since most of them, i.e. as many as 15, were in the south and the middle west, 12 in the north-west and 8 in the west. The greatest number of places that have disappeared were in the following states: Georgia (6), Pennsylvania (4), Arkansas (3), and Michigan (3).

TABLE 1. THE PRESENT STATE OF RESEARCH ON AMERICAN PLACE-NAMES OF POLISH ORIGIN

	Total number of places under scrutiny	Existing places with names of			Places no longer existing	Information not available
		Polish origin	other origin	uncertain origin		
Number of places	228	67	24	28	50	59

The data illustrating the present state of research (Table 1) lead to the conclusion that there is still much work to be done on the problems we have discussed, since the origin of more than 1/3 of the places has not yet been settled (i.e. places with names of uncertain origin or about which "information is not available"), and for most of these places there is little or no documentation available.

TABLE 2. THE RESULTS OF RESEARCH ON PLACES WHOSE NAMES APPEAR AT LEAST TWICE

	Number of places	Existing places with names of			Places no longer existing	Information not available
		Polish origin	other origin	uncertain origin		
Warsaw	34	12	—	5	7	10
Poland	28	4	2	10	7	5
Pulaski	25	17	1	—	1	6
Sandusky	12	1	—	5	2	4
Wilno	7	2	—	—	4	1
Wanda	6	—	3	—	1	2
Cracow	5	2	—	—	2	1
Sobieski	4	3	—	1	—	—
Kosciusko	3	2	—	—	—	1
Boles	3	—	—	1	—	2
Cestohowa	2	1	—	—	1	—
Vistula	2	—	—	—	—	2

Most of the settlements investigated are very small places, not only in comparison with metropolises in the United States but also with settlements in Poland. The total number of inhabitants of the five biggest towns with Polish names amount only to a few thousands and the largest of these is Pulaski in Pulaski county, Virginia, with 10,000 inhabitants. In some cases the name is applied only to a few

TABLE 3. LIST OF TOWNS AND SETTLMENTS PROVED TO BEAR NAMES OF POLISH ORIGIN

states	numbers indicating the place-name on the map	place-name	county
Ariz. Arizona	3	Polaco	SantaCruz
Cal. California	2	Modjeska	Orange
Fla. Florida	3	Korona	Breward
Ga. Georgia	1	Pulaski	Candler
Ill. Illinois	2	Mt. Pulaski	Logan
	3	Poland	Randolph
	4	Posen	Washington
	5	Posen	Cook
	6	Pulaski	Hancock
	7	Pulaski	Pulaski
	8	Radom	Washington
	11	Warsaw	Hancock
Ind. Indiana	2	Kosciusko	Kosciusko
	7	Pulaski	Pulaski
	10	Warsaw	Kosciusko
Io. Iowa	3	Pulaski	Davis
Ky. Kentucky	3	Pulaski	Pulaski
	5	Warsaw	Gallatin
La. Louisiana	6	Warsaw	Franklin
Mich. Michigan	5	Posen	Presquelsle
	6	Pulaski	Jackson
Minn. Minnesota	9	Opole	Kittson
	12	Sobieski	Beltzami
	15	Wilno	Lincoln
Miss. Mississippi	1	Kosciusko	Attala
	2	Pulaski	Scott
	5	Wiczynski	Washington
Mo. Missouri	2	Krakow	Franklin
	3	Pulaski	Ripley
	4	Pulaskifield	Barry
Neb. Nebraska	1	Boleszyn	Valley
	2	Chojnice	Howard
	4	Krakow	Nance
	5	NewPosen	Howard
	8	Tarnow	Platte
	9	Warsaw	Howard
N. M. New Mexico	1	Wilno	Grant
N. Y. New York	6	Pulaski	Oswego
	8	South Warsaw	Wyoming
	9	Warsaw	Wyoming
N. C. North Carolina	2	Warsaw	Duplin
N. D. North Dakota	4	Poland	Walsh
	5	Warsaw	Walsh
O. Ohio	3	Poland	Mahoming
	5	Pulaski	Williams
	6	Pulaskiville	Morrow
	12	Warsaw	Coshocton
	16	Zaleski	Vinton

c. Table 3

1	2	3	4
Pa. Pennsylvania	4	Pulaski	Beaver
R. I. Rhode Island	1	Sobieski	Clearfield
S. C. South Carolina	1	Pulaski	Oconee
S. D. South Dakota	1	Kosciusko	Day
Tenn. Tennessee	2	Pulaski	Giles
Tex. Texas	1	Cestohova	Karnes
	3	Kosciusko	Wilson
	4	Panna Maria	Karnes
	5	Paveleksville	Karnes
	6	Pulaski	Karnes
	8	Warsaw	San Augustine
	9	Warsaw	Henderson
	10	St. Hedwig	Bexar
Va. Virginia	2	Pulaski	Pulaski
	3	Warsaw	Richmond
Wisc. Wisconsin	7	Lublin	Taylor
	9	Poland	Brown
	14	Sobieski	Oconto
	15	Torun	Portage

houses concentrated at a cross-roads, to a small settlement, a railway station or a trading center which is neither a village in the Polish sense, nor a settlement, but which consists of a postoffice, a general store, and a gasoline station, and which is, in fact, a service center for farmers scattered over a large surrounding area.

Further research will undoubtedly call for some modifications of the data presented in Table 2, since all the settlement points that have been marked on the map as "uncertain" will fall into one or other of the remaining groups. At the same time, it may prove possible to trace some other places bearing Polish names, or to cast a different light on those that have already been examined.

Institute of Geography
Polish Academy of Sciences Warsaw

Department of English Language
M. Curie-Sklodowska University, Lublin

REFERENCES

[1] Baldwin Th., Thomas J., *Gazetteer of the U. S.*, Philadelphia 1854.
[2] Barnes W. C., *Arizona Place Names,* Unio. Ariz. Bull. Gen., 2.
[3] Bolek F., *Osiedla zalozone przez Polakow w Stanach Zjednoczonych* (Settle-

ments Founded by Poles in the United States), Polsk. Przegl. kartogr., 32. 1930, pp. 203-214.

[4] Chappin W., *A Complete Reference Gazetteer of the United States of North America; Containing a General View of the United States,* New York 1839.

[5] Dworaczyk E., *The First Polish Colonies of America in Texas,* San Antonio 1936.

[6] Espenshade H. A., *Pennsylvania Place Names,* The Pennsylvania State College Studies in History and Political Sciences, 1, 1925.

[7] Gannett H., *American Names, A Guide to the Origin of the Place Names in the United States,* Publ. Aff. Press 1947.

[8] Gudde E. G., *1000 California Place Names,* Univ. Calif. Press 1959.

[9] Haiman M., *Z przeszlosci polskiej w Ameryce* (From Polish Past in America), Buffalo 1927. [10] Haiman M., *Polacy wsrod pionierow Ameryki* (Poles Among the Pioneers of America), Chicago 1937.

[11] Haywood J., *Gazetteer of the United States of America Comprising a Concise General View of the United States,* Philadelphia 1854.

[12] Holt A. H., *American Place Names,* New York 1938.

[13] Iwanicka-Lyra E., *Liczba i geograficzne rozmieszczenie Amerykanow polskiego pochodzenia w Stanach Zjednoczonych* (Sum. Number and Geographical Distribution of Americans of Polish Origin in the United States of America), Przegl. geogr., 37, 1965

[14] Kane J. W., *The American Counties,* New York 1960.

[15] Kruszka W., *Historia polska w Ameryce* (Polish History in America), Milwaukee 1937.

[16] Kruszka W., *Historia Polska w Ameryce.* Poczatek, wzrost i rozwoj dziejowy osad polskich w Polnocnej Ameryce (Polish History in America. Beginning, Growth and Historical Development of Polish Settlements in North America), Milwaukee 1905.

[17] McArthur L. A., *Oregon Geographic Names,* Oregon Hist. Soc., 1944.

[18] Meany E. S., *Origin of Washington Geographic Names,* Univ. Wash. Press, 1923.

[19] Niklewicz F., *Dzieje pierwszych polskich osadnikow w Ameryce i przewodnik parafii polskich w Stanach Zjednoczonych* (History of the First Polish Settlers in America and the Guide of Polish Parishes in the U.S.A.), Milwaukee 1927.

[20] Niklewicz F., *Polacy w Stanach Zjednoczonych* (Polish People in the U.S.A.), Green Bay 1937.

[21] Niklewicz F., *Przewodnik polsko-amerykanski* (Polish-American Guide), Green Bay 1923.

[22] Okolowicz J., *Wychodzstwo i osadnictwo polskie przed wojna swiatowa* (Polish Emigration and Settlement Before the World War), Warszawa 1920.

[23] *Origin of Nebraska Place Names* (compiled by the Federal Projects) Lincoln 1938.

[24] Peterson C. S., *Bibliography of County Histories of the 3050 Counties in the 48 States,* Baltimore, 1944.

[25] Read W. A., *Florida Place Names of Indian Origin and Seminole Personal Names*, Baton Rouge 1934.

[26] Read W. A., *Indian Place Names in Alabama*, Baton Rouge 1937.

[27] Read W.A., *Louisiana Place Names of Indian Origin*, Univ. Bull. Louisiana 1927.

[28] Scott J., *A Geographical Dictionary of the United States of North America*, Philadelphia 1805.

[29] Stewart G. R., *Names on the Land*, New York 1945.

[30] Szawleski M., Wychodzstwo polskie w Stanach Zjednoczonych Ameryki (Polish Emigration in the U.S.A.), Lwow-Warszawa-Krakow 1929.

[31] Wells H. L., *California Names*, Los Angeles 1934.

[32] Wasowicz J., *Nazwy geograficzne pochodzenia polskiego* (Geographical Names of Polish Origin), Czas. geogr., 26, 1955.

[33] Wisniowski S., *Radom i Kalisz w Ameryce* (Radom and Kalisz in America), Tyg. ilustr., 59, 1876.

[34] McNally Rand and Company, *Commercial Atlas and Marketing Guide 1960*, ed. 91, New York-Chicago-San Francisco.

[35] McNally Rand, *Road Atlas*: United States, Canada, Mexico.

[36] Standard Oil Company Maps.

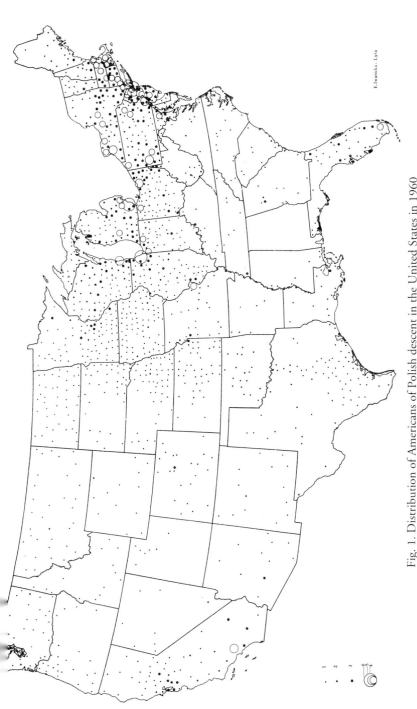

E. Iwanicka - Lyra

Fig. 1. Distribution of Americans of Polish descent in the United States in 1960

1 – less than 500 persons in a country, 2 – 500-1000 persons, 3 – 1000-10 000 persons, 4 – 10-50 thousand persons, 5 – 50-100 thousand persons, 6 – more than 100 thousand persons

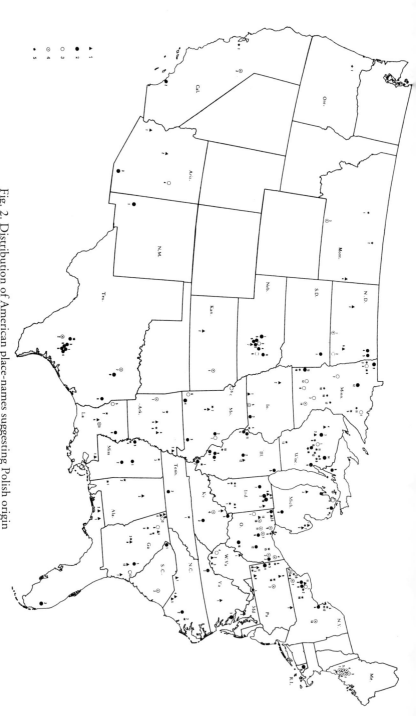

Fig. 2. Distribution of American place-names suggesting Polish origin

1 – places no longer in existence, 2 – existing places, 3 – places with names incorrectly interpreted as being of Polish origin, 4 – origin of the place-name heterogeneously interpreted, 5 – information on the origin of the place-name not available, numbers indicate place names listed in Table 3

▲ 1
● 2
○ 3
⊙ 4
∗ 5

Appendix I

A BRIEF HISTORY OF POLISH SPORTS IN AMERICA

by Tom Tarapacki

Reprinted by kind permission of the *Polish American Journal*

If there has been one aspect of American life, in which Polish Americans have been able to make a substantial impact over the past 80 years, it has been sports. Their tremendous success in athletics gave Polish Americans status, wealth, and influence that they could not attain in any other profession. The positive achievements of Polish Americans helped counteract some of the negative stereotypes that existed, while creating many new opportunities.

Coming mainly from peasant stock, most Polish immigrants to America around the turn of the century were quite used to vigorous physical activity and many possessed the strength and stamina to succeed in athletics. Considering that the alternative for most of them was back-breaking labor in a factory or coal mine, they were certainly motivated to perform well in athletics. In addition, many of the barriers that made if difficult for Polish-Americans to compete in other professions were comparatively lacking in sports.

In many cases sports was not viewed as a career in itself, but rather as a means of getting a college education. For example, when baseball great **Stan Musial** was leaving high school, his father wanted him to accept a basketball scholarship to the University of Pittsburgh. When "Stan the Man" decided to pass up college for a baseball career, the two had a serious rift. Another baseball great, **Carl Yastremski**, attended Notre Dame at his father's insistence. He left after one year to play professional baseball, but not until his father extracted a pledge that his son would finish his college education (which he did).

KETCHEL CAPTURED BOXING LAURELS

Stanley (Kiecel) Ketchel could probably be considered the first Polish-American sports hero. His rise to the world middleweight championship in 1908 coincided with the rise of prominence of sports in America. This son of Polish immigrant farmers was not only a great boxer but also a colorful character who was shot to death at the height of his career.

There were others who rose to prominence shortly after the turn of the century. **Joe Pliska** starred for Notre Dame's first undefeated football team in 1913. **Stanislaw Cyganiewicz**, a Polish-born wrestler known as Zbyszko, became a world champion in the 1920s. Golfer **Al (Watras) Watrous** won the Canadian Open in 1922 and was a member of the U.S. Ryder Cup team.

In the 1920s baseball became America's pastime, and Polish-Americans were among the stars. Future Hall of Famers **Stan Coveleski** and **Al (Szymanski) Simmons** led the way for numerous Polish-American baseball standouts over the years, including, **Ted Kluszewski, Whitey Kurowski, Steve Gromek, Frankie Pytlak, Jim Konstanty, Eddie Lopat, Ron Perranoski, Bill Mazeroski, Richie Zisk, Tom Paciorek, Carl Yastremski, Mark Fidrych,** and **Phil** and **Joe Niekro.**

POLES EXCEL ON GRIDIRON

Frank Pekarski became the first Polish-American chosen for the college football All-America team in 1914 and was followed by many more as Polish-Americans became a potent force in the sport. Notre Dame, being a Catholic University, attracted a large number of Polish-American athletes who helped make it a perennial football power. In the '40s, Polish-Americans **Johnny Lujack** and **Leon Hart** were among the "Fighting Irish" who won the Heisman Trophy, awarded annually to college football's top player.

It was during that time that players like **Alex Wojciechowicz, Chet Mutryn, Ed Danowski, Joe Tereshinski, John Strykalski, Bill Osmanski,** the **Modzelewski brothers, Bill Swiacki, Johnny Mazur, Frank Dancewicz, Ziggy Czarobski,** and Heisman Trophy winner **Vic Janowicz** helped make Polish names virtually synonymous with football. Ironically, the single person probably most responsible for this was football great **Bronko Nagurski** who was actually of Ukrainian heritage.

Some time passed before Polish-Americans were able to advance to decision making positions in sports. It wasn't until the 1960s that a significant number of Polish-Americans assumed head coach and managing positions. These included **Hank (Wilczek) Stram, Frank Kush,** and **Walt (Miska) Michaels** in football and **Danny (Orzechowski) Ozark** and **John Goryl** in baseball. However, many successful Polish-American athletes used their sports careers to take advantage of opportunities in business, politics, and other endeavors: basketball great **Tom Gola** became Controller of the city of Philadelphia; football standout star **Frank Tripucka** operated a very successful beverage distributorship; Canisius College basketball star **Henry Nowak** became a U.S. Congressman representing Buffalo; former Yankee shortstop, **Tony Kubek** became a network baseball broadcaster.

Polish-Americans have tended to favor football and baseball, but they have excelled in nearly every sport. They include: **Tom Gola, Bob Kurland,** and **Vince Boryla** in basketball; **Ed (Tyranski) Tyson** in softball; **Norm Schemansky** and **Stanley Stanczyk** in weightlifting; **Steve Stanko** and **Frank Zane** in bodybuilding; **Billy Golembiewski** and **Ed Lubanski** in bowling; **Bob Toski** in golf; **Matt Cetlinski** and **Chet Jastremski** in swimming; **Frank (Pajkowski) Parker** in tennis; **Walter "Turk" Broda** and **Peter Stempkowski** in hockey; **Steve Mizerak** in billiards; and **Tony Zale** and **Henry Chemel** in boxing.

WOMEN EXCELLED AS WELL

Women's athletics have tended to lag behind men's athletics in this country, particularly on the professional level. Still, going back to **Stella (Walasiewicz) Walsh**, the sprinter who won gold in the 1932 Olympics, Polish-American women have had an impact in athletics comparable to that of their male counterparts. They included female baseball pioneers **Sophie Kurys, Loretta (Jasczak) Jester,** and **Connie Wisniewski**; college basketball stars **Carol Blazejowski** and **Mary "Mo" Ostrowski**; bowler **Ann Setlock**; figure skater **Janet Lynn (Nowicki)**; and **Stasia Czernicki**, a holder of numerous records in candlepin bowling.

POLAND'S LOSS IS AMERICA'S GAIN

Poland has produced many great athletes over the years. **Janusz Peciak** was the gold medal winner in the modern pentathlon in the '76 Olympics; **Jozef Schmidt** won gold in the triple jump in both '60 and '64; **Irena Szewinska** was a track star who competed in 5 Games, winning 7 medals in 5 different events; **Jacek Wszola** won Olympic gold and silver in the high jump; **Zdzislaw Kryskowiak** and **Bronislaw Malinowski** were gold medal-winning steeplechasers; **Wladyslaw Kozakiewicz** and **Tadeusz Slusarski** won gold in the pole vault; and **Janusz Kusocinski** set an Olympic record in the 10,000 meter run at the '32 games that stood for 16 years. Political divisions and economic problems have often hampered Poland's sports development, especially in the post war-era. They also caused Poland to lose many top athletes and coaches to other nations. Assisting the U.S. effort in the last Olympiad were a slew of Polish-born coaches, including Peciak heading the American modern pentathlon team. **Zenon Babraj** and **Kris Korzenowski** in rowing, **Andrzej Bek** in cycling and **Paul Podgorski** in canoeing and kayaking.

Still, some top Polish athletes have emerged in recent years, though many of them have had to do the bulk of their training abroad. These include figure skater **Grzegorz Filipowski**, female marathoner **Wanda Panfil** and **Arthur Wojdat** who in 1988 became the first Pole to win an Olympic medal in swimming. Since the 1970s, Poland has been a power in what is probably that country's most popular sport, soccer. The Polish team came out of nowhere to finish third in the 1974 World Cup, and won gold at the 1972 Olympics. **Kazimierz Deyna** and **Grzegorz Lato** were among the top players produced by Poland. Deyna went on to play professionally in England and the U.S. and set a North American Soccer League record in 1983 when he scored 5 goals and 4 assists in one game.

Today, Polish-American athletes continue to be successful on the playing fields. **Don Majkowski** and **Steve Wisniewski** in football, **Kelly Tripucka** and **Frank Brickowski** in basketball, **Doug Drabek** and **Mike Bielecki** in baseball, and **Wayne Gretzky** and **Ed Olczyk** in hockey, runners **Bill** and **Gerald Donakowski**, figure skater **Tonia Kwiatkowski**, college basketball player **Tracy Lis**, boxer **Bobby Czyz** and car racer **Alan Kulwicki** are among the most prominent names in their sports today. But recent years have seen Polish-Americans become "superstars" in the front office as well. **Dave Dombrowski**, former general manager of the Montreal

Expos, now heads baseball's expansion Florida Marlins; **Mike Krzyzewski** is head coach of the Duke Blue Devils, the 1991, men's NCAA basketball champions; **Billy (Paczkowski) Packer** broadcasts college basketball for CBS-TV. It is especially significant that these men were not star athletes who were able to use their famous names, but instead relied essentially on talent and hard work to attain their achievements.

Polish-Americans continue to excel in sports, as they have throughout the past 8 decades. They have used the opportunities created by athletics, particularly the educational opportunities, to attain success in almost every aspect of what has become a billion dollar business in this country. They have made their presence felt not only as athletes, but also as owners, managers, coaches, broadcasters, and in almost every possible aspect of the billion dollar business of sports.

GREATEST MOMENTS

Here are some great moments in Polish-American sports history:

1908–Stan (Kiecel) Ketchel, just 21 years of age, defeats all contenders to assume the vacant Middleweight Boxing Championship.

1917–Frank Rydzewski of Notre Dame earns All-American honors in football.

1920–Stan Covelski wins three games as the Cleveland Indians capture the World Series, allowing a total of just two runs for an ERA of 0.67.

1929–Al (Szymanski) Simmons leads the Philadelphia A's to the first of three consecutive pennants, earning MVP honors with his 365 average, 34 home runs and 157 RBI'S.

1932–Stella (Walasiewicz) Walsh wins the Gold Medal in the women's 100-meter dash at the Los Angeles Olympics.

1938–One of Fordham's famed "Seven Blocks of Granite" and a future Hall of Famer, Alex Wojciechowicz is made the first pick in the NFL draft by the Detroit Lions.

1941–Ed Sadowski, one of the new wave of bigger centers at 6'5" and 220 lbs., leads the Detroit Eagles over the Oshkosh All-Stars to win the World Professional Basketball Championship.

1947–Quarterback Johnny (Luczak) Lujack of Notre Dame, who led the Fighting Irish to a 20-1-1 record and three national championships during his varsity career, wins the coveted Heisman Trophy.

1948–Tony (Zaleski) Zale, still fighting at age 35, recaptures the Middleweight Boxing title by knocking out Rocky Graziano in the 3rd round of their fight in Newark, New Jersey.

1950–Casimir "Jim" Kostanty of the Philadelphia Phillies, baseball's first superstar relief pitcher, wins the National League MVP Award.

1954–Standing just 5'8" and 127 lbs., Bob (Augustoski) Toski wins golf's World Championship, the sport's first $50,000 event.

1960–Bill Mazeroski hits the most famous home run in baseball history, a dramatic 9th inning homer in the 7th game of the World Series that helps the Pittsburgh Pirates defeat the New York Yankees.

1967–Carl Yastremski of the Boston Red Sox wins the coveted "Triple Crown" by leading the American League in hitting, home runs and RBI's, a feat no player has accomplished since.

1973–The National Polish American Sports Hall of Fame and Museum is established in Orchard Lake, MI, and makes baseball great Stan Musial its first inductee.

1978–Although some critics say that he's too small and too slow to play pro hockey, 17-year-old Wayne Gretzky signs a lucrative contract with the Indianapolis Racers of the World Hockey League.

1984–Polish born coach Eddie Borysewicz leads the U.S. cycling team to the country's first Olympic medals in the sport since 1912, including a gold by sprinter Mark Gorski.

1985–New York Yankee Phil Niekro, 47, wins his 300th career game and becomes the oldest player to pitch a major league shutout when he defeats the Toronto Blue Jays in the final game of the season.

1989–An interception by rookie linebacker Bill Romanowski helps San Francisco defeat Cincinnati in Super Bowl XXIII.

1991–Coach Mike Krzyzewski leads Duke to victory in the NCAA men's basketball tournament with a stunning upset of unbeaten University of Nevada-Las Vegas in the semi-final and a 72-65 win over Kansas in the championship game.

Appendix J

POLISH FOLK DANCE GROUPS

Compiled by Stas Kmiec
reprinted by kind permission of the *Polish American Journal*

The following listing of Polish dance groups in the United States was compiled from the responses to a questionnaire distributed to 100 dance groups, and the telephone contacts with another 28. We thank the ensembles for their cooperation in responding. Our apologies to any Polish groups we may have missed.

AUSTIN POLISH DANCERS, contact: Ron Houston, 1306 Arcadia, Austin, TX 78757.

BABURKI POLISH FOLK DANCERS AND SINGERS, St. Barbara's Parish, Emery Ave., Houtzdale, PA 16651. (814) 378-8347.

BIALY ORZEL DANCE TROUPE, INC., 1349 Broadway, Buffalo, NY. (716) 897-3594.

CENTENNIAL DANCERS, contact: Joanne Ygeal, 10480 Bassett, Livonia, MI 48150.

CRACOVIA DANCERS, contact: Bruce Cantreel, 1621 Wayne Ave., Dayton, Ohio 45410.

CZERWONE MAKI, Marian Siedlarczyk-Werner - Director, 2021 Thornleigh Rd., Midlothian, VA 23113.

DAWNE TANCE ENSEMBLE, Washington, D.C. 14716 Locustwood Lane, Silver Spring, MD 20905. (301) 236-6753.

DOLINA POLISH FOLK DANCERS, 2239 Stinson Blvd. NE, Minneapolis, MN 55418. Director: Edward J. Rajtar.

ECHOES OF POLAND SONG & DANCE ENSEMBLE, INC., 3030 Hopewell Place, Toledo, OH 43606. Director: Paulina Tul-Ortyl.

GORALE POLISH FOLK DANCERS, 1435 W. Cerritos Ave. #40, Anaheim, CA 92802. Director: Rick Kobzi.

GWIAZDA POLISH FOLK DANCE ENSEMBLE, 60 Charter Oak Ave., Pulaski Plaza, Hartford, CT 06106. (203) 563-9117. Choreographer/Director: Carol A. Oleasz.

HEJNAL POLISH-AMERICAN DANCERS of Long Island, 1859 Carroll Ave., Merrick, NY 11566. (516) 868-3048.

ZESPOL REGIONALNY "HYRNI", contact: Janina Duda. 4302 W. 55th St., Chicago, IL 60632.

JANOSIK DANCERS, 706 Lincoln Ave., Willow Grove, PA 19090. Morley Leyton, Director.

KARUZELA POLISH-AMERICAN FOLK ENSEMBLE, 312 Dickson Ave., Pittsburgh, PA 15212. (412) 761-4538. Artistic Director-Paul Miara.

KOPERNIK POLISH FOLK DANCERS, 2098 W. Hamton Rd., Binghamton, NY 13903. (607) 723-8042. Valentina Kozlowski, Director/Choreographer.

KOSCIUSZKO POLISH DANCERS, Virginia Cegelski-Guyette, 25 Newell Rd., Schenectady, NY 12306. (518) 393-9033.

KRAKOW POLISH-AMERICAN DANCERS of Milwaukee County. Annette Kuligowski, Director (414) 383 7177

KRAKOWIACY POLISH FOLK DANCERS of Western New York, 730 Orchard Park Rd., West Seneca, NY 14224. (716) 674-9243. Eugenia Zastepowska-Smith, Director/Choreographer.

KRAKOWIAK POLISH DANCERS of Boston, INC., 538 Mt. Hope St., N. Attleboro, MA 02760. (508) 695-3898. Jacek Marek, Artistic Director and Choreographer.

KRAKOWIAK POLISH DANCERS of Fall River, 11 Rodney Ave., Somerset, MA 02725. (508) 674-3186. Phyllis Babiarz, Director.

KRAKOWIANKI of St.Stanislaus Church, contact: Kasia Kramarczyk, 3 Rabbit Rock Rd., E. Haven, CT 06513.

KRAKUSY POLISH DANCE COMPANY, 3223 South Beverly Drive, Los Angeles, CA 90034. Marylka George, Director/Choreographer.

LAJKONIK POLISH FOLK DANCERS, 1976 Malvern Rd.,

Columbus, OH 43221-4125. (614) 486-5572. Artistic Director:Alexander Dukat.

LASOWIACY DANCERS, 5211 West Dakin St., Chicago, IL 60641. Joyce Szarowicz, Director.

LEHICI DANCERS of Chicago, 4016 N. Central Park, Chicago, IL 60618. Director Ted Wiecek.

LOWICZANIE POLISH FOLK DANCE ENSEMBLE, 291 Moscow St., San Francisco, CA 94112. Ania Slonia, Director.

"LUBLINIACY"-The Lublin Polish Song and Dance Ensemble of Haverhill-Boston and "Little Lublin" Children's Group, 186 Broadway, Haverhill, MA 01832. (508) 374-8005. Stanislaw Kmiec (founder, artistic director, choreographer).

MAREK POLISH FOLK DANCE ENSEMBLE, Box 111, Lopez, PA 18628. Ferdinand Marek, Director.

MATUSZ POLISH DANCE CIRCLE, 641 Leonard St., Brooklyn, NY 11222. (718) 389-8977. Artistic Director/Choreographer: Wladzia Jaworowska.

MAZOWSZE PNA 513 Children's Group, 212 Brentwood Dr., Wallingford, CT 06492. (203) 949-1578. Victoria Zolkiewicz, Director.

MAZUR POLISH DANCERS of Milwaukee, Inc., P.O. Box 1136 Milwaukee, WI 53201. (414) 384-5499. Prof. Alfred Sokolnicki, founder, choreographer emeritus; Choreographer, Jerry Kucharski.

MICHAS POLISH FOLK DANCE ENSEMBLE, 704 Pinetree Dr., Virginia Beach, VA 23452. (804) 486-7349. Michael Levinsky, Director.

OJCZYZNA POLISH FOLK SONG & DANCE ENSEMBLE, 2233 Rogene #101, Baltimore, MD 21209. (301) 358-3157. Dennis Klima, Director/Choreographer.

ORLETA POLISH DANCERS, 16 Clemens Ave., Trumbull, CT 06611. (203) 268-4801. Donna Knapczuk, Director/Choreographer.

"PIAST", 49 Perry Ave., Worcester, MA 01610 (508) 791-5461.

Rev. Anthony Czarnecki-Founder/Director; Edward Hoffman-Choreographer.

POLANIE POLISH DANCERS, 1053 NE 92nd St., Seattle, WA 98115. (206) 526-8765. Basia McNair, Director.

THE POLISH AMERICAN FOLK DANCE COMPANY, INC, 1001 Lorimer St., Brooklyn, NY 11222. (718) 389-1141. Artistic Director and Choreographer, Stanley Pelc.

POLISH BENEFICIAL CHILDREN'S DANCE GROUP, 2595 Orthodox St., Philadelphia, PA 19134. (215) 743-6955. Mary Dajnak, Choreographer.

POLISH FALCONS OF AMERICA. Nest #880, 5159 S. Long Avenue, Chicago, IL 60638. Eugenia Krzyzanski-Director.

POLISH FALCONS OF AMERICA. District #2-Nest #725, 3049 N. Pierce St., Milwaukee, WI 53212. Marian Hansen-Director.

POLISH FALCONS OF AMERICA. Nest #880, 24 Elmvale Place, Pittsfield, MA 01201. Catherine Mlynarczyk-Director.

POLISH FOLK DANCERS OF SAN ANTONIO, Jo Ann Witek, 107 Briarglen, San Antonio, TX 78218.

POLISH HERITAGE DANCERS, Karolina Lipinska, 4729 Oregon St., San Diego, CA 92116.

POLISH HERITAGE DANCERS, 321 Butternut St., Utica, NY 13502. Director/ Choreographer Valerie Kosuda-Elacqua.

POLISH INTERCOLLEGIATE CLUB of Philadelphia, (P.K.M. DANCERS) 9150 Academy Rd., Philadelphia, PA 19114. (215) 624-9954. Richard Klimek, Director.

POLISH NATIONAL ALLIANCE DANCE GROUP, contact: Sandy Schuster, RR #3, Box 107, Grafton, ND 58237.

POLISH ROMAN CATHOLIC UNION TEACHERS' ENSEMBLE, 5661 Norborn Ave., Dearborn Hts., MI 48127. Shirley Galanty-Director.

POLISH SATURDAY SCHOOL DANCE GROUP, 109 Rosemead Lane, Cheektowaga, NY 14227. Helena Golebiowska, Instructor.

POLONAISE DANCERS of PNA Council 27, 13 Mertensia Lane, Henrietta, NY 14467. (716) 334-2147.

POLONAISE DANCERS, contact: Stella Lamarch, 115 Vincent St., Inkster, MI 48141

POLONAISE FOLK DANCERS, 61-60 56th St. Rd., Maspeth, NY 11378. Carole Buchalska-Golis, Director.

POLONIA SONG & DANCE ENSEMBLE, 454 Melrose Ave., Ambridge, PA 15003. (412) 266-5746. Timothy Kuzma.

POLONIA FOLK DANCE ENSEMBLE, 261 Northwind, El Paso, TX 79912. (915) 833-1476. Contact: Cristina Robbins.

POLONEZ DANCERS of P.N.A, 6322 W. Fletcher St., Chicago, IL 60634. Anthony Dobrzanski, Director.

ZESPOL POLONEZ, 3831 Aberdeen Way, Houston, TX 77025. (713) 664-1305. Bozena Solecki, Director and Choreographer.

POLSKIE ISKRY, 11932 Shetland Rd., Garden Grove, CA 92640. (213) 537-0436. Eugene Ciejka, Director/Choreographer.

POLSKIE MAKI Dancing School-Polish Roman Catholic Union of America, Sharon Baker, 23345 Panama, Warren, MI 48091.

POZNAN DANCERS-Polish Women's Alliance Group 242, 20830 Country Club, Harperwoods, MI 48225 (313) 886-3018.

RADOMIANIE, 1738 N. Lafayette, Dearborn, MI 48128. (313) 561-4391. Suzan Marzec, Choreographer/Artistic Director.

RZESZOWIACY, 1317 N. Ashland Ave., Chicago, IL 60622. Bishop Bronislaw Wojdyla, Artistic Director and Choreographer; Bozena Nizanska, Guest Choreographer.

RZESZOW DANCERS-Alliance of Poles of America, Group 174, 8136 Bernice, Centerline, MI 48015. (313) 756-9584. Verna Bienkowski (Director); Marcia Lewandowski (Choreographer).

ST. MAXIMILIAN KOLBE DANCERS, P.O. Box 1901, Riverhead, NY 11901. (516) 722-5261. Christine McKay, Choreographer. Wanda Walinski, President.

SLOWIANIE SONG AND DANCE ENSEMBLE, 27736 Santa Ana, Warren, MI 48093. Sophia Filus, Director.

SOLIDARITY DANCERS, 5 Villa Park, Cheektowaga, NY 14227. (716) 656-8553. 23 St. Felix, Cheektowaga, NY 14227. (716) 894-7516. Janet Biniszkiewicz, Choreographer.

STAROPOLSKA-Dances of Old Poland, 3164 Frankford Ave., Philadelphia, PA 19134. (215) 426-8641. Director, Mary Dajnak.

THE SYRENA POLISH FOLK DANCE ENSEMBLE, INC, 3352 North Hackett Ave., Milwaukee, WI 53211. (414) 964-8444. Ada Dziewanowska, Artistic Director and Choreographer.

TATRY DANCERS, (313) 274-0183. Rose Ann Lackey, Director; Barbara Raczynski, Karen Ozimek, Choreographers.

UNION OF POLISH WOMEN IN AMERICA-DEB DANCERS, 1424 E. Columbia Ave., Philadelphia, PA 19125. (215) 739-5569. Theresa Shewaski, Director; Andrzej Wojciechowski, Choreographer.

VISTULA POLISH DANCE COMPANY. Polish Arts and Culture Foundation, 1290 Sutter , San Francisco, CA 94109. (415) 474-7070. Dr. Jean M. Novak, Artistic Director

WARSZAWIANKI. Polish Women's Alliance Council 38, 11426 Grayfield, Detroit, MI 48239. (313) 534-4850. Angela Skorski, Dance Instructor.

THE WAWEL FOLK ENSEMBLE, 5128 Casmere, Detroit, MI 48212. Contact (313) 885-7209. Director, Marcia Lewandowski.

THE WAWEL POLISH FOLK DANCERS, 616 Eleventh Ave., New Hyde Park, NY 11040. (516) 437-9310. Donna Kalinowska-Kaye, Artistic Director, Choreographer).

"WESOLY LUD" POLISH FOLK DANCE ENSEMBLE of the Polish Roman Catholic Union of America-Chicago, 8534 S. Latrobe, Burbank IL 60459. (708) 422-6102. Michalina Binkowski-Jaminski, Artistic Director/Choreographer; Richard Jaminski, Associate Director.

WICI SONG AND DANCE COMPANY, 555 N. Williams Drive, Palatine, IL 60067. (708)358-0538. Regina Oryszczak, Director/Choreographer, Magda Solarz, Choreographer.

WINDS OF POLAND DANCE AND SONG ENSEMBLE-"POLSKIE WIATRY". St. Mary's College, Orchard Lake, MI 48324. (313) 683-0524. Sylvia Meloche-Chang, Director; Jacek Marek, Guest Choreographer.

WISLA DANCERS, 7060 W. Talcott St., Chicago, IL 60631. Shirley Dudzinski, Director.

WISLA SONG AND DANCE ENSEMBLE, 1300 E. Lafayette #810, Detroit, MI 48207. (313) 259-1738. Martin Pack, Artistic Director and Choreographer.

ZESPOL ZAKOPANE, A. Tokarz, c/o Universal Trade Center, P.O. Box 1172, Calumet City, IL 60409.

ZEBRANIE PNA District 2, 212 Brentwood Dr., Wallingford, CT 06492. (203) 949-1578. Director, Victoria Zolkiewicz.

INTERNATIONAL GROUPS WITH POLISH REPERTOIRE

BRIGHAM YOUNG UNIVERSITY INTERNATIONAL FOLK DANCERS, 259 Richard's Bldg., Provo, Utah. (801) 378-1211. Ed Austin, Director. Perform the Krakowiak and Lublin Dances.

KHADRA International Folk Ballet, (415) 626-7360. Mari Nijesson, Director. Stylized Polish Dances. 1182 Market St., Suite 215, San Francisco, CA 94102.

MANDALA FOLK DANCE ENSEMBLE, P.O. Box 246, Cambridge, MA 02139. (617) 868-3641. 25 dancers and 6 musicians with the following Polish dances in their vast International repertoire: National Dance Suite (Polonez, Mazur, Kujawiak, Oberek)-Jas Dziewanowski; Zywiec Mountain Suite-Jacek Marek; Podkoziolek Kujawski-Jas Dziewanowski; Rzeszow Suite-Regina Laskowski; Opoczno Suite-Andrea Majewska.

NEW YORK FOLK BALLET, 314 W. 58th St., Suite 3B, New York City, NY 10019. (212) 307-5251.Caroline Thorn Binney, Director/Choreographer.

SLAVIC FOLK DANCE ENSEMBLE of Oakland University Foreign Language Dept. Dr. Helen Kovach-Tarakanov, Oakland University, Rochester, MI 48063. Greg Denike, Artistic Director.

TAMBURITZANS Duquesne University, 1801 Boulevard of the

Allies, Pittsburgh, PA 15219. (412) 434-5185. Paul G. Stafura, Managing Director.

POLKA DANCE GROUPS

FREE SPIRIT DANCERS, A. Rasinski, 911 Sibley Rd., Baltimore, MD 21204.

JUBILEE DANCERS, 33 Exeter Ave., Edison, NJ 08817. Marie and Casey Costa, Directors.

KOLKO POLEK, Mary Matala, 534 Birchwood Sq., West Seneca, NY 14224.

KAROLINKA POLKA DANCERS, 48 Wickhampton, Goshen, NY 10924.

POLKA DOLL AND GUYS, Linda Nimiec, 33 St. Stephen's Lane, Schenectady, NY.

POLKABRATION, Steve Coblisz, P.O. Box 1394, Schenectady, NY 12301-1394.

STAR DANCERS, 968 Osborne Ave., Riverhead, NY 11901. Dorothy Szot, Director/Choreographer, Ken Wilkowski, Choreographer.

RESOURCES:

Dance Records and Syllabi: Folk Dances from Poland (volumes 1-3); Silesian Dances; Rzeszow Dances; Easy Dances of Poland; and other cassettes and records available. Contact: Ada Dziewanowska, 3352 N. Hackett Ave., Milwaukee, WI 53211. (414) 964-8444.

Basia Dziewanowska: Polish Folk Costume/Art Specialist and Lecturer. Polish costumes, footwear, and dance recordings. Polish Folklore Family Camp, 41 Katherine Rd., Watertown, MA 02172. (617) 926-8048.

Books on Polonaise and Mazur: R. Cwieka, 1375 Clinton Ave., Irvington, NJ 07111.

Coming soon . . . Book: Dances and Costumes of Poland by Ada Dziewanowska. This definitive reference guide will include the national dances, and among the regions included are Rzeszow, Sacz, Kurpie, Lowicz, Opoczno, Silesia, Wielkopolska, Lublin, and Kaszuby.

("Having read a preview manuscript, I can confirm that this book will be an excellent resource for any folklorist"-S. Kmiec) The book will be distributed by Hippocrene Books, 171 Madison Ave., New York, NY 10016

Bibliography

BOOKS AVAILABLE IN BOOKSTORES AND PUBLIC LIBRARIES CONCERNING POLES IN NORTH AMERICA. A SELECTED LIST.

Bakanowski, Adolf, *Polish Circuit Rider*, Cheshire, CT.: Cherry Hill Press, 1971.

Baker, T. Lindsay, *The First Polish-Americans. Silesian Settlements in Texas.* College Station, Texas: Texas A & M Press, 1979.

Bukowczyk, John J. *And My Children Did Not Know Me: A History of Polish-Americans.* Bloomington, Indiana: Indiana University Press, 1987.

Brozek, Andrzej. *Polish-Americans l854-1939.* Warsaw: Inter-press, 1985.

Budka, Metchie J.E. ed. Charles Morley, Trans, and ed., *Portrait of America. Letters of Henryk Sienkiewicz.* New York: Columbia University Press, 1959.

Drzewieniecki, Walter. Polonica Buffaloniensis: *Annotated Bibliography of Source and Printed Materials Dealing With the Polish American Community in the Bufffalo, New York Area.* Buffalo: Buffalo and Erie County Historical Society, 1976.

Greene, Victor. "Poles" In: *Harvard Encyclopedia of American Ethnic Groups.* Cambridge, MA: The Belknapp Press of Harvard University Press, 1980.

Golab, Carolina. *Immigrant Destinations.* Philadelphia: Temple University Press, 1977.

Haiman, Miecislaus. *Polish Past in America, 1608-1865.* Chicago: Reissue, Polish Museum of America, 1974.

Haiman, Miecislaus. *Kosciuszko in the American Revolution.* New York, Polish Institute of Arts and Sciences, 1943.

Haiman, Miecislaus. *Poland and the American Revolution.* Chicago: Polish Roman Catholic Union of America, 1932.

Hoskins, Janina W. *Polish Genealogy and Heraldry: an Introduction to Research.* Washington, D.C: Library of Congress, 1987.

229

Kajencki, Francis Casimir. *Poles in the 19th Century Southwest,* El Paso, Texas: Southwest Polonia Press, 1990.

Kula, Witold, et al., *Writing Home; Immigrants in Brazil and the United States 1890-1891.* Boulder, Colorado: East European Monographs, 1986 CCX.

Kulikowski, Mark. *A Bibliography of Polish Americans,* 1975-1980. Unpublished, 1981. (Available at Lockwood Memorial Library, SUNYAB).

Kuniczak, Wieslaw. *My Name Is Million- An Illustrated History of the Poles in America,* New York: Doubleday & Co.,

1978. Miaso, Jozef. *The History of the Education of Polish Immigrants In The United States,* New York: The Kosciuszko Foundation, 1977.

Mocha, Frank, ed. *Poles In America/ Bicentennial Essays,* Stevens Point: Worzalla Publishing Company, 1978.

Niemcewicz, Julian Ursyn. *Under Their Vine and Fig Tree. Travels through America in 1797-1799, 1805.* Elizabeth, New Jersey: Grassman Publishing Company, 1965.

Pienkos, Donald E. *P.N.A.; A Centennial History of the Polish National Alliance of the United States of North America.* New York, N.Y. Columbia University Press., 1984. *One Hundred Years Young: A History of the Polish Falcons of America, 1887-1987.* New York: Columbia University Press, 1987. *For Your Freedom Through Ours: Polish American Efforts on Poland's Behalf, 1863-1991.* New York: Columbia University Press, 1991.

Polish American Studies; Polish American Historical Association.

Renkiewicz, Frank. *The Poles in America, 1608-1972: A chronology and Fact Book,* Dobbs Ferry, NY: Oceana Publications, 1973.

Sandberg, Neil C. *Ethnic Identity and Assimilation: The Polish American Community. Case Study of Metropolitan Los Angeles.* New York: Praeger Publishers, 1974.

Seroczynski, Felix T. "Poles in the United States." *The Catholic Encyclopedia.* New York: Robert Appleton Company, 1911.

Thomas,William I. & Znaniecki, Florian. *The Polish Peasant In Europe and America, New York:* Octagon Press, 1974.

Wytrwal, Joseph. *Behold! The Polish Americans.* Detroit: Endurance Press, 1977.

Zurawski, Joseph W. Polish *American History and Culture: A Classified Bibliography,* Chicago: Polish Museum of America, 1975.

List of Illustrations

1) Forest Lawn Memorial Park-Hall of the Crucifixion-Resurrection, Glendale, CA
2) The Crucifixion of Christ by Jan Styka (Central section), Glendale, CA
3) Arden-Helena Modjeska ranch home, about 1898. Santiago Canyon, CA
4) Polish National Home, Hartford, CT
5) Pulaski Monument, Hartford, CT
6) Wanda Landowska Center (Oak Knoll). Lakeville, CT
7) St. Stanislaus Church, Meriden, CT
8) Pulaski Monument, Meriden, CT
9) First Katyn Monument in the US, Sacred Heart Cemetery. New Britain, CT
10) Popieluszko Monument, Walnut Hill Park. New Britain, CT
11) Popieluszko Monument Marker, Walnut Hill Park, New Britain, CT
12) Noah Webster Statue by Korczak-Ziolkowski., West Hartford, CT
13) The Pulaski Monument as reproduced on the cover of "Pulaski March" published in 1879 in Savannah for the Centennial Celebration
14) Polish Roman Catholic Union of America building which houses the Polish Museum in Chicago
15) Polish Museum in Chicago-Main Exhibit Hall
16) Polish Museum in Chicago-Art Gallery
17) Polish Museum in Chicago-Paderewski Room
18) Polish Museum in Chicago-The Kosciuszko Collection
19) The Polish Highlander Community Center in Chicago
20) Copernicus Cultural and Civic Center-Solidarity Tower-Chicago
21) Copernicus Cultural and Civic Center-Gateway Theater-Chicago
22) Copernicus Statue on Solidarity Drive in Chicago
23) Kosciuszko Statue on Solidarity Drive in Chicago
24) "Polish Village" in Chicago
25) The Shrine of Our Lady of Czestochowa, in Merrillville, IN

26) Shrine Chapel of Our Lady of Orchard Lake, MI
27) St. Mary's Preparatory Classroom Building, Orchard Lake, MI
28) St. Stanislaus Kostka Roman Catholic Church, St. Louis,MO
29) The Stan Musial Statue, St. Louis, MO
30) The Katyn Memorial in Jersey City, NJ-Sculptor Andrzej Pitynski. Unveiling ceremony on Sunday May 19, 1991
31) "The Liberation" monument at Liberty State Park, Jersey City, NJ
32) Adam Mickiewicz Monument in the Polish Room, Buffalo, NY
33) The Polish Community Center,The statue of Chopin in the Mazur Gallery, Buffalo, NY
34) The Chopin Monument, Buffalo, NY
35) Statue of John Paul II, Villa Maria College in Cheektowaga, NY
36) Marcella Sembrich Memorial Studio, Bolton Landing-On-Lake-George, NY
37) Kosciuszko Foundation, New York City
38) Main Hall and Art Gallery, Kosciuszko Foundation, New York City
39) Polish Institute of Arts and Sciences, New York City
40) Polish Consulate General, New York City
41) Jagiello Monument, Central Park, New York City
42) Paderewski by Malvina Hoffman, New York City
43) Paderewski plaque at the Buckingham Hotel, New York City
44) Church of St. Stanislaus B. and M., New York City
45) St. Patrick's Cathedral on Pulaski Day, New York City
46) Empire State Building on Pulaski Day, New York City
47) Polish Scouts marching on Pulaski Day, New York City
48) Pulaski Day in New York City
49) President Walesa visits the Polish exhibit on Ellis Island, NY
50) Polish American Museum in Port Washington, NY
51) Mr. and Mrs. Henry Archacki at the Archacki Archives, Port Washington, NY
52) Boleslaw the Brave greeting Otto III. A.D. 1000, Le Moyne College, Syracuse, NY
53) Granting of the Charter of Jedlnia. A.D. 1430, Le Moyne College, Syracuse, NY
54) The Relief of Vienna. A.D. 1683, Le Moyne College, Syracuse, NY

55) The 3rd of May Constitution. A.D. 1791, Le Moyne College, Syracuse, NY
56) Aerial view of Fort Ticonderoga, Ticonderoga, NY
57) Kosciuszko Garden, West Point, NY
58) Kosciuszko Monument, West Point, NY
59) National Shrine of Our Lady of Czestochowa, Doylestown, PA
60) National Shrine of Our Lady of Czestochowa, Original Chapel. Doylestown, PA
61) The Heart of Jan Paderewski in the National Shrine, Doylestown, PA
62) Henry Archacki speaks at the official Paderewski ceremony
63) Cemetery and "Winged" Hussar Monument (by Andrzej Pitynski) at the National Shrine of Our Lady of Czestochowa. Doylestown, PA
64) Thaddeus Kosciuszko National Memorial, Philadelphia, PA
65) The Twins, Philadelphia, PA
66) Statue of General Tadeusz Kosciuszko, Philadelphia , PA
67) The Kopernik Monument, Philadelphia, PA
68) Statue of General Casimir Pulaski, Philadelphia, PA
69) Gesu Church, Philadelphia, PA
70) St. Stanislaus Cathedral of the Polish National Catholic Church, Scranton, PA
71) Polish National Union of America, Scranton, PA
72) Josef Casimir Hoffman Marker, Aiken, SC
73) Town marker and the church, Panna Maria, TX
74) The historic oak and marker, Panna Maria, TX
75) The historic marker-close-up. Panna Maria, TX
76) "First Poles" Marker, Jamestown, VA
77) The Kosciuszko Monument, Washington, DC
78) The Pulaski Monument, Washington, DC
79) Dedication of Memorial Marker to identify resting place of Ignacy Jan Paderewski, May 9, l963 by President John F. Kennedy. Arlington, VA
80) Norwid Memorial Marker, Harper's Ferry, WV
81) A view of Kaszuby, Ontario, Canada
82) Poland's Milenium Monument (part), Kaszuby, Ontario, Canada
83) Cathedral Under the Pines, Kaszuby, Ontario, Canada
84) Three Crosses Mountain, Kaszuby, Ontario, Canada

85) Polish Cemetery Memorial, Niagara-on-the-Lake, Ontario, Canada

86) Monument to General Haller, Niagara-on-the-Lake, Ontario, Canada

87) Site of the Battle of the Windmill, Prescott, Ontario, Canada

88) Church of the Mother of God, and Statue of John Paul II, Calgary, Alberta, Canada

89) Stamps issued by the US Post Office to commemorate Poles and Poland

90) Postcard commemorating Casimir Pulaski. First day of issue, October 11, l979

COVER ILLUSTRATION: Statue of King Jagiello in Central Park, New York City

PICTORIAL CREDITS

1, 2: Courtesy of Forest Lawn Memorial Park
3: Courtesy of Helena Modjeska Foundation
4, 5, 9, 10, 11, 12: by Alan Chaniewski
6: Courtesy of Denise Restout
7, 8: © Gary E. Dara
13: Courtesy of Walentyna Janta Polczynska
14 to 18: Courtesy of The Polish Museum in Chicago
19, 20, 22, 23, 24: Courtesy of Kathryn G. Rosypal, Executive Editor of *Narod Polski*
21: Courtesy of Copernicus Cultural & Civic Center
25, 30, 31, 38, 40, 42, 43, 44, 45, 46, 47, 48, 49, 51, 61, 62: © Jerzy Koss
26, 27: Courtesy of Orchard Lake Schools
28, 29: Courtesy of Polish American Cultural Society of St. Louis
37, 39, 57, 58, 59, 60, 63, 77, 80: Courtesy of *Nowy Dziennik*
32, 33, 34, 35: Courtesy of Michael Pietruszka
36: Courtesy of Marcella Sembrich Opera Museum
41, 76, 79: Courtesy of the J. Pilsudski Institute
50: Courtesy of the Polish American Museum
52 to 55: Courtesy of Le Moyne College
56: Courtesy of Fort Ticonderoga Museum
64 to 69: Courtesy of Polonia Federal Savings Association of Philadelphia
70, 71: Courtesy of Polish National Catholic Church
72, 90: Courtesy of Dr. Leonard Kosinski
73 to 75: Courtesy of Wladyslaw Wantula
78: Courtesy of Ludwik Zeranski
81 to 88: Courtesy of Stanislaw Stolarczyk
89: Polish Heritage Publications
COVER ILLUSTRATION: © Jacek Samotus/Polish Heritage Publications

Index of Towns

Index of Names and Sites

Index compiled by Teresa Juszczak

246

NEW POLISH INTEREST BOOKS FROM HIPPOCRENE BOOKS, INC.

"A giant in the field of Polish subject books"
—Polish American Cultural Network

QUO VADIS?

Henryk Sienkiewicz
$22.50 hardcover, 470 pages. ISBN 0-7818-0100-1

In a new American translation by Rev. Stanley F. Conrad, Poland's—and the world's—greatest bestseller comes alive for a new generation of readers. The Larousse Encyclopedia calls QUO VADIS? "One of the most extraordinary successes registered in the history of the book."

For Polish-American readers this new highly readable translation of a beloved book is a special celebration of a classic reborn, an opportunity to read, to reread and to give a book that has no equal as a story of love, devotion and courage. Set at the time of Emperor Nero, and his persecution of the Early Christians, QUO VADIS? helped the author win the Nobel Prize for Literature in 1905.

Rev. Stanley F. Conrad, of Waco, Texas, began translating the novel nearly 20 years ago, and only upon his recent retirement was he able to complete this immense task.

THE TRILOGY by Henryk Sienkiewicz

in a modern translation by W. S. Kuniczak

WITH FIRE & SWORD
$24.95, 1130 pages. ISBN 0-87052-974-9

THE DELUGE (2 Volumes)
$45.00, each volume 752 pages. ISBN 0-87052-004-0

FIRE IN THE STEPPE
$24.95, 750 pages. ISBN 0-7818-0025-0

THE TRILOGY COMPANION
$10.00, 80 pages. ISBN 0-87052-221-3

The greatest literary undertaking in the history of Polonia, sponsored by the Copernicus Foundation of America, is now complete. The enormous eight-year labor of translator W. S. Kuniczak, has brought the strongest chorus of praise from the book reviewers of America bestowed upon a Polish literary work in a century.

Called a "Polish Gone With The Wind" by Norman Davies in his full page review in the New York Times, which also termed it:"one of the most glorious epic journeys in literature," THE TRILOGY became a bestseller in America.

The readers of the Trilogy will find most helpful THE TRILOGY COM-
PANION which offers informative chapers on the historical context of the
work, and its principal characters, as well as a bibliography and a map.

POLISH HERITAGE COOKERY
Robert and Maria Strybel
$29.95 hardcover, 882 pages, with line drawings. ISBN 0-7818-0069-2

Today's Polish cuisine is a blend of hearty peasant dishes and more elegant
gourmet fare, assimilating a broad cross-section of cultural influences
(Lithuanian, Ukrainian, French, Italian, Jewish, Bohemian, Bavarian, etc)
without losing its distinctly Slavic flavor. A middle-of-the-road cuisine, it
does not require exotic, expensive or hard-to-get ingredients.

POLISH HERITAGE COOKERY is the most extensive and varied Polish cookbook ever published in English, with over 2200 recipes in 29 categories, written especially for Americans, with American weights, measures and
temperatures. Each recipe is listed under its American and Polish name.

It is arranged in 29 categories — from hors d'oeuvres, soups, meat, poultry,
wildfowl, game, fish, grain dishes, potato dishes, noodles, dumplings, and pan-
cakes—to vegetables, salads, home canning, desserts and beverages including
homemade cordials and spirits, sausage making, bread baking, spices and more.

Included are the elegant cuisine of Old Poland, the simple peasant cookery, and everything in between. The book is interlaced with cultural notes
and historical backgrounds on Polish foods and eating habits. Both traditional and simplified versions of Polish classic recipes are provided, together
with countless hints and shortcuts to achieving traditional flavors using
convenience items and modern appliances.

Today's health-minded habits inspired the authors to create a section
called "Cuisine Neo-Polonaise:" lower in fat and cholesterol. Good nutri-
tion is constantly stressed throughout the book.

"Cuisine Neo-Polonaise"recipes for traditional Polish dishes include cream
sauces and rich pastries with ingredients that are lighter-tasting, lower in fat
and cholesterol and often easier to prepare.

Like "Joy of Cooking" to which it has been compared, POLISH HERI-
TAGE COOKERY is a family affair. Robert Strybel is a native of Michigan
and lives and cooks with his wife, Maria in Warsaw. He is a syndicated
columnist and his "Polish Chef" recipes reach 250,000 readers every month.

THE GLASS MOUNTAIN
Twenty-Six Ancient Polish Folktales and Fables
Told by W. S. Kuniczak, Illustrated by Pat Bargielski
$14.95 hardcover, l60 pages, 8 illustrations. ISBN 0-7818-0087-0

For the young, and the young of heart, these fanciful tales have eternal
themes of love, good conquering evil, sibling rivalry, punishment for greed,

and life happily ever after. To read these tales is to be taken on a voyage to a place long ago and far away. The illustrations by Pat Bargielski are simply enchanting.

W. S. Kuniczak is the acclaimed and much-honored translator of the Sienkiewicz Trilogy, and the author of his own trilogy about Poland in World War II, The Thousand Hour Day, The March and Valedictory.

PAN TADEUSZ
Adam Mickiewicz
Polish and English text side by side
Translated by Kenneth R. MacKenzie
$19.95 paperback, 553 pages. ISBN 0-7818-0033-1

Poland's greatest epic poem in what is its finest English translation, originally published in England, is now available in North America. For English students of Polish, for Polish students of English, this classic poem in simultaneous translation is a special joy to read.

POLISH TRADITIONS, CUSTOMS, AND FOLKLORE
Sophie Hodorowicz Knab
With an introduction by Rev. Czeslaw Krysa
$19.95 hardcover, 300 pages. ISBN 0-7818-0068-4

This unique reference book is arranged by month, showing the various occasions, feasts and holidays. Beginning with December which includes the Advent, St. Nicholas Day, the Wigilia, nativity plays, carolling, as well as the New Year Day celebrations, and those of the shrovetide period to Ash Wednesday, Lent, celebration of spring, Holy Week customs; superstitions, beliefs and rituals associated with farming; Pentecost, Corpus Christi, midsummer celebrations, harvest festival customs, wedding rites, nameday celebrations, birth and death. Line illustrations complete this rich and varied treasury of folklore.

The author is a noted lecturer and writes a syndicated column on folklore. Rev. Krysa, who is Associate Professor at the S.S.Cyril and Methodius Seminary in Orchard Lake, Michigan, is an authority on Polish folklore and winner of the Oskar Kolberg award for 1991, Poland's most prized award in Ethnography and Folklore.

AMERICAN PHRASEBOOK FOR POLES
ROZMOWKI AMERYKANSKIE DLA POLAKOW
Jacek Galazka
$7.95 paperback, 141 pages. ISBN 0-87052-907-2

"The book meets in an extraordinary way the needs of today's world. And it is so practical; from the laundromat to a hospital visit, it anticipates the situations likely to confront the arriving Pole who does not speak the language. Because English is so popular a language, the phrasebook may turn out to be the essential travel companion anywhere in the world." —Nowy Dziennik (Polish Daily) New York

The phrasebook contains 65 sets of conversations, from arrival at the port of entry to looking for work, accommodation, schools; from shopping, traveling by subway, bus, train and plane, to making phone calls, using the post office or a bank, ordering food and drink in restaurants, coping with health problems and other emergencies, and much more.

• •

For a complete catalog of Polish interest books write to Hippocrene Books, Dept PH, 171 Madison Avenue, New York, NY 10016. We will also gladly send a catalog to your friends.

To order books contact your local bookseller, or write to Hippocrene Books, Dept PH at above address, enclosing your remittance for the books, including $3.50 to cover UPS shipment and handling for the first book, and $1.00 for each additional book sent to the same address.

• •

POLISH HERITAGE ART CALENDAR

Published since 1986, this monthly wall calendar (12" x 12") offers full color reproductions of masterpieces of Poland's best known painters whose works can be found in museums and private collections throughout the world.

In addition to paintings from the National Museums of Warsaw, Poznan and Krakow, the calendars have drawn on such public and private collections as The Polish Museum in Chicago, The Kosciuszko Foundation in New York, The J. Pilsudski Institute in New York, The Orchard Lake Gallery in Orchard Lake, Michigan, and a number of private collections including the well-known Fibak gallery and the Jordanowski collection.

Among the painters represented are: Jan Matejko, Jacek Malczewski, Alfred Wierusz-Kowalski, Jozef Brandt, Wojciech and Juliusz Kossak, Julian Falat, Jozef Chelmonski, Leon Wyczolkowski, Piotr Michalowski, Jan Stanislawski, January Suchodolski, Wladyslaw Slewinski, Henryk Siemiradzki, Witold Wojkiewicz, Jozef Mehoffer, Aleksander Gierymski, Stanislaw Kamocki, Olga Boznanska, Stanislaw Wyspianski, and many others.

The calendar is available in July. For full information on the current edition, its cost and back issues, write to Polish Heritage Publications, 75 Warren Hill Road, Box 71P, Cornwall Bridge, CT 06754.